LEMON

For Kim…

Forever Chasing Your Shadow

PROLOGUE
'RAIN'

It was a monsoon. Well, a mon-maybe-soon.

The rain had rained down for three solid days and three solid nights. Puddles the size of small lakes had formed in cul-de-sacs and well-tended gardens had turned into deadly quicksand.

A small, energetic Jack Russell dog, called Toby, had already drowned trying to leap across the front lawn of a neighbouring garden.

Many years from now, archaeologists would dig up Toby's remains and marvel at how the signs of panic were *still* etched on the canine's skull, even though it was devoid of tissue and bone.

The simple fact that a local radio weather announcer had cheerfully said - *"Mr Norman Dew, of Worcester, has just phoned in and asked if any heavy rain is on its way. Well, thanks for the call but there's no need to worry!"* - was, of course, a sure sign for everybody listening to start worrying.

Mr Arthur Plinth, a resident of Mulberry Road and head honcho of the Neighbourhood Watch, was sitting in his 'drawing' room and peering out of his window.

A window, he had just decided, that would benefit greatly from a pair of windscreen wipers.

As the rain streamed down his double-glazing he caught sight of a big, black car. It was stopping outside his house.

'Are you expecting visitors, Helen?!' he shouted.

Helen, his wife of ten years, was in the cupboard under the stairs. She didn't hear him.

He shouted again.

She still didn't hear him.

So, he turned back to try and see through the rivers of water that were running through his double-glazed vision.

He caught sight of his next-door neighbour being unceremoniously bundled into the back of said big, black car by two burly gentlemen, neither of whom would've looked out of place at an inaugural convention for Fairytale Giants. He didn't think anything of it.

This was a mistake.

Anyone who spots a big, black car pulling up *should* be suspicious. Two burly men getting out should confirm that suspicion. And a man being bundled unceremoniously into the back seat of aforementioned car is cause for a Police Rescue operation. Unfortunately, Mr Arthur Plinth never watched any American gangster movies, even *though* he ran the Neighbourhood Watch.

The rain still beat down with a relentless enthusiasm. The sky was still overcast and grey. The clouds were still gathered together like dirty cotton-wool balls. The thunder still rumbled like the approach of a gang of Hell's Angels. And the lightening flashed down like God's discotheque.

It was pure sympathetic background material for English A-level students everywhere.

CHAPTER 1
'YOU REALLY GOT ME'

Spencer Tracy was wondering what exactly had made him think it was a good idea to walk to the corner shop.

He'd needed some semi-skimmed milk. Not desperately. He could have made it last for the next couple of days but... well... he was a compulsive tea drinker. A fourteen cups a day man. He'd thought a walk might do him good. How wrong that sentiment would turn out to be.

Spencer Tracy was named after *the* Spencer Tracy - a famous Hollywood movie star of the 1940s and '50s. His parents had been big black-and-white movie fans. Sadly, he was as far removed from *the* Spencer Tracy as Sean Connery was from acting without his Scottish accent.

He was called 'Spence' at work by his fellow staff, and called 'You there, what's your name again?!' by his Head of Department.

However, his older brother had been named Dick Tracy, so he was thankful for small mercies.

Spence was wet through and, although physically impossible, getting wetter. His carton of semi-skimmed milk was soggier than a carton of semi-skimmed milk should be. He trudged slowly off the main street and into Mulberry Road.

Not far to go, he thought to himself.

Visibility was low and his fringe was hanging like tassels in front of his half-closed eyes. A chilly wind was picking up and cutting through his clothes like a crazed ex-wife. If he didn't catch pneumonia from this little 'walk', he mused, then the Earth was genuinely flat.

As he approached the last house before his own he looked up and caught a glimpse of Mr Arthur Plinth, his next-door neighbour, at the front window. Spence raised a waterlogged sleeve to attempt a half-hearted wave, which turned into a feeble Nazi salute (very apt, he thought, as the Neighbourhood Watch was run on similar lines), and Mr Plinth turned his face away.

Spence heard a faint sound of a powerful engine nearby. After taking a couple more steps he realised that it was at his side. He stopped as the big, black car crawled into view beside him. The darkened window opened a tiny fraction. Spence assumed they were lost and were about to ask directions.

A voice spoke.

Spence couldn't hear it. The rain had flooded his eardrums and his hearing was, at that moment, severely drowning.

Then, both of the two front doors of the car opened and a pair of big, burly men climbed out. Spence had an aversion to big, burly men. Without saying a word, they grabbed him by each arm and threw him against the car. It hurt. The back door with the fractionally opened window was whipped open. Spence caught a glimpse of the interiors and didn't much fancy a closer look. It was dark. And Spence *had* seen some American gangster movies.

Dazed and confused, and before he could make up his own mind, his mind was made up for him and he was roughly thrown inside the car. It smelled of leather.

'Good afternoon.' said a rich, silky voice. It was the sort of rich, silky voice that oozed effortless charm.

'Hello.' squeaked Spence, with the sort of voice that oozed effortless idiocy. He got comfortable and looked up.

The man who sat next to him had rather a severe face. He had cruel lips, cheekbones that you could ski off, and a long, thin nose that gave his features a rodent-type quality. His hair was fair and slicked back off his forehead and his eyes were a piercing, cold blue.

'We meet at last Mr Dicks. Or may I call you Philip?' he said.

'You can, but it's not my name.' answered Spence, nervously.

'Of course it isn't.' chuckled Spence's passenger. 'Of course it isn't.'

'No, it isn't.'

'In the very same way that my name *isn't* Lord Pembridge.'

'Isn't it?' enquired Spence.

'Of course it is.' snapped Lord Pembridge.

'Would it be too impertinent a question to ask why I have been kidnapped?' asked Spence, not at all comfortable with the situation.

Lord Pembridge laughed. It was a rich, silky laugh to accompany his rich, silky voice.

'You know full well.' he whispered, mysteriously.

'No, honestly, I don't.' replied Spence, beginning to squirm as he felt the ever-growing pool of water he was creating and, subsequently, sitting in. This was the rain dripping off him and not the fact he'd lost control of his bodily functions. That wouldn't happen for at least a few pages yet.

'Don't play games with me, Mr Dicks' snarled Lord Pembridge.

'I'm not.' said Spence, innocently.

'We shall see. We shall see.' hissed Lord Pembridge.

Spence thought it best to shut up for now and see where he was being taken. He couldn't look out of the windows as they were too dark to view the passing landmarks. So, he sat back - feeling damp, soggy and cold - and did what he always did in times of extreme stress.

He went to sleep.

*   *   *

Deep in an underground chamber sat Lemon.

She was a strikingly attractive female of the species. Her hair was lemon-coloured, hence her moniker, and she was as fresh-faced and as innocent looking as a small child. She seemed untouched and unsullied by modern times. There was something otherworldly about her. She was the human personification of a jar of honey.

She looked around the chamber, her head turning as if in slow-motion, and her eyes scanning the dark recesses. She relaxed back into her chair.

A computer, sat ominously beside her at a table, clicked and whirred into action. It bleeped alarmingly as if to catch her attention. She swivelled round and her fingers became a blur over the keys. She stopped as quickly as she had started and studied the screen. Her delicate hand clenched into a ball and banged down on the table.

Lord Pembridge had made an error.

This was unacceptable.

She sat back again in her chair, becoming as motionless as the air before a storm, and waited for his imminent arrival.

*   *   *

Spence was woken abruptly by the car stopping… abruptly.

He was thrown forward and his face became one with the partition that separated the driver from the passengers. He bit into his lip and felt the warm blood trickle into his mouth. Lord Pembridge had braced himself and grabbed Spence by the shoulder, pulling him back into the seat.

'Idiot!' Spence had heard him mutter.

It wasn't the first time Spence had heard someone mutter that in his presence. And it probably wouldn't be the last.

'Step out of the car.' snapped Lord Pembridge, as light suddenly shone through the interior. The bigger of the two burly men from earlier had opened the back door.

Spence, still somewhat fazed from waking up suddenly and then biting his lip, half-climbed, half-fell out of the car. It was still raining. But, the sun was peeking through the curtain of grey and a few dappled rays hit the ground and showed promise.

'Where are we?' he mumbled, still trying to stem the flow of red from his bottom lip. He got no answer. Instead, the biggest of the burly men, who had so kindly opened the car door for Spence, now ever-so-kindly bent one of Spence's arms halfway up behind his back. The pain was intense and Spence had no time to let out anything but a small yelp. Any breed of canine in earshot would have known what it meant.

Underfoot were a thousand tiny gravel stones that made the snap, crackle and pop sound of a certain breakfast cereal as Spence was force-led away from the car. He glanced around like a scavenging vulture to take in his surroundings.

It was the country. Rain stung his eyes as he strained to see.

It was the country... and then some.

He was aware of a long, long driveway leading up to a long, long house. It was to this house he was being shepherded.

Some houses are big and some houses are small. This house definitely fell into the former of the two categories. It probably toppled over into the 'bloody massive' category, if truth be told.

The steps leading up to it were opulent and grandiose, to match the house. It would've looked positively awful if the steps had been shabby and tattered. These were the sort of pointless things that were racing through Spence's mind as he stumbled up the first slippery, rain-soaked step. The other burly man came to his aid. He did this by grabbing Spence's free arm and attempting the same twist that his counterpart had graduated with honours at.

Spence grimaced as the muscles and tendons in his shoulders jostled for position and swapped places with each other. Lord Pembridge couldn't have been too far behind as he heard the smooth tones bark some kind of direction.

In through the double oaken doors they strode, straight along a highly-polished and sparsely-furnished passage, down two flights of marble stairs with matching banisters, and into a dingy-lit cellar with the obligatory wine-racks stacked with dusty bottles.

Spence was pushed roughly into a wooden chair that creaked alarmingly. He checked to see if his arms were still nestling in their sockets.

They were... just.

He peered into the semi-darkness. He had seen the wine stacked in rows and the slabs of flagstones that made up the floor. What he now caught a glimpse of was a bank of computer screens, set in a protective circle around a human form - like some kind of moat - and winking and teasing in the grey light. He knew about computer screens. He worked at one.

Spence was a man at one with Data Input.

He was also a man at one with World of Warcraft and Final Fantasy.

Lord Pembridge had sidled up to the computer moat and was talking to the female castle sat inside it.

And what a castle she was, thought Spence; sleek, beautiful, well-built, and with a fine pair of turrets.

Lord Pembridge was very animated which seemed to juxtapose the serene calmness of the fair-haired fortress. Spence couldn't quite make out what was being said but it didn't look good. He considered making a break for the exit but took one look at the two burly men by his side and didn't fancy them playing Ping-Pong with his head.

Why had he been brought here? Was he going to die? Who had chosen him as the candidate for whatever he was going to be the candidate for? Had someone found out that he hadn't paid his TV licence? Had he changed the litter for Eric, his cat?

All these thoughts flashed through Spence's muddled brain as he shivered slightly with the chill air that blew through the cellar.

He sneezed.

Everyone turned to look at him for one hour-long second. He made a mental note not to sneeze again. He was still wringing wet and now he was catching a cold. This was turning out to be somewhat of a bad day.

A gunshot sounded.

This, thought Spence, has now successfully passed the 'somewhat of a bad day' qualifying rounds and gone on to compete in the final of the 'worst day ever' race. If he hadn't been so wet already, he would've wet himself some more.

A body hit the floor. It didn't slump. It *hit* the floor with a resounding slap.

Spence realised that he had his eyes closed. His brain was screaming at him to open them and his bodily functions were pleading with him to ignore any advice from the brain.

And then he heard somebody in the cellar laughing. It sounded like a beautiful set of fairy-bells pealing like there was no tomorrow. It was a warm, sweet, sensual laugh. Not a laugh of a madman or a crazed killer. It was soothing and comforting.

He slowly opened his eyes to see who was laughing. His bodily functions braced themselves.

The fair-haired angel behind the flashing computer screens was laughing. She was also holding a revolver that was smoking as vigorously as a post-coital cigarette.

On the flagstones below the computer banks lay a crumpled heap; a crumpled heap that would bear the headstone description of Lord Pembridge. He had a gaping hole in his head.

Subsequently, this gave room for his brains to escape. And escape they had. They'd really made a break for it.

And so did Spence's breakfast.

The combination of regurgitated Cornflakes and escaping brains was something that didn't look unlike a Chicken Tikka Masala.

'Leave us.' said the laughing killer, waving the revolver in the direction of the stairs as an indication for the two burly men. Like a pair of lumbering mutant zombies, they left.

Spence wished he had been leaving with them. Once more he thought about making a break for it but his legs had all the consistency of a jelly that had been left out in the sun on a July afternoon.

The fair-haired temptress put down her revolver. It made a clattering noise as steel scraped against steel.

Spence jumped. He tried to speak, maybe plead for his life, maybe appeal to her better nature, maybe, maybe, maybe... but his mouth felt like the bottom of a bird cage and his tongue had become impotent all of a sudden. He gurgled and dribbled like a baby.

'I am Lemon.' said the fair-haired one, finally putting a name to herself for Spence to toy with. 'I apologise for your rough and shoddy treatment, Mr Tracy.' she added, almost sincerely.

Almost.

Spence muttered something unintelligible.

'We have made a slight error.' she continued, 'and we are truly sorry.'

'How do... you know... who... I... am?' mumbled Spence, trying so hard to speak the language that he was most fluent in and sounding like a bad Captain Kirk impersonator.

Lemon didn't answer; she just smiled sweetly.

'That man...' Spence pointed to the deceased Lord, '...called me... called me Philip... Philip Something?' stammered Spence, his mind spinning like a carousel.

'Philip Dicks is the man we wanted.' said Lemon. 'You are not him.'

'I know that.' snapped Spence, starting to regain his wherewithal. 'I could've told you that. In fact, I told him that.'

'Oh, you want me to explain?!' Lemon realised.

'It would help.' muttered Spence.

'I don't think it would.' said Lemon, her smile vanishing. She picked up the revolver and shot Spence.

He collapsed in a heap on the floor.

The heap that was once called Lord Pembridge.

CHAPTER 2
'DAZED AND CONFUSED'

It was Sunday morning. This meant that Spence's alarm clock went off at 10.00am instead of the 9.00am wake-up call on Saturday and the 7.30am wake-up call on weekdays.

'Morning, Gromit - time for walkies!! Come on, Gromit - don't be a lazy bones!! Morning, Gromit - time for walkies!! Come on, Gromit - don't be a lazy bones!!' bleated the alarm clock, in sing-song Northern tones.

Spence's fist crashed down onto Gromit's head. He wouldn't be going for 'walkies' today. His bleary eyes opened and he took in the familiar surroundings of his familiar bedroom. He pulled back the duvet and swung his legs out of bed, followed by the rest of him.

He caught sight of himself in the full-length mirror that stood adjacent to his bed, wobbled his potbelly, and leant on his roller-exerciser. He'd been roller-exercising for at least three years and his stomach wasn't getting any flatter. It was getting fatter. This was a physical impossibility. Perhaps he was doing it wrong?

Spence *used* to be well-toned and thin, until he'd taken a job as a Data Input Operator for a big corporation and slowly watched his muscles metamorphose into fat. His sideboards needed trimming and were now growing in the shape of Italy. His hair was a mess. And that's how Spence liked it. It was trying to grow all one length but hadn't managed it yet.

If you asked a hairdresser what style Spence's hair could be best associated with, they'd fall about laughing at the usage of the word 'style'. He had been 'Emo' before the whole misunderstood Goth scene had come into fashion (and would probably stay 'Emo' after the misunderstood Goth scene had long gone *out* of fashion).

'Damn clock.' he muttered, picking the battered speaking alarm clock up off the floor where it had fallen. He put it back on his bedside table, amongst the half-eaten packet of Milk Chocolate Hob-Nobs, the pouch of cherry tobacco, the embossed lighter that hadn't worked for the last few months, and a coffee cup that had a new sort of bacteria cultivating inside it.

The words 'tidy' and 'up' were omitted from Spence's dictionary. Most words concerning the general health and cleanliness of a human being were also omitted. Spence had a very small dictionary.

Spence gave up looking in the mirror. It disturbed him. He always had this image in his head of Brad Pitt and it was a big disappointment to see Brad Pitt playing the part of a scruffy tramp. And playing it very well.

He bent down to pick up a pair of trousers off his floor - a floor carpeted with clothes. If a huge explosion hit Burtons Menswear, it would look not unlike Spence's floor. In fact, if a big explosion hit Oxfam, the result would be much the same.

As he bent down, he remembered Lemon.

A wave of panic shot over him and the room span. He slumped down against the edge of his double bed, shivering with shock. It all came back to him like a unexpected Inland Revenue claim. Great chunks of flashback flew through his startled memory and embedded themselves in his brain. He recalled the kidnapping, the death of Lord Pembridge, the soggy semi-skimmed milk carton, and his own death.

He paused.

His own death?!

It didn't add up. Or subtract. Or divide. And it equalled nothing. A big, fat nothing.

If I'm dead, thought Spence, then Heaven looks pretty much like my bedroom. Considering he didn't believe in Heaven, this was a troubling thought. After all, even though he didn't *believe*, he still expected Heaven to be clean, tidy and predominantly white. He pinched himself to check if he was awake. He glanced in the mirror again. Yes. It was him.

A scratching sound erupted from outside of his bedroom door and Spence's heart missed a beat. Several beats, in fact. More beats than Ringo Starr missed when performing live.

'Who is it?' enquired Spence. He had meant to enquire this in a butch, testosterone-filled, powerful voice. And not like the Bee Gees. He had failed.

There was no sound from outside the door now.

Spence stood up, unsteadily. He pulled his bedroom door open with more bravado than he owned. There was nobody there. Something brushed against his legs and he screamed very loudly.

And fainted.

*   *   *

'Don't try and bargain with us, Mr Dicks.' snorted Lemon.

'Well, don't play games with me.' snapped Philip Dicks.

'Games? What games?' enquired Lemon, with the voice of an angel.

Philip looked into Lemon's eyes. Deep blue crystal pools. He bathed in their glow for a second.

Hypnotised.

He snapped out of it when he felt the cold, hard steel of a gun barrel pressed against the underneath of his chin.

Lemon and Philip Dicks were no more than an inch away from each other's face. He clenched the muscles in his jaw.

'If you don't tell us what you've done with the parcel, then you die.' breathed Lemon, into the face that was so close to her own.

'I haven't got it.' hissed Philip Dicks. He could see his own reflection in the sparkling lakes of Lemon's eyes.

'I grow tired of this.' whispered Lemon, her hot, sweet breath washing over her captor's senses. He felt the barrel push harder into his skin. 'We have checked your mail. We have monitored your mail. We have controlled your mail. You received no parcel.'

Philip allowed a smirk to flicker across his face. God, she was beautiful.

Lemon smiled.

Philip leant forward that final inch to snatch a kiss from a pair of seductive alien lips. It was as if everything was happening in slow motion. It was the last thing he did.

He died with her shimmering face imprinted on his brain, a split second away from that elusive kiss.

Lemon licked her wet lips and her face felt warm.

Warm with fresh blood.

*   *   *

Spence's ceiling seemed a long way away and very, very unfocused. He could just about make out his light bulb. And then it all became very clear. His breathing sped up as he un-fainted.

Eric, his cat, was licking his face. A trickle of fresh blood was seeping from where his cheek had connected with the harder edge of his bedside table.

'Eric, you bugger!! You scared the pants off me.' he sighed, stroking his aged moggy. 'Don't ever scratch at my door again.' he added, as Eric sauntered off.

It was a futile command and one that Eric wouldn't obey. The frayed carpet around Spence's doorframe was proof of that.

Spence took a few deep breaths and his head throbbed. He clambered up his bed and stood up straight. His back hurt. He had a friction burn on his knee. But, his cheek had stopped bleeding, thanks to Eric's healing tongue. And then the phone rang.

His answer-machine clicked into action.

'Hello, this is Spencer Tracy and don't even think of making a joke. Sorry I'm not in at the moment, I'm probably waiting to see who you are. Please leave a message and vital statistics after the irritating snatch of Tchaikovsky's *Romeo And Juliet* and, of course, the tone... cue music...'

The music played.

The tone toned.

A pretty voice spoke.

'Hello, Spencer - it's Jody. Pick up the phone.'

Spence grimaced with pain as he tried to hurry out of the bedroom.

'Pick up the phone, Spence.'

He made a meal of getting down his flight of stairs.

'I know you're listening, Spence.'

He tripped over the sleeping form of curled-up Eric.

'Oh, you arse. Ring me back now.'

Spence dived for the receiver and missed.

'Bye.'

He was successful at the second attempt.

Click....

Hmmmmmmmmmmmmmmmmmmmmm.

21

'Hello? Hello? Jode?!' huffed Spencer.

He heard the dialling tone and punched her number into his novelty phone. It was the shape of a pineapple. And the novelty was that he ever used it. The few guests he ever had were somewhat surprised, originally, to see a pineapple hooked up to an answer-machine. It was a damned realistic novelty phone. Spence hated the telephone and had steadfastly failed to move with the times. That's why he had bought an answer-machine instead of a mobile.

This was a mistake.

It meant he had to use it twice as much now, ringing back all the people that left messages. He used to just ignore the phone ringing. Now, he couldn't. It caused him a lot of grief, especially as he couldn't resist listening to it whenever someone left a message - just incase he wanted to speak to them. Then, it was a game of *'Catch The Caller'* and he usually ended up on the losing side.

Spence waited patiently as Jody's phone rang. He knew she would now take ages to pick it up, on purpose. Finally her voice came on the line.

'Hello, Jody. It's Spence. You just rang. What did you want?'

'Money.'

'And...'

'I wondered if you wanted to come over for Sunday lunch.'

'Why?'

'Oh, well, if *that's* your attitude...'

'No, no - I'd love to.'

'See you at 12.30, then. Now, sod off.'

'And goodbye to you too, sweetie.'

Spence put the slice of pineapple back to make it whole. He rubbed his face and considered a shave. It was only Jody he was seeing. No need.

So, he made his way back up the stairs, stopping momentarily to apologise to Eric, who was still looking cheesed off with being used as a football. Spence stroked him a couple of times and told him in soothing tones:

'Never get in my way when I'm running for the phone, you huge bag of dirty fur!'

Eric retaliated by attacking Spence's hand with teeth and claws. This was Eric's way of showing affection. It was also Eric's way of showing who was the Master in their volatile relationship.

Jody Marianne Lane, the disgruntled telephone caller, was a quite stunning individual. She was raven-haired, pocket-sized (but perfectly formed), and fiercely intelligent. In short, she was exactly the sort of woman that would steer well clear of Spencer Tracy.

She had met him at Oxford University, where she was studying Philosophy. He, on the other hand, was visiting a cousin who happened to be her flat-mate.

Spence had never gone to University - he preferred the University of Life (and he hadn't achieved very good grades there, either). Oddly, they'd hit it off instantly.

Opposites attract, so they say. Often, in disbelief, whilst desperately trying to find some sane reason for the coupling they're talking about.

Jody and Spence had been together, in what most friends called a seriously *un*steady relationship, for five years.

Then, they'd split up.

Spence was trying to work his way up from a Data Input Operator and Jody was trying to talk her way out of a top job with the Ministry of Defence. She lived in a house that was five minutes walk from Spence's house, purely by accident.

They hadn't really kept in touch for a couple of years after they had split up. Then, they'd bumped into each other in the local park.

And, from then on, they saw a lot of each other.

Spence didn't want to spoil their friendship with another relationship attempt and nor did Jody. So, they just slept with each other instead.

Spence dressed in a hurry. And it showed.

He slipped into a pair of checked trousers, buckled up his belt to try and hide his stomach, spent an age deciding whether to leave his white, grubby T-shirt un-tucked (finally deciding to tuck it in), and searched his room for his trusty black overcoat, which he'd purchased from auction when a local Theatrical Costumiers had gone bankrupt. He cursed himself for not buying a new pair of laces for his boots (both laces had snapped months ago and he was three 'eyes' short of comfortably keeping them on his feet) but wore them nevertheless.

He stood before the full-length mirror, hoping to have all the panache and elegance of an 18th Century gentleman.

Sadly, he had all the panache and elegance of a 21st Century scruff.

The clock said: 11.17am.

And then Lemon came back to him again.

Once more he was looking down a revolver and being shot. It had been one hell of a realistic nightmare. And that's all it could have been.

A nightmare.

He sloped out of his bedroom and down the stairs - taking care to avoid Eric, who had decided to test Spence by falling asleep on the fifth step up from the bottom of the stairs - to the kitchen. He made for the refrigerator and swung it open.

Sure enough, inside - amongst the other dairy products - was the carton of semi-skimmed milk that he'd purchased yesterday. It showed all the signs of being caught in a downpour as the colours had run and it was in danger of releasing its contents. His brain did back-flips and failed to dismount properly.

It had all been so... well... *real*.

He picked up a banana and unzipped the skin. He went through yesterday's post.

There was a British Telecom telephone bill (final demand), the South West Gas bill (final demand), the rent for the house (final demand), a letter from Auntie Nancy (the postmark said it had been posted three weeks ago but the unreadable hand-writing had baffled the Post Office so much that they'd hired a Calligraphy expert to decipher the address), a Reader's Digest envelope (suggesting that he open it 'URGENTLY' and he could, in all likelihood, win the best part of £20,000 - give or take £20,000 - but he'd *definitely* be entitled to the free gift of a toaster... if he purchased £25 of merchandise from the catalogue enclosed within a week of opening it), and a parcel bearing his address *but* for the attention of a Mr Philip Dicks.

Nothing too interesting, then. He threw the post back across the top of the breakfast table.

*   *   *

'He did *what*?!!' screamed Lemon.

'He posted it to himself.' stammered Suzanne Addison.

'So, why didn't we know about it?' hissed Lemon, from behind her protective ring of flickering computer screens. Suzanne's heart was speeding up to a crescendo.

'Lord Pembridge monitored the out-going post. We monitored the in-coming.'

'I know.' snapped Lemon.

'He addressed it to himself but used a different house.' explained Suzanne, sweat trickling down her spine. 'Lord Pembridge found out the address and picked up the man who rents the house.'

'I know.' said Lemon, realising her mistake.

'But, it wasn't Philip Dicks.' said Suzanne.

'I know.' repeated Lemon.

'Oh.' was all Suzanne could muster in reply.

'You can go.' said Lemon, her voice barely audible against the humming of her precious computers.

Suzanne Addison didn't need to be told twice. The quicker she could get back upstairs to the offices in The Manning Estate, the safer she felt.

Lemon sat in relative silence and contemplated.

Lord Pembridge had patched through to her computers an address when he had picked Spencer Tracy up. She had found out who this person was, knew it wasn't the address of Philip Dicks - which she had been closely monitoring - and shot Lord Pembridge for his incompetence.

Wrong move.

Then, fired a shot at Spencer Tracy, which had missed him. This was a deliberate action. From what Lemon had seen of her accidental captive, she knew he would faint at the sound of another gun-shot... especially when the barrel was pointed at his head. There was no point killing a innocent nobody, who probably had a special somebody that would miss him and alert the Police. He had then been discreetly returned to his home.

Another wrong move.

Spencer Tracy was obviously not as innocent as his read-out had shown her. He must have been connected with Philip Dicks.

But how?

She needed that computer disk before it got back to Delgado. It was imperative. If Delgado and the M.o.D. got their hands on the disk, her whole operation would go up in smoke.

She tossed her fair-hair off her face and stared at the closest computer screen. Technology was never wrong.

Was it?

*   *   *

Spence scrambled for the post again. Mr Philip Dicks? He recognised that name. It rang a distant bell in the cloisters of his memory. But where had he heard it before? Perhaps it was the last person who'd rented the house? After all, he'd only been residing in it for a year. He turned the parcel over and over in his hands, almost willing it to speak to him.

Needless to say, it didn't.

Eric began to 'miaow' from the direction of the stairs. Spence ambled out of the kitchen to see if he was okay.

He was asleep.

Spence had a feeling that Eric did this on purpose, just to annoy him. And it worked *every* time. He stroked Eric half-heartedly and decided to get to Jody's house early for once. And she'd give him a decent reason for opening the parcel. He had considered opening it himself for a second but knew the guilt would eventually consume him if he had.

Plus, Jody had a better kettle than he had, one that produced more steam. He threw the empty banana skin in the general direction of the bin and checked his pocket for his house-keys. He decided to let Eric continue his nap as he opened the front door and stepped out into Mulberry Road.

The sun was shining but was as weak as Spence's willpower. Murky clouds were gathering for some kind of general meeting in the sky and a chill wind whipped the trees into a frenzied hoedown. He fiddled with the buttons on his overcoat (discovering that he'd lost another two after the incident with the Tesco shopping trolley), did it up as best he could, and set off for the main road.

Sunday was the only day you *wouldn't* see Mr Arthur Plinth (next-door neighbour and beloved leader of the Neighbourhood Watch) watching the world of Mulberry Road pass by from his front window.

Sunday was God's day. And Mr Arthur Plinth was a religious man.

Well, religious in the sense that he religiously watched the horse racing every Sunday on the television. He wasn't adverse to a 'little flutter'. And he wasn't adverse to losing the majority of his 'little flutters'.

Spencer Tracy glanced at the front window of No.169 and saw no sign of his next-door neighbour. He vaguely recalled Mr Arthur Plinth being in his nightmare.

Another flashback.

Spence took a deep breath and concentrated on the concrete path. He narrowly avoided colliding with a streetlight.

*   *   *

Lee Morgan drove an Aston Martin. Somebody else's Aston Martin.

The lock of an Aston Martin was child's play to an experienced crook. Lee cheerfully broke the 40mph speed limit and shot over the red light at the crossroads. A flash of the Speed Camera glared twice at the car as he passed it. Lee laughed. He wouldn't be the one receiving the fine. He screwed up the fax from Lemon and lit it with the dashboard lighter. It burnt quickly, as each flame competed with the other to win the race towards Lee's fingers. As they got within sight of their goal, he flicked the paper out of the window and watched it flutter and separate in the wind. In a matter of seconds he had left it far behind.

He swerved to avoid a cyclist and missed the turning to Mulberry Road. One handbrake turn and a startled cyclist heading for a hedge corrected his mistake. He decreased the speed of the Aston Martin and pulled up three houses short of No.171.

Fumbling around in the glove compartment, he discovered a couple of unwrapped cigars. He usually smoked roll-ups but... well, a cigar or two wouldn't hurt. He chewed on the end of one and pocketed the rest. Using his own lighter this time, he made the cigar end glow a fiery red for a second and then took a huge drag.

The smoke wafted around his mouth and little wisps escaped down his throat and out of his nostrils. The nicotine shot through his bloodstream like a knife through butter. He kicked open the door and stepped out into the grim cul-de-sac. He hated town houses. He'd been brought up in one. A horrible two-up, two-down. He blew smoke rings into the wind and watched as they were torn apart.

*   *   *

'Bloody fast cars.' muttered Spence, as an Aston Martin ran over a red light and tore across the semi-deserted crossroads.

Two other cars braked hard, screeching to a halt, and probably used more colourful adjectives than the scruffy pedestrian.

Spence turned right at the traffic lights and headed up into Hillview Estate. Another 30 seconds and he was standing at Jody's front door.

He rang the bell.

The door opened before the last electronic peals faded away.

'You're early.' muttered Jody, glancing at her watch.

'And not for the first time.' chuckled Spence, winking. Jody forgot to laugh at his joke. After all, it was the 78th time she'd heard it. And it hadn't been funny the first time.

She turned and walked back up the hall, into her kitchen. Spence stepped off the drive and into her house. He closed the door and wondered how many times he had closed that particular door.

Quite a lot.

It was the sort of useless thinking that Spencer's brain mused over.

Quite a lot.

'Are you vegetarian this week?!' shouted a voice from the kitchen.

'Meaning what?' shouted back Spence, sauntering in the general direction of the kitchen. He left the parcel he was carrying on the little table that seated the telephone.

Even though he felt at home with Jody, there was always that couple of minutes of politeness, that couple of minutes of awkwardness, that couple of minutes of intense nervousness before the friendship rhythm kicked in. Perhaps it was sexual tension. Perhaps it was sexual anticipation. Perhaps it was sexual desperation. Whatever it was, in Spence's mind, it *had* to be sexual. He reached the kitchen as Jody answered his question.

'Well, do you want traditional Sunday lunch or vegetarian Sunday lunch?'

'Do I have a choice?' asked Spence, leaning casually against the doorframe.

'No.' was Jody's matter-of-fact reply. Spence stopped leaning casually on the doorframe.

'Oh.'

'I'm doing a Nut Loaf.' explained Jody.

'Whatever turns you on.'

'Did you bring any wine?' asked Jody, shutting the oven door and throwing the oven gloves in the direction of the cutlery draw. She looked at Spencer's empty hands.

Spence shrugged apologetically.

'You *never* bring any wine.' frowned Jody.

'Then, why bother asking?'

'To prove to myself that all men are selfish, unthinking, incapable automatons.'

'Glad to be of service.'

'Have you ever bought a bottle of wine in your life, Spence?'

'Yes.'

'When?'

'When I said "Yes", I meant "No".' muttered Spencer.

Jody half-smiled.

'I hate you. D'you know this?' she teased.

Spence nodded, with a smirk creeping across his face.

'In my opinion, people who don't bring wine when coming for a meal, should be taken outside, lined up against a wall, and shot.' Jody continued.

Her world view was somewhat governed by the fact that she was a lover of the squashed, fermented and corked grape-in-a-bottle-juice.

'Oh, you want me to explain?!' Lemon realised.
'It would help.' muttered Spence.
'I don't think it would.' said Lemon, her smile vanishing. She picked up the revolver and shot Spence.

Spence heard the shot again and again, echoing around the empty cavities in his brain. The colour drained from his face. His mouth became dry. His eyes stared through Jody.

This unnerved her.

'What's the matter?' she asked, 'Spence, you don't look too good.' she added, with genuine concern. Spence snapped out of it.

'I was born that way.' he quipped. It was a pathetic attempt to appear at ease again. The colour returned to his cheeks, in glorious monochrome.

'Do you feel okay?' asked Jody, walking over to her dinner guest and brushing his fringe out of his brown eyes. She looked into his Chocolate Button-like orbs, trying to figure him out. Spence attempted a smile. He grimaced instead.

'Go and sit down.' ordered Jody, steering him out of the kitchen and into her spacious dining room. He took the weight off his legs with relief, as he perched on one of the matching chairs that surrounded the dinner table like a cordon of soldiers.

'I'm all right, Jode. Honestly.' said Spence.

Jody looked at him quizzically. He attempted another smile.

Success.

Jody was half-convinced.

'Just go and see to lunch.' he added.

'Are you sure?'

'I'm fine. I just felt a bit faint, that's all. I didn't eat breakfast.' lied Spence.

*   *   *

Lee Morgan took a last long pull on the cigar and cast it asunder. He took out a bunch of keys from his pocket. After the fifth try, he found the right one.

The door to 171 opened with ease.

A fat, scruffy cat shot out of the door as it opened and cannoned through Lee Morgan's legs. He made an attempt to kick it.

And missed.

He glanced inside the house. He knew there was nobody home.

He'd rung from the car-phone that came as a complimentary item with the Aston Martin.

An answer-machine had answered.

He'd knocked on the front door several times.

Nobody had answered.

There were two full milk bottles in a small, replica crate by the side of the doorstep.

To be honest, Lee Morgan didn't much care if there was anyone home or not. He'd have been happier if there had been. He liked the sound of someone's nose breaking. The satisfying crunch of splintering bone sent shivers down his spine and rocketed his adrenaline into temporal orbit.

He was an all-round bad egg. With salmonella included.

He stepped inside the rented abode and slammed the door shut. The entire glass portion of the panelling shook alarmingly. He knew what he was looking for and set about his search immediately. He began to turn the house upside down.

Figuratively speaking, of course.

CHAPTER 3
'FIRE-STARTER'

Spencer Tracy was feeling much better. Two tumblers of Jack Daniels had seen to that. It was always a good idea to have a drink before your Sunday lunch, especially if cooked by Jody. Cooking wasn't Jody's strong point. She was to cooking what Delia Smith was to Karate. Spence didn't mind. He could eat anything. Any food was good food, as far as he was concerned.

Whilst the food was cooking away, Spence and Jody had sat and drank. They hadn't really talked much. The radio was on and that had distracted them enough. Spence was in need of a cup of tea. He didn't mind whiskey, in large or small quantities, but he craved tea. He suddenly realised that he hadn't actually had a cup of tea yet.

And this was Sunday.

This was the one day in which he drank a lot of tea, usually.

And it was now 12.18pm.

It was Sunday afternoon and he had yet to consume his first cup of tea of the day. This, in Spence's eyes, was a grave mistake.

'I'm going to make a pot of tea.' said Spence, standing up.

'What for?' asked Jody. Spence had broken her concentration. She lost the thread of Desert Island Discs and now probably wouldn't know the reason behind Tom Baker's choice of "I'm Going To Spend My Christmas With A Dalek".

'To drink.' replied Spence.

'Can't you wait until after dinner?'

'Not really.'

'Spence.' warned Jody.

'Okay, okay. I'll wait.' grumbled Spence.

'What *is* the matter with you?'

'Nothing.'

'You're such a grumpy sod today. Anyone would think you had actually had something interesting to moan about.' scoffed Jody.

Spence didn't reply.

'So,' Jody continued, 'Are you going to ask me how my interview went?'

'What interview?'

'The internal one.'

'What?'

'I told you a couple of days ago. Dad's trying to get me out of one section of the Ministry and into a so-called 'easier' section. I think he just wants me behind a desk, out of harms way. I can't see why he's bothered. I'm perfectly happy where I am.' said Jody.

Spence half-listened.

He'd heard enough about the Ministry of Defence to last him a lifetime. He could probably make a pretty tidy packet from certain tabloid newspapers. The amount of stuff she told him was ludicrous. He was sure she told him because he wasn't interested. As soon as he heard anything about the Ministry, he'd store it in the 'Recycle Bin' section of his memory, which then would be deleted at the end of every day.

'So, I presume you didn't accept/take/were given the job – delete where applicable.' muttered Spence, trying to appear interested, if only for the sake of keeping Jody in a good mood. After all, he was intending *some* kind of recreational exercise that afternoon.

'I refused it.' said Jody, triumphantly.

Spence knew she was proud of this. Unfortunately, he didn't know why.

He wished more of his time had been spent actually listening to her previous conversations and made a mental note to press the restore button when going into the 'Recycle Bin' at the end of every evening.

'Congratulations.' smiled Spence, weakly.

'God, you're a moody bugger.'

'Sorry.'

'You will be.'

'No, seriously. I'm sorry.'

'Okay, apologies accepted.' said Jody, ruffling Spence's hair, as if he was a little child. Mentally, that wasn't far off the truth.

'And I suppose you're now going to ask me how my promotion aspirations are faring?' muttered Spence.

'No.'

'Good.'

'I'll go and get the dinner.' said Jody, getting up to leave.

'I was passed over again.' muttered Spence.

Jody made a split-second decision. She could either sit down, let Spence pour out all of his angst - most of it brought on, it was only fair to say, by his inherent laziness and cynical outlook, or go and check on dinner.

She went to check on the dinner.

Spence's head hung low. He was seeing if he could touch the tabletop with his fringe. Why, he didn't know. It was something to do.

His mind flashed back to the nightmare. The room he was in metamorphosed into a cellar. He stood up, his heart racing, and the cellar became a room again. This was seriously freaking him out. It was so real that it felt surreal.

He rubbed his hands down his trousers to wipe off the sweat from his clammy palms. He walked over to the patio doors and stared out at the garden. There was nothing interesting to look at. A garden was a garden to him. Sure, it was beautiful and tranquil but he just couldn't get motivated about one. He glanced to the side and caught his reflection in the pane of double-strength glass that made up one of the patio doors. He didn't look good. So, he strolled over to the bookcase and perused the titles. He knew most of them off by heart. He'd *bought* most of them.

And there was the photo in the frame.

Him and Jody.

They had their heads pressed together, slightly off-centre framing due to holding the camera at arm's length in order to take the picture of themselves, with smiles as wide as the Watford Gap. It was as infectious as measles. He grinned. And his stomach turned over.

God, he loved her. And he knew she loved him. But, there was no way they could start again. Too much water under the bridge. It was Niagara-bloody-Falls.

'It's fine.'

Spence spun round. 'What is?' he gasped.

'The dinner. It's fine'. said Jody.

'Good. Excellent. Great.' stuttered Spence, moving away from the bookcase. Jody moved towards him. They met somewhere in the centre of the room and hugged; squeezing the breath out of each other. They looked like the two wrestling champions of the world, in a stalemate situation.

They did this sometimes, for no reason other than they could. It was like they needed to connect or they'd drift too far apart. It was weird. But, it worked.

And that was all that mattered.

'I needed that.' said Spence, as they released their vice-like grip on each other's torso.

He felt alive again. Refreshed. Like he'd *really* woken up and found everything was okay with the Earth today. Jody smiled.

They sat down on the sofa and cuddled close.

The sounds of BBC Radio Four wafted around the room like a pungent scent. Tom Baker had chosen a Gregorian chant as his final song on Desert Island Discs.

*   *   *

Lee Morgan had ransacked the whole of the downstairs and had found nothing. He was, to put it mildly, cheesed off. He sat on the first step of the stairs and rolled up a cigarette. Half the tobacco ended up on the carpet and disappeared.

Camouflage. The carpet was the same colour. Very nice.

He fumbled in his pockets for a lighter, and found nothing. This was getting to be a habit. He cursed loudly and ambled into the kitchen, turned the grill on, and lit his cigarette from there. He very nearly lost his eyebrows. Still, it was lit. He sucked deeply. It began to calm him down.

Lee Morgan wasn't the most relaxed of men. He was as highly-strung as a tennis racket. If somebody had tried to massage him at this point, they would've broken their fingers. Or *he* would've. He leant against the work surface and his elbow rested on the pineapple. It clicked into action.

Beeeep...

'Spencer, this is Stuart... Stuart Rix. Got a poetry gig lined up on... um... the 8th of this month. At The Toad & Toucan. Excellent if you could be there. Brilliant. Give me a ring. See you soon. Right.... er... bye!'

Beeeep...

'Hello, Spencer - it's Jody. Pick up the phone... Pick up the phone, Spence. I know you're listening, Spence... Oh, you arse. Ring me back, now. Bye.'

Beeeep... Be-beep.

The tape rewound itself.

Lee Morgan hastily jotted down the messages. Not for Spencer, obviously. The number of crooks that clean you out, but also check your answer-machine messages for you and leave a note, was pretty low.

Lee Morgan pocketed the note, thinking it might be of some vague interest to his employer. He then picked up the pineapple and threw it at the far wall, ripping the plug out of the socket in the process.

It shattered.

Well, after all, it was only a cheap novelty item. It certainly wasn't built to last. And nowhere in the manufacturer's brief did it say: 'Must be able to withstand walls'. It was a mindless act of vandalism on Lee Morgan's part. And it made him very happy.

He picked a ripe apple from the fruit bowl and bit into it with all the venom of a snake. Mingled with the taste of cigarette smoke, surprisingly it didn't taste that nice. He threw that in the same direction as the fake pineapple. It splattered spectacularly and showered him with tiny chunks of Golden Delicious. This had not been his intention. And it made him less happy.

He cursed, for - at a rough estimate - the 89th time that day, and made his way out of the kitchen and up the stairs. He stubbed his cigarette out on the banister in frustration.

This was slowly turning into a search. He had figured it would be a smash-and-grab. He hated searches. It meant having to actually... well... search. And he had better things to do. He couldn't think of any at the 'better things' at that precise moment, but he knew there *were* better things he had to do. Anything was infinitely more pleasurable than searching through this rubbish-tip of a house.

The door to Spencer Tracy's room was slightly ajar and Lee Morgan kicked it open with such ferocity and power that one of the hinges gave up on life. The door tilted, as if under the influence of alcohol. He spotted a cricket bat nestling in one corner, with a pair of grass-stained white trousers hanging off the handle. His eyes gleamed. He could do some *serious* damage to the room with a cricket bat.

And this made him happy again.

*   *   *

'This is a really pointless conversation.' laughed Spence, not realising the irony in his sentence. Every conversation between him and Jody was a pointless conversation. In fact, if they ever found a point, it would be sandpapered, filed, varnished and smoothed out to nothing by the time they reached it. Spence half-heartedly hit Jody with the closest cushion he could find. Jody retaliated with a neighbouring cushion.

'You have just described every conversation I've ever had with you!'

'True! Oh, so true!' said Spence, melodramatically falling to the floor. He was showered with cushioned blows.

'Cease this punishment!' cried Spence, in his best mock-Roman Emperor voice. He snatched the cushion off Jody and wrestled her to the floor, tickling her sides.

'Have you heard of a knee-jerk reaction?' cried Jody, suppressing her giggling squeals.

Spence shook his head and carried on torturing his feeble captive.

'I have the knee,' explained Jody, pointing to her knee. 'You are the jerk' she continued, 'And *this* is the reaction...' she finished, kneeing Spence in the stomach.

He doubled up and fell off her.

She pounced.

The captor became the captive.

It was a move of athletic precision. The Ministry of Defence had not trained her to be a Tea-Lady, unless all M.o.D Tea Ladies had a black belt in Martial Arts.

'I submit, I submit!' submitted Spence, winded slightly from the surprise attack. He kept forgetting that Jody was so competitive. A simple childish fight turned into a full-blown competition. One day he'd learn Karate too. One day he'd beat Jody. One day he'd discover the whereabouts of the lost city of Atlantis.

'I win.' smiled Jody, helping him up off the floor.

'Haven't you ever heard of a tactical retreat?'

'You didn't retreat, you gave up.' scoffed Jody. Spence began to regain regular breathing.

'I didn't give up. I retreated, to fight another day.' explained Spence, flopping back down on to the sofa.

Jody grinned a knowing grin. Her hands were on her hips, her legs apart, and Spence had an unnerving image of Wonder Woman. It was quite a nice unnerving image. Jody tossed her raven tresses back off her face and licked her lips.

Spence crossed his legs.

'I'd better go and check on dinner again.' said Jody.

'Yeah, do that.' nodded Spence, folding his arms and trying to look nonchalant. His Inner Caveman told him to sling her over his shoulder and carry her to the nearest cave. His hot-blooded male instincts told him not to bother carrying her anywhere. His sensitive, caring, understanding instincts had a bucket of cold water handy.

Jody walked out of the room, unharmed, for the time being. He was sure he could smell burning. And it wasn't him.

'Oh, my God!' shouted Jody, from the kitchen.

42

Spence uncrossed his legs and waddled to the kitchen. Smoke was billowing out of the kitchen and into the hall. Spence brushed the swirls of grey away from him and peered into the smog. He saw the oven door open, Jody wearing a pair of oven-gloves, and a tray of smoking, charred remnants that in no way resembled Nut Loaf.

Jody despairing looked at him with all the innocence of a small child with a mouth covered in chocolate.

'Slightly overcooked.' was Spence's verdict.

She coughed in reply.

*   *   *

The bedroom was now - officially - a wreck.

Lee Morgan stood panting, brandishing the cricket bat in the same way as an ancient warrior brandished a bloodstained sword. He was grinning in a slightly manic air and his eyes were so enlarged that his eyelids were having trouble keeping them in their sockets.

He still hadn't found the package yet but was finally enjoying the search. He charged across the landing to the bathroom. It took him less than a minute to demolish that. He made a point of smashing the tiles along the wall too. Just incase the package was hidden behind them, of course. There was method in his madness.

Or was that the other way round?

He brushed the sweat off his forehead with the back of his wrist and wiped it down the front of his shirt. He liked sweating. Proper work required sweating.

And he was good at sweating. His body odour was proof of that.

He put a huge dent in the bathroom door with another gigantic swing. This was more like it.

One more room to go.

He lurched into it. It was a sort of study. It would soon be a sort of mess. Gleefully, he took note of an expensive PC, an expensive stereo, and an expensive Home Cinema system.

He hoped it was insured.

Nah, he didn't.

$*$ $*$ $*$

'Haven't you got a fire alarm?' asked Spence, opening the kitchen window as wide as he could.

Jody kicked the oven door shut and plonked the tray of what-once-was Nut Loaf into the sink.

'Yes. Of course.' smarted Jody, turning on the tap. As the torrent of water hit the charred remains of Sunday dinner it sent more reams of smoke billowing into the atmosphere. 'It's just that I could never be bothered to buy any batteries.' she added.

Even the vegetables had boiled dry.

And she'd forgotten to put the roast potatoes in. A tray of them sat, looking slightly embarrassed, on the kitchen table.

Spence noticed this.

'You've forgotten to put the roast potatoes in.' said Spence, picking them up and juggling with them.

Jody started to look as frazzled as her Nut Loaf.

'I know.' she hissed, 'There's no need to remind me.'

'We could order a pizza.'

'On a Sunday?'

'Sure... I know the number.' smiled the deeply concentrating Spence, losing control of the air-born potatoes and letting them fly off to different directions of the kitchen.

'Be free, my beauties!' he cried, watching them hit the floor and bounce quite spectacularly.

He stood up.

'I could use a bit of sympathy.' muttered a disgruntled Jody, wrenching the tap to shut the flow of water off.

'And I could use a bit of pizza.' replied Spence, strolling back into the hall.

He went to the little table, bought specifically for the telephone, and picked up the receiver.

He dialled Pacino's-Dial-An-Italian-Pizza, from memory, and waited for the cod Italian accent that would undoubtedly answer.

'Pacino's. Whatta can I do-a for you, senor?'

The Italian accent had a hint of West Midlands about it.

'One Family Meal Deal.' said Spence.

'One-a-Fameel-Meal Deal, coming-a right up.' said the pathetic accent.

'Thanks.'

'Whatta flavour pizza, you want-a?'

Spence caught sight of the package he'd brought round to Jody's house.

It was addressed to Philip Dicks. He knew this.

Suddenly, he heard voices. One was pure silk, the other was his...

'We meet at last, Mr Dicks. Or may I call you Philip?'
'You can, but it's not my name.'
'Of course it isn't. Of course it isn't.'

'Whatta flavour pizza, you want, mate?'

'What? Sorry?'

'Listen, just tell me a flavour, right?' said the now distinctly Brummie voice.

45

'Er, whatever. You choose. Just deliver it to 4 Noakes Road, Hillview Estate.'

Spence slammed the phone down and gripped the table. His legs had gone distinctly Strawberry Jelly-like.

He turned the parcel over to read the name again.

It *was* Philip Dicks.

But, it was Spence's address...

'Philip Dicks is the man we wanted. You are not him.'

'How long are they going to be, Spence?' said Jody, right in his ear.

His nerves reacted violently. He jumped violently and knocked the little table over.

It startled Jody too.

'Christ, Spencer! What the hell did you do that for?' she gasped.

'Sorry, sorry.' mumbled Spence, 'You startled me a little, that's all.'

'I wouldn't like to be around when you get startled a lot.' said Jody, picking up the table and the telephone. 'What's this?' she asked, as she stooped to recover the parcel.

She turned it over in her hands and read the label.

'It's your address.' she noted.

'I know, I know.' mumbled Spence, taking a deep breath to calm himself down.

'Who's Philip Dicks?'

'Philip Dicks is the man we wanted. You are not him.'

'Well, it's obviously not me.' snapped Spence, viciously snatching the parcel out of Jody's hands. He put it back on the telephone table.

'Why bring it round here, then?' asked Jody, suspiciously.

'I don't know.' sniffed Spence, grumpily.

'Open it.'

'I don't want to.'

'Open it.'

'You do it, if you want to so desperately.' muttered Spence, feigning a distinct lack of interest.

Jody chuckled under her breath.

'Okay. I will.'

Obviously, this was the reason Spence had brought it round. He wanted *her* to open it, to relieve him of the guilt factor.

Once it was opened, he could look at the contents, but actually opening it...

'On your head be it.' said Spence, 'I should, of course, have put it back in the post, really.' he added, fiddling with the pockets in his overcoat.

Jody took the parcel into the kitchen. She sat at the table and reached for the knife.

Spence 'casually' leaned against the doorframe. He was trying to create a distinct lack of interest.

And failing miserably.

*   *   *

It was no use.

The parcel, the package, the whatever, just wasn't there. The house was a tip.

Lee Morgan kicked the upturned armchair in frustration. This wouldn't go down to well with his Boss. She didn't appreciate failure, even if the failure wasn't his fault.

This should've been a simple job. This Spencer Tracy character was pretty clever. He'd made Lee Morgan look stupid.

And Lee Morgan hated looking stupid.

His Social Care Worker had called him 'stupid' once and he'd never let her forget it.

Well, a scar down your cheek is a constant reminder not to do it again. He'd been on remand for this little incident and it wasn't long before he became known for 'getting things done' around the neighbourhood.

He'd never killed anyone, as he did have some vague morals and ethics floating around in his poor excuse for a brain. He believed, as long as he didn't actually kill someone, then what he did was perfectly acceptable.

After all, people heal.

So, Lee Morgan had failed. He'd have to report to his Boss with empty hands.

He wasn't too happy again.

His long-departed Dad had impressed on him his own personal motto to 'Always Fight Fire With Fire' and, although this was why he was the main reason he was thrown out of the West Glamorgan Fire Brigade, he stuck by this steadfastly.

He casually lit a match and dropped it on one of the scattered cushions. It smouldered, spluttered and caught fire.

Lee Morgan walked out of the house, down Mulberry Road, into his 'borrowed' Aston Martin.

He slammed the door shut, by-passed the ignition again, and screeched off.

Two smoking tyre tracks lay parallel on the cement and were the only evidence left of Lee Morgan's visit.

CHAPTER 4
'GIMME SHELTER'

Jody had wasted no time ripping open the parcel addressed to Philip Dicks. Spence wasted no time moving from his position at the door to a more convenient position, looking over her shoulder.

At point-blank range.

It could've been a moment of nail-biting tension. It could've all happened in slow motion. It could've explained a lot of things.

But, this was real life.

Jody stuck her hand inside the package and pulled out a folded piece of paper. There was nothing else inside but a lot of bubble-wrap. She casually threw that on the floor.

Unfortunately, she didn't notice the computer disk that was wrapped so tightly in the packaging. This was probably the biggest mistake of her life - apart from that one-night stand with Anthony Truscott, of course. Someone should have told her he liked to say his own name in bed.

Weird.

Spence waited for her to open the piece of paper. She felt his breath on her neck. She took her time.

On purpose.

She felt Spence's breathing speed up. It was rather a pleasant feeling. She slowly unfolded the piece of paper.

In capitol letters, scrawled in fading blue biro, was one word…

'DELGADO'.

Nothing else.

Spence and Jody looked at this one word for longer than necessary, as if they were expecting to learn something else from it. And it obviously wasn't going to talk. Not even under extreme staring. This one word was a tough cookie.

'Delgado?' huffed Spence, proving his ability to read a word when he had to.

'Intriguing.' added Jody, thinking exactly the opposite. There was another bout of staring. Still, the one word remained true to itself. It was as silent as a particularly silent thing that had just acquired a certificate in silence from the University of Mime.

'That's it?' moaned Spence, snatching the piece of paper from Jody's grasp. He turned it over. The other side was blank.

'What was the point of that, then?' asked Jody.

'Sorry?'

'Why did you bring that parcel here, Spence?' asked Jody.

'I thought I knew the name.' muttered Spence, still waiting for the one word to crack under the pressure of the interrogatory stare.

'From where?'

'I had a... at least I *think* I had a... well, I *know* I had a...'

'Had a classic case of not being able to finish your sentence?' interrupted Jody.

'A dream. A nightmare. I don't know. Something. Anyway, I remember that name from it.' said Spence, stumbling through his memory.

'Delgado?'

'No, no. The name on the parcel. Philip Dicks.' Spence corrected.

'You had a dream about Philip Dicks and then received a parcel addressed to him.' summarised Jody. 'Do you know this man?' she asked.

'No, I didn't. And I don't. What I mean to say is... I didn't have a dream about Philip Dicks, I don't think.'

'You don't think?'

'I don't know.'

'You don't know?'

'I don't think I don't know. Oh, this is confusing me now.'

'You're confused? How do you think I feel?' scoffed Jody. She swivelled round on her stool to look at Spence, standing behind her. He was still staring at the paper.

'It all seemed so real.' muttered Spence.

'Why don't you go home, Spence? Have a lie-down. A nap. You look like you could use one. Mind you, you always look like you could use one.' said Jody.

'If I could just remember the whole thing? It keeps coming back to me in small, fractured pieces.' sighed Spence.

He folded the piece of paper and stuffed it in the back pocket of his trousers. He looked at Jody. She smiled half-heartedly. He leant down and kissed her lightly on the lips.

'I think I'd better go home.' he said, without any real conviction. His eyes seemed glazed and his mind seemed elsewhere.

Jody tried not to seem too concerned.

'Good idea.' she said, cheerfully. There was a stagnant pause.

'What is?' asked Spence, scratching his head and grimacing.

'Just go home, Spence. I'll call you tonight. See how you are.' said Jody, in the best soothing tones she could muster. Spence answered as if he hadn't heard what she had just said.

'Yeah, right. Bye, then.' he muttered.

He walked out of the kitchen. She heard the front door open and close.

Spencer Tracy had left the building.

$$* \qquad * \qquad *$$

Lemon was still waiting for Lee Morgan's report.
How long did it take to search a house?

She sat patiently inside her ring of computers. The
light from the monitors gave her face an eerie glow in the
dingy darkness of the cellar. No-one was there to see the
effect. She tuned in to the hum of the machines and let
herself be taken along with it. What was an annoying
drone to anyone else was soothing and relaxing to Lemon.
Thoughts strolled through her mind, at leisure.

Important thoughts.

Upstairs, in the centre of Manning Estate, was the
Library. Four walls decorated with books; all leather-
bound, all in alphabetical order, all brand new, all
untouched and unread.

A long, wooden, highly polished table stood in the
middle of the library. Twice the length of an ordinary,
long, wooden, highly polished table. It was the sort of
table that would have important meetings held around it.
It was the sort of table that would have enormous
banquets held on it. It was the sort of table that destroyed
Brazilian Rain Forests.

At that moment, two women were sat at the North
end of the table. One was a smartly dressed, middle-aged
executive. The other was Suzanne Addison, personal
assistant to Lemon. Not that Lemon really needed a
personal assistant. But, Suzanne Addison was a hard
worker and loyal. It was the type of job description that
made the boring work worthwhile.

'If I am to understand this,' said Suzanne, leafing
through the sturdy document that was in front of her,
'You want these terms and conditions agreed *before* your

company re-joins us?' she asked. It wasn't really a question, more of a formality. The smartly dressed, middle-aged executive closed her briefcase and nodded.

'Just a precaution.' she said, smiling at Suzanne.

'I don't think that's a problem.' said Suzanne, getting up. 'If you just stay here a moment or two, I'll get them signed now.' she added.

'Oh, there's no rush.'

'We'd rather it was dealt with swiftly.' said Suzanne, returning the earlier smile. 'Make yourself comfortable.' she added, marching from the room with the document.

The smartly dressed, middle-aged executive looked around the Library. Making oneself comfortable in a room like this was like laughing at a Charlie Chaplin film.

Impossible.

Suzanne marched forcefully until she came nearer the cellar. Her confidence seemed to fade and she assumed the poise and appearance of a nervous wreck, which was something that happened to most of the staff when appearing before Lemon. She coughed unnecessarily as she descended the cellar steps. Lemon looked up, her concentration broken, as Suzanne approached.

'A document to be signed.' said Suzanne, holding out the document. Lemon narrowed her eyes. There was a frightened pause by Suzanne Addison. Lemon didn't respond. 'I have the representative in the Library.' added Suzanne, breaking the silence.

'What do they want?' asked Lemon, her voice so mellow it was hypnotising.

'The usual. Assurances, guarantees, agreements.' said Suzanne.

'Why do they want these?' asked Lemon.

'I'm not sure. Something to do with the risks.'

'Why now? Why not at the start of our relationship?' asked Lemon. Her voice was soft. This cushioned the questioning. This didn't help Suzanne Addison. She knew she was sweating, in a cool, air-conditioned, underground cellar.

'I think they think we're taking on too much.' muttered Suzanne, realising that she was still holding the document out in front of her as her muscles began to complain. She rested her arms as she filed the document under her right arm.

Lemon slowly smiled.

Suzanne was taken in by it. It was such a beautiful smile.

'Take care of her.' said Lemon.

It was such a beautiful smile.

'And that's our answer?' asked Suzanne.

It was such a beautiful smile.

'We can do without an investment that needs answers.' sighed Lemon.

It was such a beautiful smile.

*   *   *

As Spencer Tracy came out of Hillview Estate, back on to the main road, he could see great columns of smoke emanating from behind the closest houses.

He didn't think anything of it.

Somebody was having a barbecue, perhaps.

To feed about a thousand people.

Or a bonfire.

A *massive* bonfire.

Still, it wasn't any concern of his. He had more important things to worry about. And that's what he was doing.

Worrying.

He was trying to piece together this reality-based dream he'd had, or hadn't had. There must have been some sort of plot. Or not.

There was something he had missed out. Something important. What was it?

He kicked at a loose stone in his path and it flew across the road, skidding and bounding. If he could just sit down and go through it properly. He wished he hadn't gone to see Jody after all. After that first flashback, he should have rested and thought. Resting and thinking were two actions that were alien to Spence. It had been a long time since he actually had to rest and think. That was something you were taught at school. And he'd never listened to anything they'd tried to teach him at school.

That was why he ended up as a Data Input Operator.

He stopped automatically at the place where he normally crossed the road. As he looked up he heard a wailing noise.

Sirens.

He hated sirens. They unnerved him.

He sauntered across the road, which was surprisingly quiet until his stomach rumbled louder than a hibernating Grizzly Bear who's just been disturbed by a swift boot up the backside.

It was Sunday lunchtime. Perhaps that was why it was quiet. Well, he couldn't exactly rest and think on an empty stomach. He'd order a pizza. No, he'd done that at Jody's house.

Bugger.

The sirens had got louder when two massive Fire Engines roared past, causing a considerable follow-through wind. His fringe whipped his forehead, his hair flashed through several new styles (most of them better than the one he had) - settling on a 'wild and unkempt'

55

look - and he shivered. He watched the Fire Engines turn up a side-road not to far away. The columns of smoke had obviously got out of hand. Someone had put one too many sausages on the barbecue, or poured petrol on the bonfire in an attempt to make it burn better.

There was something of a Pink Floydian glow from the street that the Fire Engines had entered. And the columns of smoke had turned into plumes. Not a good sign. The sirens had stopped though. That, at least, pleased Spence. He blew on his hands to try and get some feeling back. It was as cold as an Eskimo's codpiece. His overcoat had about as much warmth in it as a Venture Scout's fire and he was beginning to shiver.

He finally got to Mulberry Road and turned up into it. Looking up the road he saw two Fire Engines, jets of water, a huge fire and the shell of a house. He gulped.

It was his house.

Well, not his house exactly. He rented it. But, it felt like his house. It was his home.

Correction; it *had* been his home.

He found himself running up the street as if his life depended upon it. His overcoat flapped about him like Batman's cape and faces of neighbours blurred into a continuous line. They were all stood about, morbidly watching (and enjoying) his rented home burning to the ground. He brushed them aside and was caught by a big Fireman.

'Where do you think you're rushing to, sir?' he warned. 'House on fire, is it?' he added, somewhat sarcastically.

'Yes.' said Spence.

'Yes?' repeated the Fireman, letting go of Spence's midriff.

'This is my house.' gulped Spence, his eyes fixed on the not-so-towering inferno and his statement still using the word 'house' in its present tense.

'Oh.' said the Fireman, 'I'm sorry, sir. Very sorry.' he added, sincerely. Spence didn't reply. He just stared. And was stared at.

The Fireman left him alone and went to shoo away the band of spectators. Suddenly, Spence stopped staring and started to panic. He ran back to the Fireman, gripped him by the arm and swung him round to face him. It was almost choreographed.

'There wasn't... there wasn't... a... cat?' stammered Spence, failing to couple words together to make a coherent sentence.

'There wasn't a cat?' repeated the Fireman, slightly confused but able to string the sentence together rather better than Spence.

'Wasn't there?'

'Wasn't there what, sir?'

'A cat.'

'A cat, sir?'

'Inside.'

'Inside... the building?'

'Yes, yes.'

'No, sir. I don't think so.'

Spence breathed a sigh of relief. Eric must've escaped. He hoped. He didn't much like the 'I don't think so' part of the Fireman's answer. It was like in Chemistry class when Mr Edwards had said...

Mixing Copper Sulphate and Hydrochloric Acid whilst heating it over a Bunsen Burner is ineffective. Probably.

It was the 'probably' part that Spence had heard and he'd been the only one that day to keep his eyebrows.

It took three-quarters of an hour for everything to come to a smouldering finish; the last flickering flames, the last droplets of water, the paperwork and the condolences.

And then it began to rain again. Just to add some much needed irony to the proceedings.

Spence's rented abode was no more. He stood in the middle of the charred foundations, surrounded by rubble, and got wet.

Very wet.

*   *   *

Lemon had received a fax from Lee Morgan. It wasn't very appealing. She put it through the paper shredder. This seemed to satisfy her.

Still, she had a few leads from that Welsh cretin. At least he'd been thorough, if nothing else. This was turning out to be more complicated than she had wished for. This Spencer Tracy character *must* be stopped. He obviously had the parcel. He obviously was in league with the recently deceased Philip Dicks. He obviously was more devious than he had first appeared. He obviously had to be dealt with. And obviously soon.

Obviously.

She swivelled round in her chair, majestically. Facing one of her beloved monitors, she began to type. She needed to find out about Jody Marianne Lane. This was the link. A weak spot maybe. Her fingers caressed the keyboard like a lover and there was hardly any sound as she typed. The computer banks got turned on by Lemon.

And vice versa.

*   *   *

Eric jumped off the roof of the shed belonging to Mr Arthur Plinth and wife, Helen. He began to land on all fours, as all cats do. They take it for granted.

Except Eric didn't land on all fours.

He landed on his back legs and went into an improvised parachute roll. Eric was the exception to the 'all fours' rule. He'd never mastered it; never been born with it. It was something he just couldn't do. And it annoyed him. He stood out in the cat world.

If there had been cat scientists, they would've had him in for laboratory tests. Cat University lecturers would have lectured about him. Cat professors would have written papers on him. Cat bullies would have teased him at school for being 'different'. Cat Circus owners would have hired him as a novelty act. But none of this happened because, well, cats aren't human.

It wasn't as if Eric hadn't tried. He had. The trouble was that there were no correspondence courses teaching you how to do it, no teachers of the ancient art that he could take twice-weekly evening classes with, no adverts promoting an instructional DVD of '*The All Fours Theory: A New And Improved Method*', with matching bestselling book.

So, Eric just looked undignified. And he didn't do a lot of climbing. He was your basic ground level cat. Had to be.

The fire had surprised him.

Luckily, he had avoided going back into the house after Lee Morgan's arrival. He didn't fancy a kick up his ample rear end. He had mooched around, miserably.

He'd made a half-hearted attempt to catch a sparrow. The sparrow had been so surprised to escape so easily that it had flown into a fence, broke its neck, and died. Eric had made a mental note to attempt to catch sparrows half-heartedly more often. He had scanned the street for any sign of Spencer Tracy.

No luck there.

Eric marked his territory on Lee Morgan's Aston Martin. Usually he would have gone for the tyre, but this time he fancied the look of the door-handle. It was something that Lee Morgan was bound to touch.

If cats could grin from ear to furry ear, Eric would've been doing it. But, of course, they can't. Don't believe everything you read in stories. Cats don't grin, they sneer. It's akin to their general nature. Cats are surly, cunning, devious and very, very, very selfish. Not unlike a teenager. Eric was all of these and more.

He did love Spencer Tracy, though. Grudgingly.

He'd then scratched his claws along the side of the Aston Martin.

Accidentally, of course.

He knew that Mrs Beevers at No.165 kept a saucer of milk out for the hedgehogs. The hedgehogs that never came.

Eric had been drinking the milk ever since he and Spence had arrived in Mulberry Road.

Poor Mrs Beevers was convinced that the hedgehogs were living in Mulberry Road, right next to a busy main road that carried a lot of trucks, cars, motorbikes, and heavy goods vehicles. Hedgehogs, of course, love busy main roads, don't they?

Eric had made his way to Mrs Beevers' back garden. He found the saucer of milk. Full cream milk.

If there had been any hedgehogs, they would've died of cholesterol long before they died of flatness on the main road. Eric felt his arteries clenching as he lapped it up. There was also a plate of soggy bread. Mrs Beevers couldn't work out why the hedgehogs drank but never ate.

Perhaps they were Lindsay Lohan hedgehogs. Eric really appreciated Mrs Beevers' concern for wildlife.

After his daily treat, Eric had looked for a nice bush to nap under. It was whilst he was doing this that he heard the screech of tyres and smelt burnt rubber.

Lee Morgan had left.

He also smelt smoke. He made his way through the adjacent back gardens and climbed up on to the shed at No.169. It was his favourite vantage point. He spotted the fire inside his home, through the facing window. This was going to annoy Spencer Tracy, he was sure of that. That was when he had attempted to jump off the roof of the shed. Sometimes he plain forgot that the 'all fours' rule didn't apply to him.

Ouch.

If cats had osteopaths, he'd have needed one.

*   *   *

It was now 2.30pm.

Spence was starving.

He was also gasping for a cup of tea. There was not a lot else he could do here. Someone had rung his landlord, which saved him the job. He had given Jody's address to the Fireman, for them to contact him if they needed to. So, that seemed the obvious place to go back too. And the 'Family Meal Deal' would've arrived by now.

He half-jogged, half-ran back to Jody's house. She had gone out.

Typical.

He stuffed his hands in his pockets to find his set of keys. He was convinced he had Jody's back door key on it. He happened upon the piece of paper from the parcel again.

Delgado.

What did it mean? And did he really want to know? He crumpled it up, in a vain attempt to fold it, and pushed it back into his trouser pocket. At last he found his keys.

Sure enough, amongst his front door and back door key (no longer needed now), a school locker key he'd kept for posterity, a bicycle lock key for a bicycle lock that could never be cut through - not even by a oxyacetylene torch - which was of no use to him as his bicycle had been stolen years ago (complete with the lock and the railing he'd secured it to), miniature keys that he'd found on the road side and had kept for a talking point if conversation flagged, a token key-ring depicting a well-known cartoon character, and a small novelty torch fashioned in the shape of a Sonic Screwdriver - which shone out a pin-prick beam of light that was, frankly, of no use on a dark night, was the key he'd been looking for.

Jody's side-door key.

He'd had it made last week. After discreetly 'borrowing' Jody's side-door key. He'd then lost the original after the copy had been made. This meant that he was the only one with a key to her side-door. As well as anyone who happened to have picked up the lost original.

He went down the side of the house and came to the gate, which was locked.

With a padlock.

That he didn't have the key to.

So, he tried to climb over and got stuck on the pointy bits that lined the highest point of the gate. This was awkward. He didn't want to struggle too much because of the danger to the soft, fleshy, dangly bits that were worryingly close to being speared.

On the other hand, he didn't particularly fancy being stuck on top of Jody's gate until she came back home again.

And it was still raining.

Eric liked the wet. Most cats didn't. But Eric did. He was rather an outsider to the cat world. He had difficulty landing on all fours and he liked water. This was plain odd to most cats. He'd spotted Spencer Tracy in the crowd that had gathered to see the burning of home and had just sat and watched him. He didn't look very happy. Eric thought it best to keep his distance at the moment. He wondered if these humans who sprayed water for a living knew that the fire had been started deliberately.

Probably not.

And he couldn't tell them.

Well, he *could*, but they'd only think he was asking for someone to scratch him under the chin and give him a few strokes. And make stupid noises. And speak to him as if he was a six month-old baby.

So, he decided to keep quiet for now. Until he had an itch under his chin and fancied a bit of stimulation.

He followed Spencer Tracy as he walked away from Mulberry Road. It was his guess that he was going to Jody's house. He liked Jody. She ignored him, didn't attempt to stroke him, but also fed him vast amounts of food. She was a good woman in Eric's feline eyes.

So, Eric slunk along behind Spencer Tracy and crept behind the large oak tree that stood in the middle of Jody's front lawn. He watched, with amusement, as his Master attempted to climb over the side alley gate. He was obviously quite desperate to find some shelter from the rain. There was a ripping sound, a shouting in agony sound, and a sickening thump as Spencer Tracy managed to finally get past the gate obstacle.

If cats could snigger, Eric was sniggering.

CHAPTER 5
'BORN UNDER A BAD SIGN'

Spencer Tracy was wet.

Dripping wet.

He was also lying on his back and in considerable pain. His trousers were ripped in exactly the place where you really don't want trousers to rip. He had just developed a headache and he'd somehow managed to re-open the little wound on his cheek that he'd acquired from his bedside table earlier on in the day. He'd also lost his bunch of keys. He could only assume that they'd fallen from his grip when he had fallen from the gate.

This wasn't one of his best days.

Firstly, he had this irritating recurring nightmare which might or might not be true. Secondly, his home had been burnt to the ground. Thirdly, he had spectacularly dived off a seven-foot gate. Fourthly, he had mislaid the bunch of keys that would have enabled him to get inside Jody's house and, fifthly; he was being rained on. This was obviously God's punishment for a lifetime spent failing to attend regular Church services. He did, indeed, work in mysterious ways. As did Spence's egotistical cousin Lionel Dale, who the Taxman had yet to catch up with.

Spence wondered whether he could have avoided all of this by looking at his horoscope for the weekend. What would it have said?

'Sagittarius: Avoid leaving your house this weekend or having surreal dreams. Tall gates are put in your path. Don't climb over; go round. Insure your home contents due to likelihood of freak fire. Feed the cat. And, by the way, don't incur the wrath of God - go to Church for once.'

Fat chance.

He was tired, hungry, soaked and seriously fed-up. Oh, *and* he was in pain. A lot of pain.

Yippee.

He slowly and surely, and more than a little gingerly, got to his feet. The majority of his body hurt. The rest of it was numb with cold, including his brain. He leant against the wooden gate to catch his breath and several splinters embedded themselves into his buttocks. This *really* wasn't one of his better days.

'Ow, ow, ow, ow, OW!!' he cried. He ignored the splinters and scouted around for the bunch of keys. They were nowhere to be seen and had either been (a) stolen by a magpie, (b) sucked through a hole in the space/time continuum, or (c) he'd managed to drop them on the *other* side of the gate. The gate that he'd just climbed over.

Unsuccessfully.

He could feel the wind whipping around his gaping trousers. He was now angry. Well, angry wasn't really the right word.

Furious.

Bloody furious.

Bloody, bloody furious.

Bloody, bloody, bloody furious.

You get the picture.

The wooden gate was like a red rag to a bull. He took a few steps backwards, snorted, and charged at it - lowering his shoulder in the process and bracing himself for the impact.

Someone on the other side pulled the gate open.

Spence charged through the open gate, slid on the bunch of keys he had been looking for, and hit the green, plastic dustbin. This was the same green, plastic dustbin that had wheels and an inability to stay stationary when crashed into. It trundled off into the oak tree with Spence clutching on to it for dear life.

Spence hit the oak tree at the same time as the green, plastic dustbin. The green, plastic dustbin bounced off.

Spence didn't.

His only consolation was that he was knocked unconscious instantly.

Eric - Spence's old but wise cat - sauntered out from behind the oak tree to survey the crash. He saw Spence's prone figure and hopped on to the breathing torso, got comfortable, and settled down for a nap.

Jody Marianne Lane stood, her hand still on the brass handle of her wooden gate, surveying the wreckage from a distance. Out of all the possibilities she could imagine happening when opening your side gate, this was probably not in the Top Ten. It would've had trouble scraping into the Top Forty. Perhaps she was imagining it. If she screwed her eyes shut for a couple of seconds and then opened them again, perhaps it would go away.

She tried.

After the flashes of white faded when she eventually opened her eyes again and the focus facility completed the task it was designed for, the picture was still exactly the same.

Although Eric now had *his* eyes closed, dozing off on his unconscious owner's prone body, and was purring like a small engine.

Jody let go of the brass-handled gate and it swung closed, with a resounding clunk. Carefully avoiding the puddles that had formed on her drive, she made her way over to Spence. The grass was muddy and squelched underfoot. All the careful avoidance of puddles was now made redundant as her shoes were encased in thick, brown, sticky sod.

It was going to be easier for her, she reckoned, to drag Spence in through the front door - rather than drag him through the side gate, down the side alley and in through the patio doors at the back. So, she skipped across to the front door, opened it wide, and skipped back to Spence's side. He hadn't moved. She put her hands under his armpits and pulled. He was a dead weight. Well, hopefully not a *dead* weight.

Inch by inch, she dragged an unconscious man - with a fat cat still cat-napping on his torso - across her front lawn and the threshold of her house. The neighbours had all ready begun to think up some juicy rumours.

Once she got them both safely inside, she dumped Spence unceremoniously in the hall and slammed the door shut to keep out the driving rain and wind. She shook her hair and let droplets of water fly and then slipped out of her coat. She kicked off her shoes. One of them hit Eric. He left the hall in a huff and adjourned to the kitchen area, where he found some bubble-wrap and began clawing it rhythmically; making it pop like a drumstick hitting a snare in a cheap Casio keyboard type of a steady rock beat.

Jody found an elastic band and tied her wringing wet hair into the best ponytail she could manage. She knelt down by Spence, who was nicely spread-eagled and exposing his boxer shorts for the world to take notice of, and gently slapped him round the face a couple of times.

He didn't stir.

So, she slapped him harder.

It didn't take him long to wake up. Focusing on the conscious, he got an image of Jody, looking distinctly wet. His head throbbed as much as his libido.

'Oh, my *head!*' moaned Spence, groggily.

He tried to sit up and found he was on the Waltzers at the fairground.

'Oh dear.' he whispered, as he lay back down again.

Jody smiled wryly and brushed his plastered fringe off his forehead.

'What were you doing trying to force your way into my back passage?' asked Jody.

Spence was too cold and in too much pain to think of a suitable innuendo. He conjured up the closest thing to a smirk that his face would allow.

'I'll rephrase that...' sighed Jody.

'Don't bother.' whispered Spence, 'I liked it best the first time.'

'In the minority there, methinks.' quipped Jody.

'My head hurts.' grumbled Spence.

'Well, if you want to kiss an oak tree, Nature Lover, don't attempt a Glasgow kiss.' Jody advised. 'Now, just lie here a minute whilst I get you a blanket.' she added, noting the chattering teeth.

'I'd rather have a cup of tea.' muttered Spence.

'So would I.' said Jody.

'Good.'

'I'll get you a blanket and then you can join me in a cup of tea.' she soothed.

'Do you think there'll be room for both of us?' whispered Spence, slipping slowly back into a catatonic state.

*   *   *

Suzanne Addison had received some more orders from Lemon. She was good at receiving orders. She was also good at getting something done about them. This was why she worked for Lemon. She'd had orders to follow up a name.

Jody Marianne Lane.

Lemon had wanted background. And when Lemon wanted background, she knew it meant detailed - right down to whether Jody Marianne Lane had sucked a dummy as a baby or not.

She had also been told to find out the same background detail for Spencer Tracy and to cross-reference the two. As if the two of them hadn't done *enough* cross-referencing in their time.

She set to work.

Lemon expected speed. And what Lemon wanted, she got. It was as simple as that. Employees that weren't up to speed within a day or two of arriving at the Manning Estate usually left as quickly as they arrived.

In a body bag.

This was a great incentive to all the staff. Nobody quibbled, nobody argued, nobody stepped out of line. Everyone was happy in their work, happy with their pay, and happy to be of service.

Or else.

*   *   *

After about half an hour and several cups of tea, Spence's head had stopped spinning like a carousel. However, the incessant pounding from inside his cranium suggested that Animal from The Muppets had taken up residence there.

He was now sat in one of Jody's armchairs and feeling more comfortable than when he was lay in the middle of her hall. He had vaguely explained his reason behind scaling Jody's gate and she laughed. She had laughed at the simple fact that his home had been torched and all his worldly possessions had gone up in smoke.

Yes.

Laughed.

She couldn't help it.

He downed his third cup of tea and politely asked for a bed for the night; preferably the one that Jody was sleeping in. She agreed... to him sleeping in the spare bedroom.

He decided to go and have a bath. Well, Jody decided this for him. And he wasn't going to argue with his new Landlady.

Yet.

He struggled out of the chair and ambled out of the room.

'Shout if you need me.' said Jody.

'In what way?' came back Spence's reply, from halfway up the staircase.

'In a non-sexual way.'

'So, not even a scrubbing of the back type way, then?' a hopeful voice cried.

'No.' answered Jody, grinning to herself. She took the teapot and cup back into the kitchen and made a hash of trying to prize the teabags out and throw them in the bin. She caught sight of the parcel that Spence had brought round for her to open. The name on the front seemed familiar to her too. And, now she came to think about it properly, so did the name 'Delgado' which had been on the piece of paper inside.

Why?

She didn't know. Perhaps she just *thought* it jogged a memory. For Spence's sake.

As she tried to ignore these thoughts, the doorbell ding-donged. She answered it.

At the door, soaking wet from the torrential rain, stood two big, burly gentlemen. Neither of them spoke. They looked like the sort of gentlemen who would have trouble speaking anyway. One-Syllable Grunting was more their line of communication.

'Hello.' said Jody, as politely as she could.

The two men nodded their greeting, in a menacing silence.

'Can I help you?' she added, attempting to extract some sort of answer from them.

'Does Mr Tracy reside here?' grunted Big Man #1.

'Yes.' said Jody. 'Temporarily.' she added. News travelled fast, she thought.

There was a pause in the stimulating conversation.

'We'd like to have a quiet word with him.' said Big Man #1.

'Well, I'll pass on a message to him.' said Jody, not liking the tone of the statement.

'We'd like to see him in person.' said Big Man #1.

There was another pause.

'Come back tomorrow.' said Jody, closing the door. It didn't shut. A size-13 Doc Marten boot was acting as a doorstop. Jody started to worry.

'We'd rather not.' said Big Man #1.

Big Man #2 (the silent type) pushed the door open with one shove. Jody followed the movement of the door, involuntarily.

Both Big Man #1 and Big Man #2 stepped into Jody's house.

Involuntarily.

Jody stepped in front of them.

Voluntarily.

'Now hang on a minute.' snapped Jody, angrily. 'What gives you the right to barge into my house unannounced?'

She stood her ground. The answer to her question was standing in front of her, if truth be told.

Two men built like the promise of a lifetime of steroid use; broad shoulders that looked like they'd left coat hangers in their jackets, thick necks that were wider than their actual heads, huge mutant muscles, and a grim determination to carry out whatever orders they were given.

That's what gave them the right to barge into Jody's house unannounced. Still Jody stood her ground.

'We'd like to speak with Mr Tracy.' repeated Big Man #1.

'You can't.'

The two big, burly men moved towards her.

'Because he's not here.' she added.

The two big, burly men stopped moving towards her.

'He doesn't arrive until tomorrow.'

The two big, burly men turned and left.

'Did you want to leave a message?'

The two big, burly men lumbered down the drive.

'A message I could pass on?' shouted Jody.

'We'll be back.' came the faint reply. 'Tomorrow.'

'That's what I was afraid of.' muttered Jody, to herself. She shut the door and felt herself shaking. She leant back against the wall and breathed deeply.

That wasn't nice, she thought.

Calmly, she gathered herself together and walked upstairs to the bathroom. She stood at the door and listened.

Spence was whistling. He always whistled when he was in the bath. It came from an in-built fear that locks on bathroom doors weren't that safe. Spence was probably the only human being who could actually whistle out of tune. It was a knack. And it came far too naturally.

Jody knocked gently on the door.

Spence continued whistling.

Jody knocked once again - a little louder this time.

Still Spence continued whistling.

Jody got fed up with being polite and entered her bathroom. She sat on an upturned washing basket, next to the bath.

'Aha!' cried Spence, grinning in a manner that could only be described as maniacal, 'Come to rub my back have you?' he asked, coyly. He winked like someone possessed.

Jody managed half a smile. Spence stopped winking and leant over to Jody.

'What's the matter, Jode?' he asked, genuinely concerned, and genuinely dripping water all over Jody's jeans.

'You don't owe any money, do you?' she asked, looking deep into Spence's eyes.

'Only this month's rent.' grinned Spence. 'And I'm hardly likely to have to pay that now, am I?' he chuckled. He caressed Jody's face with his hand. Jody's face got wet.

'Why?' he asked. Jody looked frightened. He wasn't used to seeing Jody look frightened. Jody was Mrs Martial Arts. Nothing frightened her.

Except the sight of him, naked in a bath, perhaps.

'I had two men at the door, asking after you.' blurted out Jody.

'It's nice to know I'm wanted.' grinned Spence, relaxing back into the bath-foam.

'That's just the point,' snapped Jody. 'Are you wanted?' she asked, leaning on the edge of the bath.

'Don't be stupid.' spluttered Spence. He flicked water at Jody in a playful and suggestive manner. Jody didn't fancy playing and his manner suggested to her that he wasn't taking this seriously. She picked up the flannel from the water and threw it at him.

It hit him in the face.

'Be serious, Spence. These were big, burly men.' she snapped. Behind the flannel, Spence panicked.

He saw the image of two big, burly men bundling him into a black car. A big, black car. This was getting too weird.

He tore the flannel off his face and jumped out of the bath. Jody was covered with dirty water.

'Where's the towels?' cried Spence, standing in all his glory, dripping wet. Jody shook the wet off her - she was still wet enough from being outside and this didn't add much to her mood.

'Spencer, you idiot!' she shouted, getting up off the washing basket and shaking herself. Spence grabbed her by the shoulders.

'Where's the towels, Jode?' he asked. Jody looked up from where she was staring. It wasn't a pretty sight... and she had seen it all before.

She pointed to the rail behind him. Spence twirled round, grabbed a towel and slung it round his waist in one fluid movement. He stormed out of the bathroom. Jody was left standing there. Not knowing quite what was going on.

'Spence?!' she cried. 'Speeeeenccccee!!' she added, with a little more effect. She heard the flurry of Spence's heavy footsteps run down the stairs.

'Where have you put my clothes?!' came the shout.

Jody sighed, flicked her hair off her face and ran downstairs after Spence. She discovered him in the kitchen, hands on his hips, frowning.

'You'll have to wear some of the clothes you left here last time you stayed for the week.' she said.

Spence rushed past her and out of the kitchen.

'And they're in the spare bedroom!' she shouted, anticipating Spence's next question. She heard Spence's heavy footsteps again, thumping up her stairs. She sat down at the wooden table and watched Eric the cat play with an orange that he'd knocked out of the fruit bowl and on to the floor.

Five minutes passed.

Spence returned to the kitchen. He had changed out of his birthday suit and into a pair of baggy red and black tartan trousers and a v-neck black T-shirt. His hair was slicked back and he was rather red in the face.

'Hello again.' he puffed, sitting down opposite Jody.

'What, if I may be permitted to ask, was all that about?' asked Jody.

'That dream I had yesterday.' answered Spence.

'What about it?'

'I don't think it was a dream.'

'I know.' said Jody.

'You do?' said Spence, rather taken aback.

'Yeah. You said it was more of a nightmare.'

'No, no, no. It was real.'

'It was a real nightmare?'

'Yes. Well, no. Yes *and* no. Look, I think it happened - that's what I'm trying to say. I think it *actually* happened.' Spence said, leaning across the table.

'I think that bump on the head may have done more damage than I at first realised.' muttered Jody, raising a quizzical eyebrow. Spence kicked the orange out of the door.

Eric trotted after it.

'The two men at the door. What did they look like?'

'I don't know. Big and well-built.' said Jody. 'Why?'

'Did they look like bouncers? Bodyguards?'

'I suppose so. I don't really know. I mean, I've never met any bodyguards.' Jody paused, her eyes staring. 'Though I did go out with a bouncer once. He was big. Mmmm. In every department.' she recalled.

'Never mind about that.' snorted Spence.

'From the basement upwards.' added Jody.

'Listen, Jody - I think I'm in some sort of trouble.' said Spence, grabbing Jody's arms and gripping them a little too tightly.

Jody snapped out of her bedroom mind and brought it back to the kitchen.

'I don't know what sort of trouble and I don't know quite why I'm mixed up with it but I am.' said Spence, succinctly.

'You're living in a fantasy world.' sighed Jody.

'I know those two men that were here.' said Spence.

'Does that mean I could've let them in, then?' said Jody, perking up a bit.

'No. I think they were the two men who bundled me into a car at the start of my dream. I mean, yesterday. Real life. Yesterday.' stuttered Spence.

'This is getting beyond a joke, Spence.' said Jody. 'And you're beginning to hurt me.' she added. Spence let go of her arms and she got up from the kitchen table. She sauntered over and switched the kettle on.

It was 7.32pm.

'Look, Spence...' started Jody, popping two teabags into the teapot. 'Why don't you just rest up? You're tired, you're in shock, you've been through an emotional upheaval, you've...'

'...not believed a word I've said.' interrupted Spence.

'That's not true.' snapped Jody.

'I think I'll just go to bed.' said Spence, grumpily. He stomped up the stairs like a small child and Jody heard the spare bedroom door slam.

CHAPTER 6
'IN THE MIDNIGHT HOUR'

Spencer Tracy was dreaming of death.

It was something he regularly dreamed of and he wasn't particularly concerned about it. From his point of view, he thought it was a better idea to dream about it than actually experience it. And, as far as he knew, no-one had actually *died* from dreaming about death.

Well, not that he'd heard about.

As long as he kept dreaming about it he wasn't going to worry unduly. When he reached the grand old age of seventy and he stopped dreaming about death, *then* he could start worrying.

Mind you, he had never really thought that far ahead anyway. Reaching the ripe old age of thirty-three had been strenuous enough. He took every day as it came, as long as it didn't come too quickly. Plus, he liked dreaming. It gave him something to talk about when he woke up.

Usually to Eric, his cat, admittedly.

Still, he was never short of an anecdote about death at parties. However, he always seemed to be short of company at parties and he could never quite figure that out.

Spence had yet to learn that death as an amusing topic of conversation was not something everybody appreciated.

Apart from Eric, of course.

Eric seemed to love hearing about it. This was probably because Eric was yearning for the day when Spence keeled over and died. Not that Eric was that sadistic. Well, sort of. He just wanted to be the first cat that out-lived his human owner... by a long, long time.

Eric was, in fact, planning to live forever.

For a start, he hadn't needlessly wasted any of his nine lives yet and figured if he could stay out of trouble he would be virtually immortal. This was what Eric was dreaming about as he lay at the end of Spence's temporary bed, curled up in a furry ball, purring contentedly like a well looked-after moped.

Spence always dreamed about death, Eric always dreamed about living. Somehow they were just *right* for each other.

There was a strange squeaking sound downstairs.

Mice?

No.

A small round hole was pulled out of the kitchen window. A black-gloved hand reached inside and unlocked the lock. As you do. The window was then opened. Unfortunately, it was only a small window.

A few choice words drifted off into the night air as the squeaking sound started again.

This time a small round hole appeared in the glass of the door. The same hand felt for the bolts. It took the person on the other end of the hand at least five minutes to realise that there weren't any bolts. And the key was in the door.

Jody Marianne Lane was to security what James Bond was to monogamous relationships.

The door was opened and into the kitchen stepped Big Man #1, closely followed by Big Man #2.

The time was 12.01am.

So, technically, they had kept to their promise of returning tomorrow. Just. They were dressed all in black, with matching gloves and balaclavas. Nice.

Big Man #1 motioned to Big Man #2 to follow him and they left the kitchen to scale the stairs. Their mission was to find Spencer Tracy. Incase it was unclear.

Up the stairs they crept, on to the landing. Now they were faced with three doors. Three identical doors. Which should they choose?

A complex game of 'Eeny-Meeny-Miney-Mo' ensued and the chosen door was opened.

It was the bathroom.

Another game was employed and a second choice was tried.

It was the right one.

Eric the cat raised one lazy eye to the sound of the door opening. He expected to see Jody. She always crept into bed with Spence on the first night of him staying there, however much she'd rallied against doing so. Eric didn't recall Jody looking like two big, burly men wearing balaclavas, though.

Unless she'd brought a friend.

Kinky.

The two intruders closed the door as quietly as they had opened it and approached the bed. Eric realised this was a good time to slink off the bed and hide underneath it. Otherwise he'd be down to a meagre eight lives.

Spence was breathing deeply and muttering. He always did this in his sleep. He'd been known to have perfectly sensible conversations with people whilst he was asleep. And they were usually more interesting than his normal conversations.

The two intruders shoved a handkerchief in his mouth and slapped him round the face. Spence awoke with a start. He was being held down on his bed by Big Man #2.

To begin with, Spence thought he had died.

The first thing he saw as he came into consciousness was a balaclava-ed head with two piercing eyes boring into him. His instinctive reaction was to say...

'Hello there, Mr Death, sir!'

This would be closely followed by an ear-splitting scream.

Unfortunately, he found no sound coming from his mouth due to a fabric-like blockage. He tried to struggle but was held in a vice-like grip. Things weren't looking too good.

'You're Mr Tracy? Right?' hissed Big Man #1, from somewhere just out of view.

Spence nodded.

It seemed the sensible option. To deny anything at this stage, thought Spence, would probably result in a lot less teeth.

'The Boss wants money.' hissed the usually quiet Big Man #2.

Sadly, Big Man #2 had something of a high-pitched voice, like he'd been inhaling helium. This was probably the reason why all the talking was left to Big Man #1. There was a certain amount of menace lost when your attacker sounded vaguely like Mickey Mouse.

If Spence hadn't had a handkerchief shoved halfway down his throat, he would probably have laughed dangerously loudly

'Within a week.' added Big Man #1.

Spence was dragged out of his bed in one muscular move and slammed against the wardrobe. His feet were at least a foot off the floor and his shoulders were brushing against his ears.

Big Man #1 was now in view and wasn't a pretty sight. Looking like Big Man #2's identical twin was something that didn't exactly fill Spence with hope. And it was cold out of bed. Especially when all you were wearing was a pair of Winnie the Pooh boxer shorts.

'I'm going to take my handkerchief back.' said Big Man #1, approaching menacingly. 'I don't expect to hear a sound from you.' he added.

Spence was too scared to let out a sound, anyway. Well, out of that particular orifice, anyway.

Big Man #1 extracted a distinctly wet handkerchief from Spence's mouth. Spence was as silent as a he could be. He even breathed quietly. His arms were beginning to hurt now from where he was gripped by Big Man #2.

There was something of an embarrassing pause.

'What money would this be, exactly?' whispered Spence, risking his life.

'The money you owe to our Boss.' hissed Big Man #1, cracking his knuckles for pure effect. It actually was quite painful for him to do convincingly, due to the beginnings of arthritis, but he soldiered on in his quest to appear menacing.

'And your Boss is?' asked Spence, getting a sudden mental image of Lemon flash in front of his eyes... the silken hair, the silken voice, the silken revolver that had shot him.

'You *know* who we're working for.' growled Big Man #2, in a distinctly high-pitched fashion.

Spence giggled. He couldn't help it.

Big Man #1 got a lot nearer all of a sudden.

'What's so funny?' he said.

'Nothing! Nothing, nothing. Honestly, nothing.' Spence panted.

'I suppose you think that torching our Boss's building was amusing.' he added.

'I didn't.' said Spence, feverishly trying to recall what happened after Lemon had shot him.

Or hadn't shot him.

God, this was *really* screwing his brain about.

'It's no use denying it.' said Big Man #1. He tapped Big Man #2 on the shoulder and Spence felt the carpet underfoot and the pressure on his arms lessen considerably. Big Man #2 had put him down.

'Just pay up or else.' menaced Big Man #1.

'Or else what?' asked Spence, innocently. He realised his shoulders were still at the height of his ears and lowered them.

'Or else... erm... *things*.' said Big Man #2, in falsetto.

'Things?' echoed Spence, in falsetto.

'If you know what's good for you, you'll pay.' said Big Man #1.

'Okay, okay, I'll pay.' said Spence, feeling cold, tired and very grumpy. He turned to the bedside table. 'Cheque or cash?' he asked.

There was a confused pause.

'Um... not *now*.' mumbled Big Man #1

'What?'

'We don't want you to pay right now.'

'Why?' asked Spence, reaching for his cheque-book.

'We're just the messengers.'

'Look, I've got a debit card - it won't be any trouble. I'll write the number on the back of the cheque. Now, who shall I make it payable to?' asked Spence, searching for a pen.

'Pay the Boss.' grunted Big Man #1

'That's her name then, is it?' muttered Spence, still searching and wondering why you could never find a pen when you needed one. And, he was sure, if he found one, it would be the one that ran out after the first two words of writing.

'Her?' chorused Big Man #1 and Big Man #2, in perfect harmony.

'Look, leave it.' said Big Man #1, backing off towards the door.

'Found one!' said Spence, triumphantly. He held a pen up at his two intruders with a huge grin on his face.

They were leaving.

'Hey, hey!' barked Spence. 'Wait for the cheque.' he cried.

'Pay the Boss, not us.' came back the reply. The door closed and he could hear muffled footsteps running down the stairs. Spence threw the pen at the closed door.

'I was intending to.' he muttered. He slumped down on the bed. Eric let out a squashed 'miaow' and shot out from underneath, the space for him to lie had suddenly become a lot more compressed.

'I hope this wasn't another bad dream.' added Spence. He got back under the covers and felt Eric settle at his feet again, using his claws.

'I'm having real trouble distinguishing between what's real and what I'm dreaming.' grumbled Spence, plumping up his two pillows. He lay on them and they became as flat as a tune sung by Rex Harrison. 'Perhaps I'm being secretly experimented on by aliens.' he mused. His eyes became heavy and sleep ambushed him.

It was 12.25am.

There was another strange squeaking sound downstairs.

Mice?

Not likely.

A small round hole, not unlike the one in the kitchen window and the side door, was being pulled out of the French windows in the dining room. Another black-gloved hand was feeling for the lock and successfully finding it. The patio doors slid open.

Two bigger, burly men entered - dressed all in black, with matching gloves and balaclavas.

The first two intruders, who had just departed, had been Spence's landlord's goons. The Fire Department had informed Mr Letts (the Landlord) that his house had been burnt down in an arson attack. Mr Letts, who had never liked Spencer Tracy anyway, had assumed it was his doing. So, Mr Letts wanted money. And he wanted lots of it.

These new intruders weren't the same two big, burly men. But there wasn't much to choose between the two couples in looks alone.

However, the main difference was that these two new intruders were a lot more dangerous. They were from Lemon, with orders to kill Jody Marianne Lane and to capture Spencer Tracy. With her dead and him vanishing, the police wouldn't have to figure over the case for too long. This gave Lemon time to quiz Spence, glean the information from him, and kill him too. And to leave Jody Marianne Lane alive was to risk discovery.

This time there would be no mistakes.

Bigger Man #1 and Bigger Man #2 went through the dining room and up the stairs. The stairs creaked alarmingly this time. These new intruders weren't too concerned with stealth. They had a job to do.

Eric heard the creaking stairs and his claws dug into Spence's bare feet.

Again.

Spence awoke with a start.

Again.

He was beginning to get used to it. There was that oppressive silence that always hangs like lead in the night and nothing else.

On the landing, Bigger Man #1 and Bigger Man #2 were faced with exactly the same problem as their earlier opposite numbers.

Three doors.

Three identical doors.

They chose right first time.

Opening Spence's door wide, they found their intended victim sitting up in bed, with his arms folded and a disgruntled look on his face.

Eric did another vanishing act under the bed to preserve all of his nine lives once more. This was the most exercise he'd had in one night. And he wasn't enjoying it.

'Come back for it, have you?!.' sighed Spence, throwing off his covers.

The two new intruders looked at each other, slightly confused.

Spence swung his legs out of bed and scrambled for the pen and the cheque book.

'I'm glad you finally made up your mind.' he added, oblivious to the words 'mistaken' and 'identity'.

The two new intruders approached, to see what Spence was doing. He seemed to them to be writing a cheque.

'Look, I'll leave the thing blank and just sign it. It'll be a lot easier. I mean, we're not sure what you're Boss is called and you didn't say how much money she wanted.' he explained.

He signed his name with a flourish on the cheque and tore it out, holding it out towards the two new intruders. They both frowned.

'Hang on!' cried Spence. 'Wasn't it Lemon?' he added. 'I'm sure she was called Lemon. Yes. She introduced herself.'

By now, the two new intruders were seriously confused.

Lemon hadn't told them to accept payment from this character. Had she?

No, she hadn't.

And yet, he seemed to be convinced that was what they had come for. Perhaps there had been new developments that they weren't aware of?

Spence held out the cheque again.

'Here, take this and be off with you. I need some sleep.' he grumbled.

Bigger Man #1 accepted the cheque.

They stood there like confused statues, at the end of Spence's temporary bed.

'Now, sod off!' snapped Spence, getting back under the covers. He was getting a tiny bit agitated with the whole charade. There was hushed mumblings from the two new intruders. Spence settled down to sleep.

Eric ventured out to take a look. He was considering climbing back on the bed but he could sense trouble. There was something not quite right about the return of the two big, burly men. Something that Eric couldn't quite put his paw on.

Spence suddenly shot up out of bed and ran at the two whispering intruders.

'I mean it! Sod right off! Both of you! You've got what you were ordered to get so you can return to the big house, your beautiful Boss, and just leave me the hell alone!!.' he yelped, waving his arms about like a windmill in a hurricane.

The two new intruders were somewhat taken aback. Perhaps there really *had* been new orders? Somehow, they'd got it wrong. It could happen.

Spence planted a hand on each of them, spun them round and pushed them out on to the landing.

'Goodbye.' he said, forcefully. 'I'm sure you can find your own way out. After all, you found your own way in.' he added, sarcastically. He seemed to genuinely know what was going on.

They'd have to chance it and return to the Manning Estate. They could always come back again. Better to be safe than sorry, especially where Lemon was concerned.

They looked at each other once again, shrugged their shoulders and left.

Spence stood, exasperated, in the doorway of the spare bedroom, and watched them stroll down the stairs.

He was tired and angry - a combination that didn't endear him to many people.

Eric sauntered over to brush against his legs. It tickled. It was Eric's subtle way of telling him to go back to bed, so that Eric could curl back up into a ball at his feet.

Plus, it would give him the third opportunity in one night to dig his claws into Spence's unprotected feet in a caring and loving way.

Spence squatted and stroked Eric. He then picked him up, which he hadn't done for ages. This surprised Eric so much that he didn't even struggle.

'Back to the land of dreams!' he whispered in Eric's ear.

It deafened Eric.

When will human beings learn, thought Eric, that cat's ears are hypersensitive?

Twats.

He was carried back to the bed and placed at the end of it. Wearily, Spence climbed back under the covers, shivering slightly with the cold.

It was still raining outside and he could hear the dull thud of a thousand droplets hitting the pavement. It was quite relaxing. He plumped up his pillows again and rested his head.

Eric attempted to dig his claws into Spence's flesh but Spence moved his feet in time. Eric was too tired to mount a second attack and he settled down for the rest of the night.

Spence muttered and grumbled to himself as he tried to get comfortable. His body was throbbing from the adrenaline and the tender areas on his upper arms had now begun to blacken.

'How long does it take for a cheque to clear?' he asked, aloud.

Eric didn't answer.

'I hope they won't be too annoyed.' he added, pulling the covers up over his head.

Spencer Tracy had a bank balance of £23.64p. And he was sure that the sum written on to his cheque by this Boss person, when they received it, would exceed this limit.

Ah well, he thought, it's not the first time I've had a cheque bounce.

It certainly wasn't. If this cheque bounced it would be the 57th one.

Something of a record, in fact.

His Bank Manager had once considered ordering a cheque book made entirely of rubber for Spencer Tracy.

Seriously considered.

The day that Account Number 476532 was closed would be a day to party.

Seriously party.

It was 12.48am.

There was yet another strange squeaking but this time it came from the landing.

Was it mice this time?

No way.

Jody Marianne Lane had finally woken up. Not from the noises made by Big Man #1 or Big Man #2, or even from the noises made by Bigger Man #1 or Bigger Man #2, or even from the noises made by Spence and Eric.

No, sir.

She had been woken by the rustling of the large oak tree outside her window.

Jody was like that.

You could let off a klaxon in the same room as her when she was asleep and she wouldn't miss a wink. But, woe betide you if you breathed in the same room as her when she was asleep. She'd be awake in a matter of milliseconds.

She had got out of bed, wearing nothing more than a lengthy and considerably stretched T-shirt, and had considered going back to bed on her own or creeping in with Spence. She favoured the latter. Spence was like an old cuddly toy. When he was there, you took him for granted. When he wasn't, you missed him. She just wanted the warm feeling of someone else lying close to her, the softness of skin on skin. She shot out of her bedroom like a jack-in-the-box and strode across the landing, listening to the floorboards playing a composition in Squeak Minor.

She listened at Spence's door and couldn't hear him snoring, or muttering. She opened the door slowly. As she poked her head inside, she noticed that Spence wasn't in his bed. He had gone. The covers were all ruffled and crumpled and folded back, so she knew he *had* slept in it.

Eric the cat was peering out from underneath the bed.

Funny, she thought, perhaps he's gone downstairs for a drink, or to the toilet. Gone to the toilet to use it and not to drink out of it, she hoped.

She decided to get into Spence's bed anyway. It would be a nice surprise for him when he came back to the spare bedroom.

Unless he'd gone to her room with the same intentions?

No, they'd have passed on the stairs.

She ducked out of the room again, shutting the door gently, and skipped back across the landing. She threw off her T-shirt and cast it back into her room.

Naked as God intended, she skipped back across the landing with a kind of bouncing motion this time. Gently opening the spare bedroom door, she strode in.

91

As she did so, she felt a sharp pain across the back of her neck and down the length of her spine, then the reeling sensation of numbed senses.

She collapsed on the bed and promptly passed out.

Now, if this had happened *after* she'd been in the room a while, she wouldn't have complained. In fact, she'd have congratulated Spence on the best sex they'd ever had.

Scarily enough, Spence had been the main cause of this sensation anyway. He was stood behind the door, holding a metal clothes rail from the wardrobe in his hand and sporting - what could only be described as - a pained expression. He looked at the naked form of Jody Marianne Lane, limbs akimbo, sprawled on the bed. She had such a great body.

Perfect arse, small waist, lovely curved back, dainty hips, short but perfectly formed legs, beautiful dark hair falling over her delicate shoulders, and a perfect lump developing on the back of her head.

Eric the cat crawled out from his second home, underneath the bed, and sat looking at Spence, his head slightly tilted to one side. He had one of his 'You Try Explaining *That* When She Wakes Up' faces on him. He used it often. He had seen Spence get into trouble with Jody a lot of times.

Spence lowered the metal rod and let it drop to the floor. It rolled towards Eric who sidestepped it like a feline Fred Astaire.

'Oh... for want of a better word... bugger.' Spence gulped.

CHAPTER 7
'LIFE IN THE FAST LANE'

Bigger Man #1 and Bigger Man #2 were dead. Lemon had killed them both, with ruthless efficiency.

All she heard were petty excuses. She was fed up with excuses. Her henchmen had come back confused and wanting the new orders.

What new orders?!

Incompetent fools.

Incompetent *dead* fools.

She was caressing the computer terminal she was working at. It seemed to glow brighter. The file she had punched up was that of Jody Marianne Lane. This girl could be a problem. Best to kill her.

Damned fools.

Such a simple task. One dead, one captured.

Failed.

Still, she had the next best thing - Colonel Jack Lane; one of the top men in the Ministry of Defence and Jody's father. He was on her side. Lemon had him eating out of her hand. This was just a temporary glitch in her plan.

Idiots.

Why did things have to start getting complicated now? Just when they were so near completion. There could be no loose ends, no mistakes, and no favours. Everything must be running as smoothly as possible before the switch.

Now, how to kill Jody Marianne Lane? That was the problem. She had wanted to make it look like an accident, or pin the blame on someone else. But now, she was getting impatient. They were so close to the deadline.

It would have to be just a simple killing. No plans, no fuss. Hit and run? Incident at work? Whatever. It just had to be done.

And soon.

*   *   *

Monday morning. 10.30am.

This was not a good time to be alive, especially at work. It was the part that meant you'd been working for at least *half* the morning, but you still had at least *another half* to go before lunch. What was it that Sir Bob Geldolf once sang, before he was knighted and had gone all Third World on everyone's arses?

'Tell me why, I don't like Mondays.'

Well, Mr Geldolf, we all *know* why Mondays are so bad, we don't *need* to ask questions and we *certainly* don't need to write songs about them.

And, worst of all, Jody had a headache. It throbbed, pulsated and pounded like a particularly nasty pimple. The lump on the back of her head was quite fetching, though. There was a definite shape to it, to the touch. Luckily, the lump was hidden by her hair but, like Jody herself, it still had delicious contours. She'd spent most of the morning so far getting people to feel it, touch it, and comment on it.

It was a busy life in the Ministry of Defence.

'Tell me why, I don't like Mondays... tell me why, I don't like Mo-oo-oon-days...' she sang, rifling through her 'IN' tray to see if she had any interesting documents to sign.

She hadn't.

She took another couple of pain-killers and gulped them down with a sip of water. Spence really was an idiot, she thought. And the story he had fed her? Well, yes, okay, the side door and the kitchen window and, yes, yes, the patio doors as well, did collaborate his far-fetched tale but she surely wasn't expected to take it seriously. Nothing had been taken from the house. The video, the television, the stereo, they were all still there. That was the main thing. And if Spence decided to pay off the would-be burglars out of his own pocket then that was fine by her.

A buzzing from her intercom stopped her thinking any more about it. She pressed the connecting button.

'Yes?' she asked.

'The Colonel's here to see you.' said her secretary.

'Okay, send him in.' answered Jody. She hastily grabbed a pile of the papers from the 'IN' tray and scattered them about her desk. She fixed her gaze on the nearest one and didn't look up when she heard the door open and close.

'Hello, Jody.' came the familiar voice.

'Hello, Dad.' grinned Jody, looking up from her 'work'. The Colonel was a rotund man, red of face and usually constantly out of breath. Today, he looked different. There was something healthier about him.

Jody smiled at her Dad. He was obviously looking after himself better. Ever since her mother, Marianne, had died two years ago, he'd been cocooned in his own world. Perhaps he was now trying to break out of it. She hoped so, for his sake and her own. Mum would always be with them in spirit.

The Colonel brushed his few remaining strands of greying hair over his increasingly bald dome.

'Working?' he asked.

Jody kept grinning. She wanted to get up and hug him. But she didn't. He'd never liked physical contact. She presumed it was because of the strict upbringing he'd had as a child and, of course, his military bearing.

95

'If you can call it working.' she chuckled, scooping the papers up together.

'I do.' he answered, rigidly. It had been a week since Jody had last seen her Dad. He was a busy man; one of the busy men in the higher echelons of the Government organisation. And the Ministry of Defence was a pretty big building.

'Did you want anything, Dad?' she asked. The Colonel just stood there, straight-backed and staring. He picked his gold watch from his tweed waistcoat and swung it round a couple of times. He caught it and looked at it.

It was 10.40am.

'Where's Spencer Tracy?' he asked.

'At work, I hope.' replied Jody. It was an odd question for him to ask, she thought. He'd never liked Spence. He hadn't thought him good enough, which he wasn't, and that was part of the reason that Jody had initially been attracted to Spence.

'What are you doing tonight?' he asked.

'I don't know.'

There was a lengthy pause.

The Colonel looked at his watch again. Jody frowned. 'Why the sudden interest in my personal life?' she enquired.

The Colonel didn't give an answer.

'You're not trying to get me another better internal job?' she asked, waiting to see his reaction.

He didn't react.

'You're not going out tonight, are you?' he asked, mysteriously.

'No. At least, I don't think I am.' replied Jody, puzzled.

'Good.' said the Colonel, pocketing his watch. He turned smartly and marched out of Jody's office. Jody leant back in her chair and raised her eyebrows. What was all *that* about? She picked up the phone and asked for an outside line. The dialling tone appeared as if by magic.

$$* \qquad * \qquad *$$

It was 10.40am.

Time for a break, thought Spence. He logged off and reached for the plate of custard creams that were by the side of his terminal.

Flicking through the internal office newspaper he spotted a picture of Mr Pertwee when he was still in school uniform. It was Mr Pertwee's birthday. He was fifty-five. The printed picture, put their as a humorous homage to the effects of growing older, must have been taken at least fifty years ago. The odd thing was, Mr Pertwee didn't look much different, if truth be told. He had the same grim determined look on his features, coupled with the same arms-folded, legs-apart stance that he adopted in times of crisis. He was even peering over his glasses, at that young age. Surely you had to *learn* that as you got past forty? Spence had never seen a five-year old child wearing half-moon spectacles before.

Mr Pertwee was Spence's Head of Department at work. The staff under his command had yet to come up with a decent nickname for him. They tended to just refer to him as 'Git'. It was fairly apt.

Spence munched on the first of his biscuits and crumbs spread over his stomach like measles. He adjusted his tie to make it looser for the seventh time that morning. He hated ties. He knew it was a physical impossibility but, somehow, all his ties continued to get tighter and tighter as the day wore on.

The phone rang.

He nonchalantly hit the receiver with his hand and it flew up in the air. His other hand caught it and the internal newspaper fluttered to the floor.

'Yello.' he chirped.

'Hello, Spence.'

Spence sat up and brushed the crumbs off his shirt. 'Look, I'm sorry about last night, I really am!' he urgently whispered.

'No, I know. No, it's not that.' said Jody.

'Oh, good.' said Spence, relaxing in his chair again. He reached for another biscuit and tried his best to eat it as quietly and discreetly as possible.

'Don't eat.' said Jody, sighing. 'I hate it when you eat on the phone.' she added.

'Sorry.' spluttered Spence, spitting bits over his computer screen. He wiped them off with one of the pages of the internal newspaper that hadn't fallen on the floor around his feet. The screen was decorated in streaks of black print.

'Look, have you got any plans tonight?' asked Jody.

'Why?'

'Well, I think Dad's going to visit. I mean, I'm not entirely sure. It was just something he said. Or didn't say. Oh, I don't know.'

'That makes two of us.' muttered Spence, slightly confused. 'So,' he said, louder, 'The Colonel is coming to dinner.'

'Yes.' said Jody.

'Well, as it happens, I'm going out.' said Spence, breathing an inward sigh of relief. He didn't really get on with the Colonel. They tended to rub each other up the wrong way. It was a sort of Tony Blair and Gordon Brown type of relationship. Polite but strained.

'Where to?' asked Jody.

'It is the 8th today, isn't it?' answered Spence, with another question. There was a faint sound of rustling papers and then Jody spoke.

'Yes.'

'I'm supposed to meet Stuart at The Toad & Toucan for another poetry reading.' said Spence.

Stuart Rix was Spence's old Geography teacher from school. He'd been absolutely rubbish at Geography.

And so had Spence.

Still, they got on famously and had kept in touch after Spence had left school. Stuart - or 'Sir Stu', as Spence called him to his face because he could never quite look beyond the teacher/pupil relationship - had regular poetry nights at The Toad & Toucan; a quaint country pub where people came to drink alcohol, smoke dope, and generally fight a lot. Spence had been invited along as the comic relief.

And, when Spence read what he thought passed as poetry, it really *was* funny.

Still, it was a good excuse to get thoroughly stoned and start a fistfight. And, plus, there was this really beautiful woman there who was something of a surrealist. The trouble was that she was Stuart's wife. Mind you, Stuart was usually too blind drunk to notice his wife and Spence discussing the merits of surrealist poetry.

Very closely.

In each other's mouths.

This was why he never invited Jody to these gigs. She'd only get the wrong idea.

Spence ran his fingers through his tangled hair and they got stuck.

'And I suppose I'm not invited.' huffed Jody, down the phone.

'I really don't think it's your scene.' soothed Spence, in calming tones.

'How would you know, considering I've never attended?'

'I just know, that's all.' snapped Spence.

'Well, if you intend to carry on staying at my house for the time being then I'm coming with you tonight.' snapped back Jody. She'd always wondered what Spence got up to at these poetry nights. And if he got up to what she *thought* he got up to then she wanted to get up to it too.

'But, you just said the Colonel was coming to dinner.' grumbled Spence, somewhat indignantly.

'He didn't actually *confirm* the booking.' Jody back-pedalled. 'And besides,' she added, 'I can easily put him off. I've only got to tell him that you're staying at the house and he won't come near the place.' she chuckled.

'Okay, fine. I get the message.' sighed Spence, resigned to the idea.

'Good.' said Jody, cheerfully.

'Look, I'll probably be working a bit late tonight. Mr Pertwee's given us all new deadlines to meet. A sort of birthday present in reverse.' said Spence.

'Is it his birthday, then?'

'Yes.' muttered Spence. 'Stupid git!' he added, through clenched teeth, as he ground the heel of his shoe into the picture of the young Mr Pertwee that was staring up at him from the internal newspaper-carpeted floor.

'Call me a stupid git again and I'll make sure your testicles can be used as ear plugs.' Jody warned.

'No, not you, Jode. Mr Pertwee's a stupid git. *You're* just an ignorant git.'

Jody ignored him, proving Spence's jocular comment. 'Do you want me to pick you up?' she asked.

'If you don't mind.' said Spence. He'd never bothered to learn to drive. He knew too many people with cars. Generous people with cars. Generous people with cars that he could rely on to give him lifts.

He'd taken up bicycling once in an attempt to be independent and fit once. It had lasted a week. He had torn his hamstring, strained his chest muscles, and had an asthma attack - which slightly baffled his Doctor as Spence didn't have asthma.

Plus, it was such a responsibility to drive. You had to be aware of other cars, pedestrians, cyclists, traffic lights, motorbikes - the list was endless. Passenger seats were made with Spence in mind, he was sure of that. Jody had a car supplied by the Ministry of Defence. It was a top-notch, high-flying, brand-spanking, shiny new car.

Jody had tried to get him interested in the size of the engine, the aerodynamics, the high-tech suspension, the power steering, etc, etc. Spence had been more interested in the in-car C.D. system with bass boost, the sun-roof, the Sat-Nav, and the excellent flashing lights of simple symbols that told you your seat-belts hadn't been fastened, or that you hadn't turned the headlights off, closed the back door, or that the petrol was dangerously low.

'What time do you want picking up?' Jody asked.

'About six-thirty.' replied Spence. 'Oh, and you couldn't pick up some new clothes at lunch, could you?' he pleaded.

'You mean, *buy* you some new clothes.' corrected Jody.

'I'll pay you back.' Spence lied. 'It's just that I'm wearing the only work clothes that were in the spare bedroom wardrobe and there's hardly anything else decent.' he explained. Jody sighed.

'I suppose so.'

'Excellent. Thanks, Jode.'

'Right, see you at six-thirty sharp.'

'Okay. Six-thirty - blunt.'

'And Spence...'

'What?'

'Get a new joke.'

'I'll work on it.'

'Bye, then.'

'Bye.'

Spence put the phone down and reached for another custard cream. He flashed his fingers over the keyboard and checked to see how much data he'd inputted.

Not enough.

If he was going to meet Mr Pertwee's deadline, he'd have to work through lunch hour. And the canteen was serving Lasagne.

So, was it to be a large helping of work or a large helping of a sumptuous Italian dish?

His Garfield tendencies won out.

By a mile.

*   *   *

The Colonel listened to the click of the receiver being replaced and the purring of the dialling tone. He turned to Jody's secretary and nodded his thanks.

She smiled back.

That's what she'd been taught. Always smile at the high-ranking men. They seemed to expect it. They also seemed to expect other things too. That's why she was still only a secretary and likely to stay one. The Colonel put his finger to his lips and winked. Obviously, listening in on Miss Lane's calls was something he always did. After all, he was a Colonel *and* Miss Lane's father. Perhaps he always did it. She'd only been there a couple of weeks, transferred from 'C' Division.

Still, it seemed rather odd.

Then again, when did anything that happened in the Ministry of Defence seem normal? Never, as far as she could remember.

The Colonel, touched her hand as a gesture of thanks. His touch was smooth and cold. She shivered slightly. He turned and was gone; striding down the corridor like a soldier.

An old, overweight soldier.

*   *   *

Lee Morgan had never killed anyone before. Not intentionally, anyway. Sure, he'd maimed and crippled plenty of people but killing? Well, it wasn't really his cup of tea. Not that he ever drank tea. But, a new fax he'd received from Lemon said just that. For him to kill somebody, that is; not drink a cup of tea.

He was sitting in a café; smoking vigorously and blatantly flouting the 'No Smoking' laws. Nobody had told him to stop. No-one dared.

He'd ordered a plate of French Fries. Well, he'd ordered 'chips'. When he'd asked for this, the waitress had looked horrified. She'd looked down her nose at him and sniffed. They were French Fries to her and all the usual clientele. 'Chips' were for common people. And, to be fair, Lee Morgan certainly fell into that category.

He looked out of the cafe window. It was a horrible day again. It was dark and dreary. A blanket of black clouds covered the once blue sky and faint rumblings of thunder could be heard. It hadn't started raining yet but it was only a matter of time. The traffic was bad, the people scurried by with a serious intent and Mother Nature obviously was in a pretty bad mood.

But, then again, so was Lee Morgan. He'd been waiting nearly half an hour for his plate of chips. He stubbed out his fifth cigarette, on the embroidered, clean, white tablecloth. He had time to kill. And someone. Someone called Jody Marianne Lane. It had rung a bell, though he couldn't remember why. The only thing that bothered him slightly was the fact that it was a woman.

Why couldn't the first person he had to kill be a man? He didn't really have any strict morals (and social graces were people you could rob rather than something you were taught) but there was something niggling him about this assignment.

Still, it was a job.

And Lemon expected results.

If he had a choice between killing Jody or disobeying Lemon, he'd always choose the former. He'd never met Jody Marianne Lane but there was no way she could be scarier than Lemon.

Or more beautiful.

He was cut short in his deep thinking by the waitress shoving a plate of very thin chips in front of him. She didn't say a word and walked off.

Stuck-up bitch, thought Lee.

He picked up a fork with one hand and alternated with the salt and the vinegar with the other. Why he'd come in this silly cafe to eat, he didn't know. It was too up its own arse for his liking. Still, he could always walk out without paying. As he always did.

But, it did have a nice view of the Ministry of Defence.

*   *   *

It was 6.30pm.

Spence had had a miserable afternoon. He'd met the deadline, wished Mr Pertwee a very happy birthday, and now he was stood outside by the main road, searching the traffic for any sign of Jody. He hoped she'd picked out some decent clothes for him to change into. The Toad & Toucan was an hour's drive away, in the middle of nowhere, and it was easier to go straight there now. They could eat when they got there.

He sat down on a nearby bollard and sighed heavily. He was joined at either side by two big, burly men. They were stood far too close to him. He got up and walked to the edge of the road again. They followed him. He decided to take the direct approach.

'Hello.' he said, as cheerfully as he could muster.

Big Man #1 produced a knife.

'Goodbye.' Spence added, swinging his briefcase into Big Man #1's stomach and launching himself at Big Man #2.

Big Man #1 doubled up and fell to the floor, Big Man #2 toppled backwards with Spence. Spence scrambled to his feet and took to his heels, straight across the extremely busy main road. He missed being hit by several cars with extremely good brakes and reached the other side safely. Big Man #1 and Big Man #2 had helped each other to their respective feet.

Spence was breathing rather heavily already. He knew he could probably out-run the two big, burly men but he would also miss Jody's lift.

Bugger.

His brain didn't think that fast. What to do, what to do? His prayers were answered as Jody's car came into view. She pulled up next to Spence. Spence wrenched the door open and dived in.

'Drive, drive!' he shouted, his voice slightly muffled as his face was pressed into Jody's lap. He hooked the handle of the car door with his left foot and pulled it closed. Jody didn't bother asking and just instinctively put her foot on the accelerator, speeding off into the traffic.

Big Man #1 and Big Man #2 made a despairing lunge at the accelerating car and missed. They dived out of the way as an Aston Martin sped up behind them, accelerating at the same speed as the Ministry of Defence car.

'Mr Letts is not going to be pleased with us.' muttered Big Man #1.

'We'll definitely get him tomorrow.' said the strangely soprano Big Man #2.

'And this time *you* can produce the knife.' snapped Big Man #1, rubbing his aching abdomen and grimacing slightly.

CHAPTER 8
'SHOT IN THE DARK'

The Toad & Toucan was a small pub in a small field, in the middle of some big countryside. It was frequented by locals and served a famous local brew called 'Old Snot' which took your breath away. And part of your liver.

The Toad & Toucan pub was made of stone and was 'Ye Olde' in the right sense. A picture of Lord Lucan hung above the wooden door, which was a slight mistake. When the new owner – Mr Miles Rossini - had re-christened the pub, he'd employed a local artist to paint a new sign. Unfortunately, Mr Rossini spoke with a heavy foreign accent and the local artist was 84-years old and profoundly deaf. He had been convinced that the pub was going to be called 'Lord Lucan' after a lengthy phone conversation. So, that's what he'd painted.

Most of the younger people who came to the pub had no idea that Lord Lucan was a famous peer who had mysteriously disappeared after a suspicious murder and had never been found. They just thought the new owner liked Freddie Mercury. As Queen happened to be the owner's favourite band, it all turned out okay in the end.

It was 7.23pm and Stuart Rix, Spence's old teacher, had drunk two pints of Guinness. He had also rolled a spliff the size of a small child and passed it around the circle of his fellow poets.

Mr Rossini turned a blind eye to his best customers smoking indoors; this was because he actually *was* blind in one eye.

The Police also turned a blind eye to the poetical puffings of The Toad & Toucan Poet Troubadours. This was because Sergeant Daniel 'Book 'em, Danno' Sherwin was one of the leading members of poetical group. He supplied the inspiration. Any 'inspiration' that he confiscated from the local students usually found its way into Stuart's expert rolling hands.

Sergeant Sherwin was also a homosexual and proud of it. The phrase 'bent copper' seemed to apply to him rather well, whichever angle you looked at it.

Outside, a car turned into the gravelled car park and its engine sighed and went quiet.

Another car engine, almost as a faint echo, did the very same thing.

Two car doors slammed - three, if you listened very hard - and footsteps approached the pub.

Spencer Tracy and Jody Marianne Lane walked into the bar. They were greeted with a rousing cheer, hearty handshakes, and a great deal of sweet smoke and alcohol fumes. Mr Rossini poured two pints of Old Snot and placed them on the counter.

'Compliments of The Toad & Toucan' he grinned.

Spence and Jody accepted them willingly. Spence leaned over the counter.

'We're staying here tonight.' he said, motioning to Jody. Mr Rossini winked the wink of an old pervert.

'Luckily, we have a room free.' he said, eyeing up Jody with his one good eye and liking what he saw. Spence smiled widely and shook the always-accommodating owner by the hand.

'And you'll be relieved to know that Mrs Rix isn't coming to read tonight. She's got a heavy cold... which, if memory serves me rightly, you had last time you came up.' added Mr Rossini, waggling his eyebrows in a most unnerving fashion.

Spence watched as Jody was led away by Stuart and sat down with the rest of the poets. They hadn't met Jody before and made the introductions before Spence had a chance to. He took a swig of Old Snot and choked as politely as he could.

It was strong stuff.

He wondered who the two attackers were that had tried to mug him. It was a close thing and he'd never been happier to see Jody.

Well, apart from that time when she'd dressed in a French Maid's outfit on his birthday.

Perhaps his cheque had bounced? Two big, burly men weren't hard to forget - with or without balaclavas. They obviously meant business. Big business. He'd have to go to the police. Something had to be done. This Lemon character wasn't going to lie down and walk away.

God, this was strong stuff.

Still, it could wait until tomorrow. I mean, Sergeant Sherwin could help but he was far too stoned. And it all seemed such a long time ago now; almost as if it hadn't happened. He was beginning to doubt it. The flashbacks had come with less frequent regularity and it all seemed so far-fetched.

Reality was something he found hard to cope with at the best of times. This was just making it worse. Well, a spliff and another pint of Old Snot would put pay to reality for a while.

*   *   *

Lee Morgan stood, arms folded, by his Aston Martin. Well, it wasn't *technically* his Aston Martin but that was just a minor quibble to Lee. He had watched his intended victim walk into the pub with, presumably, her boyfriend or her lover or her husband or whatever.

The dark of early evening had descended and the great thing about the countryside was a distinct lack of streetlights.

This was probably because there was a distinct lack of streets *to* light.

He stared at the quaint country pub for a couple of minutes, focusing his mind. An owl hooted and the trees replied with a conspiratorial whispering as the wind swept across the land with a rigid purpose. A rigid purpose, in Lee's mind, of making him damned cold.

Lee Morgan opened the door of the Aston Martin and reached inside for his camelhair coat. Well, it wasn't *technically* his camelhair coat but that was just another minor quibble to Lee.

He put it on and tried to get warm. He took out the handgun from the case and screwed the silencer to the barrel tip. It was heavy in his hands. He hoped he was as good a shot as he used to be. Shooting cats with an air pistol was a far cry from shooting a human with a hefty handgun. Still, the principle was the same. And there was a certain feline quality about his prey. He slipped the gun into the inside pocket of the camelhair coat.

It fitted almost perfectly and made a satisfying bulge.

*   *   *

'I know I've matured like a tempting fine wine,
Mellowed with age and seasoned with time.
I know I'm secure like a lock on a door,
Safe from the clutches of love once more!' the Sergeant slurred.

A round of spontaneous applause greeted the end of Sergeant Daniel Sherwin's poem.

He bowed dramatically, narrowly avoiding head-butting the microphone, and wallowed in the clapping and cheering. He left the little raised stage and sat down with the audience.

Stuart bounded back up to the microphone, clutching it as if it was about to make a hasty escape.

'Thanks, Danno! Daniel Sherwin, ladies and gentlemen! Excellent. Right, right. I think it's time for another, from me.' announced Stuart.

'Very kind of you. I'll have a Guinness!' came a quick-witted shout from the boisterous crowd. There was a ripple of applause and a communal laugh-in.

Stuart ignored the comment, as he so often did when it really *was* his turn to buy a round. He turned a couple of pages in his tattered folder and found what he was looking for.

'An Ode to Bus Route Number 24.' he announced.

The audience members who'd heard it before cheered.

The audience members who hadn't were not sober enough to do anything else but join in with the cheering.

Jody was up at the bar, ordering another couple of pints of Old Snot.

Damn, it was strong stuff.

Spence joined her and slipped his arm around her tiny waist. He kissed her on the neck. He'd meant to kiss her on the cheek but Old Snot affected your sight and balance with quite remarkable speed.

She shivered.

She felt so sensual.

Old Snot did that too. In fact, Old Snot should have been available on the NHS.

'I've booked the room here.' whispered Spence, his hand wandering over her pert behind. She grabbed his face with one hand, pulling his cheeks together and making him involuntarily pucker up. She planted a wet kiss on his lips and let him go. He reeled slightly.

'Spence, have I ever told you I love you?' she said.

Spence nodded.

'A thousand times. I counted.' he replied.

'Well, I mean it.' she said, her green eyes staring into the brown of Spence's.

'And I love you, Jode.' said Spence, sincerely.

Well, as sincerely as you *can* sound when slurring every other word.

'How well I understand you.' she grinned. Mr Rossini placed two pints of Old Snot in front of the swaying lovers. Jody threw a note at him and waved away the change.

Mr Rossini took one look at it and didn't argue.

It was a fifty-pound note.

*   *   *

It was 8.48pm, by Lee Morgan's watch.

Well, it wasn't *technically* Lee Morgan's watch, etc, etc, etc. He didn't bother to lock the Aston Martin. Well, he couldn't. He'd broken the lock.

Stuffing his hands in his pocket, Lee Morgan walked across the road and towards the lights of The Toad & Toucan. He sat on one of the picnic tables that were dotted around the side of The Toad & Toucan.

It was dark where he sat but ever-so-slightly illuminated by a nearby window. He could see inside the cosy pub. It was quite a good view. Good enough. There was a lot of noise coming from within.

He could hear a voice speaking through a microphone, incredibly muffled and inaudible. There was laughter, cheering, shouting and lots of smoke. He spotted his mark and her 'friend' at the bar. As quickly as he spotted them, they moved out of his sight.

Still, there were three windows dotted along this side of the pub and a multitude of picnic tables. He could stay there all night, if need be.

*   *   *

It was Spence's turn at the microphone. He tottered on to the small stage and rummaged through his memory for a decent poem. Why hadn't he remembered to bring his poetry book?

There had been a fire. Oh, yes.

The fire that had burned down his rented abode.

Yes. That's why.

Well, it shouldn't be too hard to recall one of his masterpieces. They were all etched on his memory, even if it was a memory that was awash with Old Snot and illegal dope.

He came up with a complete blank.

He recited a limerick. It wasn't particularly funny but he needed to stall for time. The audience seemed to like it. So, he recited another. They roared. He made one up on the spot. It went down rather well.

Not only was Spence's brain drowning in Old Snot and clouded with dope, so was everybody else's. This was going to be a triumphant return to the microphone. He finished with the rudest limerick he could recall which opened with the starting line: 'A lady was diagnosed with acute angina'... and got worse.

He left the stage to much applause and back-slapping. Yes, it felt good. He was greeted by Jody who seemed to be speaking in tongues. He replied with his own' their two tongues thrusting and parrying like a Musketeer swordfight.

Indigo Flow, the resident band of The Toad & Toucan, launched into their first song and it was loud. It was an Irish jig - their own composition - called 'Twiddle Aye Dum Dee Twiddle Aye Dee', which prised half the audience out of their seats and onto the small space of wooden floor that constituted the 'dance' area.

* * *

Inside the pub, an awful racket had started up. It could probably be referred to as 'music' - but only in the loosest possible terms. The windows were filled with people dancing. All of them looking like they had a nervous muscular disorder.

Lee Morgan frowned and reached inside his coat for the handgun. He pulled it out slowly and fiddled with it. He could see Jody and her 'friend', sitting together at a round table by the window.

Everyone else seemed to be dancing.

Her 'friend' suddenly sprang to his feet and pulled at Jody. She resisted. Her 'friend' skipped off into the crowd of mad dancers and was enveloped by them.

She was alone with her back to the window.

This was perfect.

Lee Morgan started to sweat. It was a cold night and yet he could feel the telltale tingle of trickling sweat rolling steadily down his forehead. His hands were clammy and shaking.

Come on, pull yourself together.

He steadied his hands and the gun by fixing them on the picnic table. She was in his line of fire.

Steady, steady.

The music seemed to get louder and rang in Lee Morgan's ears with an unheralded intensity. The darkness seemed to swallow him whole as his finger tightened on the trigger. The fast pounding of his heart matched the fast pounding of the drums. Everything was so loud.

An owl hooted again and startled him. It seemed so close. He peered around. There was nothing there.

The sounds of life inside The Toad & Toucan got louder and louder. He turned back to the window and concentrated on the back of the head that was outlined there.

*　　*　　*

Spence had slipped twice and fallen on his backside. The room was spinning. He was pulled round again for another quick jig. The band seemed to be very loud tonight. His ears protested at the level of noise they were being subjected to by buzzing like a maniac with a chainsaw and a neat line in decapitation.

He'd smiled at Jody twice when he had passed where she was sat, orbiting the room like an out-of-control moon.

She seemed to be happy enough.

But, that may have been the smoke and alcohol kicking in.

*　　*　　*

She wouldn't feel any pain. Lee Morgan was convinced of that. Anyway, who cares? He didn't know her. Why should he worry? He licked his dry lips and tasted sweat. He felt his stomach knot as his finger pulled back on the trigger.

It clicked.

Nothing happened.

Sod it.

The safety catch was still on.

*　　*　　*

Jody got up and staggered to the bar again. She tried to focus on Mr Rossini. Had he sprouted an extra head, grinning madly at her? Was he like a real-life Zaphod Beeblebrox?!

No, don't think so.

Though, he *was* leaving a trail of lights behind him as he moved.

She shook her head and focused on the task at hand. She ordered another pint of Old Snot. The smoke was getting to her and she felt her eyes watering. She dabbed them with her sleeve.

She felt totally gone.

Toilet.

Yes.

She could feel the pressure on her bladder and tugged at Mr Rossini's shirt.

'Toilets?' she asked, trying to make herself heard over the band.

It wasn't going to be easy.

Mr Rossini shrugged, made a gesture to his ear and carried on pulling Jody's pint.

She did a quick mime.

It was a very basic mime, which involved squatting and making a face of bladder-bursting relief. Mr Rossini got what she meant, as did everyone else who wasn't dancing, and he pointed some general directions. She nodded her thanks and lunged for the internal door.

After picking herself up off the floor, she tried again.

This time she was successful.

*   *   *

She'd moved.

Lee Morgan took a huge gulp of fresh air as he realised the necessity to breath at regular intervals. She'd got up and disappeared out of his vision. He clicked the safety catch back on and made a mental note.

The music stopped and he could hear clapping and whistling. Everything became tranquil for a brief second as the countryside became peaceful and serene again, having a short respite from the overwhelming din.

Then it started up again.

Twice as loud.

Lee Morgan just couldn't work out what the music was supposed to be. He relaxed slightly as he waited for Jody to return to her seat. It wasn't a long period of relaxation. Someone walked out of the front entrance.

He froze.

His muscles stiffened and he prepared to dive for cover. It was two people, in fact. They burst out the door, laughing and supporting each other. There was no time for him to escape.

'Hello there!' shouted one of the revellers, striding across towards the occupied picnic table. The other one followed unsteadily.

'What are you doing freezing your buttocks off out here?' said the other one. Lee Morgan swiftly adjusted the safety catch and stood up. The light from the windows was hitting his face badly. They would've seen his features by now and probably could easily identify him in a line-up.

Of course, he completely failed to take into account the fact that the interlopers into his comfort zone were absolutely plastered. They would've no more been able to identify him the next day than they would be able to tell Lee Morgan at that moment what their surnames were.

Still, Lee Morgan was edgy and his nerves were screaming at orders at his twitchy reflexes.

'Come inside, sir!' roared the closest man, plonking his hands heavily down on to the picnic table to steady himself. He was finding walking *and* talking very difficult to master. The board which he rested his full weight on was loose, still waiting to be nailed down by the landlord.

But, nobody ever sat at the picnic tables, the landlord had argued, crossing the odd job off his 'To Do' list.

The drunken man fell backwards and toppled into his equally drunken follower as the loose board shot upwards with amazing force. Lee Morgan took the full brunt of it on his chin and flew backwards, involuntarily letting go of the handgun he was holding so tightly.

He landed on the wet grass and lay still for a second.

His chin throbbed and his head span.

Little white lights flashed in front of his eyes like his own personal kaleidoscope.

Ouch.

He tried to collect his thoughts as he watched the dancing lights do a duet with the twinkling stars up above. His hand clenched and unclenched. Where was his handgun? He tried the other hand.

It wasn't there either.

The incessant cacophony of sound that emerged from the pub, as if piped through a distorted megaphone, really was beginning to irritate him. And he was mean enough without getting irritable on top of it.

He could hear the sounds of grunting and puffing from the two idiots who'd been the cause of his pain. They were obviously on their feet. He waited until they shuffled over, their two faces peering down at him.

'Are you okay, mate?' said the original buffoon who'd leant on the picnic table.

Lee Morgan reached up slowly, put a hand on the side of each of their heads and cracked them together with all the force he could muster. There was a pleasant hollow thud and the two faces staggered out of his panoramic view.

He sprang to his feet, slightly woozy and trying to shake the dizzy feeling from his head. He turned on the nearest man, who was clutching his head and down on his knees. He picked him up by the scruff of his neck and powered his fist into his midriff. The explosion of air that came from the man's mouth was like a hurricane.

Before he had chance to do anything else, Lee Morgan had brought his knee into contact with the winded man's face. His head snapped backwards with an alarming crack.

The other man, witnessing the last part of Lee Morgan's brutal attack, ran at him headfirst. Lee whipped round and faced the charging. He rolled backwards on to the floor and kicked his legs up, flinging the man over him. There was a dull thud as the flying man hit the floor.

Before he could attempt to get up, Lee Morgan was astride him. A few swift punches straight into the centre of his face put him out cold and the sound of a broken nose echoed out into the air. Lee got off him and was breathing heavily.

Rain had started to fall again. Just a light drizzle this time. He could see his breath leaving his mouth like great puffs of smoke and disappear into the atmosphere.

Where was that handgun?

He scanned the area and could see no sign of it. He realised how hot he was now and threw off his camelhair coat. It landed on his first opponent like a shroud.

Something glinted as the full moon broke through the dense clouds. Lee Morgan ran for it and scooped up his handgun like it was his baby. He checked it over. It seemed to be okay. He shook his head again as great swirls of blackness threatened to engulf his distinctly hazy vision.

Concussion?

This was just what he needed. He struggled to remain conscious. It eased again and his vision became a little clearer. He pointed the gun at his camelhair coat and shot a hole in it. The body underneath the coat jerked and then lay still.

The music from The Toad & Toucan faded, echoed, increased, faded, echoed, and increased as Lee Morgan struggled against himself with continuing discomfort. He fired a second shot through the neck of the other fool, the same jerking motion occurred and a strange gargling sound sped through his ears as the dying man expired.

What a mess. What a bloody mess. Quite literally.

He leant against the wall of The Toad & Toucan and peered into the nearest window as discreetly as he could manage. The party still seemed to be in full swing. He couldn't see Jody Marianne Lane. He couldn't see a lot as his vision narrowed into a tunnel.

He slipped the safety catch back on and pocketed his handgun. Staggering across the grass and slipping on the pool of blood seeping from the throat of the second of his corpses, his main aim was to get back to his Aston Martin. He reached it with a great deal of difficulty. He fumbled for the door handle and wrenched it open with some force.

Just... got to... get... home.

Now.

He fell into the driver's seat and slammed the door shut.

Can try... again... tomorrow.

The deep throaty roar of the engine echoed through the still air as the Aston Martin came alive. The back wheels span and gripped as the car jerked forward with a sickening motion.

Veering from one side of the road to the other, it passed The Toad & Toucan and vanished from view, deeper into the countryside. What it left behind, aside from the smell of burnt tyre rubber, was a scene of hot-blooded merriment and cold-blooded murder.

*　　*　　*

Jody returned from the toilet and felt very light-headed. She reached the bar in one long, hopeful stride and picked up her umpteenth pint of Old Snot. She struggled to keep the whole pint intact as she returned to her window seat.

Spence was still dancing.

Well, if you could call it dancing.

He was moving in time with the off-beats, which only someone with absolutely no sense of rhythm could do. The band ended their song with a heavy crashing of cymbals and gratuitous feedback.

Jody gratefully accepted a drag from a spliff that was doing the rounds and held her breath as the smoke wound down her throat and into her lungs and bloodstream. She breathed out and her senses tingled and prickled.

She passed it on.

It was surely the adult version of the Pass-The-Parcel game, with a much better prize each time the music stopped.

Spence picked his way through the jubilant crowd and made it back to be by Jody's side. He collapsed on to the seat next to her, breathing heavily and with sweat pouring down his face. His pupils were dilated and his pulse was hyper. He gulped down the remnants of whatever was in the couple of empty glasses that sat on the table.

'I'm going outside for a breath of fresh air.' said Spence, between breaths.

'I'll come too.' said Jody.

'What's the time?' asked Spence, brushing the back of his hand across his sticky brow. Jody looked at her watch a couple of times before answering.

'It's about quarter-past eleven.' she answered.

The band started a final number and drowned out Mr Rossini's attempt to call 'time' at the bar. Jody and Spence both got unsteadily to their feet and made for the exit. They reached it safely, giggling like two adolescents.

Out in the open air, the rain hit them like a cold shower and the wind blew threw their hair. They fell into each other's arms and kissed passionately, both sets of hands wandering like a polar expedition over the furthest and least visited parts of the Atlas of their bodies.

A flash of sheet lightening illuminated the nearby forest and thunder rumbled like a bad case of indigestion.

They broke off and leant against opposite sides of the doorframe, both of them panting furiously; their torsos heaving up and down like a storm-swollen sea.

'Shall we go to bed?' asked Jody, tilting her beautiful face into the rain and feeling each drop invigorate her olive skin. Spence laughed.

'Did you even need to ask?' he said, brushing his fringe out of his eyes once more.

'I was just being polite.' added Jody, grinning.

The wind blew stronger and the rain whipped against their bodies. They turned to go back inside as another sheet of pure lightening lit the area like a huge strobe light. Something caught Spence's attention, something just out of the corner of his eye.

'Hang on, there's something over there.' he said, letting go of Jody's warm hand. He stepped out into the night and made his way along the sidewall of The Toad & Toucan.

Jody sighed and followed him.

The light from inside shone out of the windows and created a stained-glass effect on the grass, whilst the muffled music and raised voices created an odd background for Spence's whim.

He nearly tripped over something as he went to investigate. He bent down and picked up a camelhair coat. Someone was underneath it; sleeping of a few pints of the local beverage, no doubt.

Spence held the garment up. The lightening flashed again for him. There was a dark stain across the fawn coat. The sleeper wasn't going to be best pleased. Even the Dry-Cleaners would have trouble getting that stain out.

Jody walked away from Spence, spotting another dormant figure not too far away. She slipped on something greasy and almost fell. This part of the grass seemed to be wetter than the rest... and a lot darker. The hairs on the back of her neck did their own gymnastic routine. Bending down, she put her fingers into the puddle and held it up to the light of the moon.

It was blood.

Christ, it was a pool of blood.

The lightening obliged again and she saw the unseeing eyes of the dead staring up at her. Her heart pole-vaulted into her mouth and her stomach did somersaults in an attempt to out-do the gymnastic routine that her neck hairs had been so good at.

Spence was standing over her.

'Stupid drunks - they're both out like a light.' he chuckled, shivering slightly. It was too cold to stay out in the open air any longer. Besides, they had a nice warm bed to christen.

The lightening flashed again and Jody stood up. She seemed serious all of a sudden.

'What's the matter?' he asked her.

She stared into his eyes with a fierceness that chilled him more than the elements.

'They're not drunk.' she said, slowly and deliberately.

'Okay, they're not drunk. They're asleep, passed out, had a fight, who cares?' re-evaluated Spence, shrugging. He grabbed Jody's shoulders but she shook him off.

'They're dead, Spence.' she paused. 'These two men are dead to the world. And I don't mean fast asleep.' she hissed.

Spence grinned at her feeble joke.

Her face was set. She wasn't joking.

His eyes ventured downwards and he saw the pool of blood discolouring the grass at his feet. The sound from the pub quietened and the intermittent lightening flashes floodlit the horrific scene with a brilliant intensity. The thunder crackled and spat like an explosion.

Spencer Tracy's colour drained from his face and he went as deathly white as the two recently deceased, drunken revellers.

'You're not going to faint are you, Spence?' said Jody, concerned.

'No.' said Spence, indignantly.

And promptly fainted.

CHAPTER 9
'LET'S WORK TOGETHER'

Monday night hadn't been kind.

After every Emergency Service had left The Toad & Toucan, it was late.

It was *very* late.

In fact, it was Tuesday.

Spencer Tracy and Jody Marianne Lane hadn't been to bed. They sat on the still-neatly made bedding in The Toad & Toucan, acres apart from each other, in a state of sober shock.

This wasn't helped much by the appearance of an identical hangover for both of them. A hangover and delayed shock go together like the Lone Ranger and Toronto.

Sobriety, eh?

It wasn't always a good thing.

Sergeant Daniel 'Danno' Sherwin would have probably been arrested if it had been a routine 999 call. He was still smoking dope when the police had arrived.

Mind you, if they'd arrested Danno, they would also have had to arrest the whole of The Toad & Toucan itself. And with two - apparently motiveless - murders on their hands, there was going to be enough paperwork as it was. No need to create even more.

Plus, the Press were all ready sniffing around like bloodhounds. Local *and* National. Any senseless killings were as essential as a full English breakfast for Mr Johnny Journalist.

The good news, if it could be classed as such, was the fact that Spence and Jody had one hell of an excuse for skiving off work today and probably, to be honest, for the rest of the week as well.

This wasn't exactly forefront in their minds, though.

A splitting headache was forefront in their minds.

But, just behind that - and niggling as much, if not more - was a fear.

It was the fear of a possibility.

The simple possibility that this was all something to do with Spence's dream

*   *   *

Mr Letts wasn't happy. This was easy to spot. When Mr Letts wasn't happy, his beard bristled. It physically bristled. You could almost hear it. He was sat behind a large desk, in a large chair, smoking a large cigar. His head was clouded in wisps of blue smoke.

Big Man #1 and Big Man #2 were stood like a two silent statues, in front of him; like two naughty students waiting for punishment from their Headmaster. And Mr Letts was making them suffer. He had already wounded them with a verbal tirade of Mount Everest proportions and was now trying to finish them off with the old 'Silence' routine.

Even though it was daylight outside, the room was half-lit and oppressively dark. This was a trait of all shady characters; a shadow-filled, oppressive, half-lit room. It could be blazing sunshine outside but inside it would be dark. It was a contractual obligation.

And Mr Letts was *certainly* a shady character.

He'd been questioned more times by the South West Police than they cared to mention. They were the Hayfever Sufferer and he was the Pollen. He got right up their nose and irritated like hell.

They hadn't pinned him down to anything yet. They *had* pinned him down... but not to any specific thing.

126

They'd discreetly kicked him a couple of times too when he'd been pinned down but nothing had been forthcoming.

Mr Letts was as slippery as a tub of Vaseline.

The bristling beard was stroked and ashes from the cigar fluttered out of it like a swarm of moths. Mr Letts leant forward and his leather chair creaked a warning. He rested on the desk, with its neat piles of paper and paperweights and pens, and looked at his hired help.

Big Man #1 and Big Man #2 didn't look back - they found the allure of the carpet much more interesting to their eyes and shuffled their feet in, what could only be described as, an uncomfortable manner.

Mr Letts rested his smoking cigar on the lip of his ornamental ashtray and smacked his lips together as if chewing on some imaginary food.

His eyes narrowed considerably - which was some achievement as they were narrow enough normally - and he drummed on the desk with his nicotine-stained, yellow-tinged fingers.

To be honest, he much preferred cigarettes but was obliged to puff away on a fat Cuban because that's what people expected. And by 'fat Cuban', it was the cigar in his mouth they were expecting and not some gay, sweaty, lard-arse called Fidel.

So, the cigar was stuffed in-between Mr Letts moustache and beard simply because that was expected of him. After all, remember, he was *officially* a shady character).

The thing that most annoyed Mr Letts was the way his entourage had been foiled, twice, by this Spencer Tracy character.

Sure, he was used to the odd cock-up (and we're not taking about Fatty Fidel the Cuban here) but this

Spencer Tracy was proving an elusive catch. He was getting slightly uneasy with the whole thing.

There must have been some motive for the arson attack, he thought. One of his houses was a pile of smoking rubble. Had he crossed swords with Spencer Tracy before, perhaps? Had he been hired by a rival firm? Was there a big insurance scam that he was blatantly unaware of? What *was* the reason?

One thing was for sure - he wanted money and he wanted it from Spencer Tracy.

He'd get it too. He was sure of that.

Mr Letts could get blood out of a stone. Enough blood for a Vampire to get seriously drunk on.

He knew that Big Man #1 and Big Man #2 were incompetent fools but he hadn't the heart to sack them. They were like the illegitimate sons he'd never had... and never wanted. They were intellectually challenged and it would've been like drowning two puppies in the sacking that he didn't want to give them.

Mr Letts stopped drumming his fingers on the table because it was starting to sound like the William Tell Overture.

Big Man #1 and Big Man #2 gave up staring at the carpet and looked up at their employer.

Mr Letts smiled a toothless grin. His gums glistened with saliva and he smacked his lips together once more.

'I will give you five days to bring Spencer Tracy to me.' rasped Mr Letts, his voice thick with years of tobacco. 'Don't try and extract money from him. Just bring him here and I'll have a word with him.' he added.

Big Man #1 and Big Man #2 nodded their understanding and turned to leave.

Mr Letts picked up his cigar again and wrapped his fat lips around it. He eased himself back into his chair and watched his adopted twins walk off. As they got to the door, he piped up a final warning.

'No mistakes this time, lads.'

'Right you are, guv'!' replied Big Man #1 - the spokesman - as he opened the door.

'And don't call me "Guv", you imbecile!' spluttered Mr Letts.

'Sorry, guv'!' said Big Man #1, cheerfully and with no sense of irony, as he left the room with his partner in crime.

'I am a respectable businessman, not a bleedin' West End gangster.' muttered Mr Letts.

The two big, burly men left his office.

'And don't slam - '

The door slammed, rattling the windows and causing a genuine Picasso print, purchased from the indoor market in 1975, to crash to the floor for only the third time that week.

' - the door.' finished Mr Letts, sighing heavily.

*   *   *

It was 11.12am and Spence and Jody were on their way home.

Well, on their way to Jody's home at least. Somewhat dazed and still in a comparative state of shock, they were silent throughout the whole car journey.

They'd been questioned by the police, given statements, had their fingerprints taken, warned not to leave the country, and generally frowned and scowled at a lot. It didn't seem like real life.

The morning always puts the night's events into a different perspective. There is something about the morning that is maternally comforting and stable. It throws you slightly off balance.

On their way home, they passed what looked like a serious accident but neither of them took much notice of it.

An Aston Martin had obviously veered off the road and down a ravine. There was an Ambulance at the side of the road, some policemen were looking at the broken railings and down below a twisted body was being pulled out of the wreckage.

Spence and Jody were too wrapped up in thoughts of last night to feel any sympathy, curiosity, sadness, or worry. Another accident was something they felt nothing for after witnessing the tragic circumstances of last night.

*   *   *

Lemon hadn't heard anything from Lee Morgan and was beginning to lose her cool. She sat motionless and straight-backed, staring at one of the blank screens that surrounded her, willing any sort of message to come through.

She would wait another 15 minutes, she decided.

If Lee Morgan hadn't filed his report by then, she would get in touch with Colonel Lane. He might know *something.*

She pressed the button that summoned her Personal Assistant.

*   *   *

It was time for lunch when Jody pulled into her drive and wrenched the handbrake for all it was worth.

Neither of them were hungry.

Spence and Jody climbed wearily out of the car and trudged indoors, like a pair of zombies. Jody headed for the kitchen and Spence headed for the nearest comfy chair.

'Are you going to make a cup of tea?' shouted Spence, from the dining room. His voice sounded odd as it burst through the bubble of silence like a sharp needle. Jody had switched the kettle on as soon as she had entered the kitchen. It was an automatic instinct. She grunted a reply and reached for two mugs.

Just to the one side of the mug-rack, on top of the pile of bubble-wrap, was the parcel that Spence had brought round, for the attention of the Philip Dicks person.

What was that name again? That one that had sounded so familiar to her?

Delbert?

Del Monte?

Davros?

'Spence, what was that name on that piece of paper?' she yelled, as the kettle began to steam and switched itself off.

'What?' was Spence's reply.

'The name on that piece of paper - the one in the parcel.' explained Jody.

'What?' was Spence's reply. Again.

Jody snatched up the parcel off the top and stormed into where Spence was sitting. She threw it at him and caught him on the bridge of his nose.

'This parcel.' she snapped.

'Ouch.' said Spence, peeling the parcel off his face and turning it over in his hands. He shrugged and dropped it to the floor. 'I don't know - I can't remember.' he muttered.

'Well, where did you put the paper?' she asked.

'In my pocket.' he replied.

'Which pocket?'

131

'Trouser pocket.'

'Which trousers?' grimaced Jody, starting to get slightly exasperated.

'The ones that I put in the wash yesterday.'

'Oh, you imbecile!' she snapped. 'That could have been important!'

Jody sauntered back to the kitchen and opened the washing machine.

Sure enough, in the moulded lump of washing that lay as a cube inside, was the pair of trousers that Spence had thrown in. She pulled them out and searched the pockets.

A soggy piece of what-once-was paper stuck to her hands and separated. There was no way she'd be able to decipher the smudged ink that once made sense. Ah well, it couldn't be helped. She had more important things to worry about.

Like where she'd put the teabags.

*   *   *

The fifteen minutes were up.

Lee Morgan hadn't reported in and Lemon had to assume that he wasn't going to. She knew she had to get in touch with Colonel Lane. Her lily-white hands hovered over a pad of yellow keys.

She pressed the fourth one and it started flashing.

The signal was sent.

*   *   *

In an oak-panelled office, deep in the bowels of the Ministry of Defence, sat the Colonel.

Colonel Jack Lane.

Jody's military father. As if you'd forgotten.

He was steadily scrawling some notes on a couple of typed reports, simultaneously.

Suddenly, he dropped the pen as if it was electrically charged and sat bolt upright in his chair. His pupils rolled upwards and disappeared. There was nothing in his eyes but whiteness. He convulsed a couple of times and his mouth twitched rapidly.

Finally, his pupils rolled back into his dead eyes and he stood up immediately.

Swivelling on his heels, he turned away from his desk and headed towards the door. He pulled it open and marched out stiffly.

It took him a couple of minutes to get outside the building and reach the nearest public telephone booth. He wrenched open the heavy door and stepped inside. A pound coin was inserted and he dialled a number from memory.

Suzanne Addison answered.

She knew what she had to ask him and waited for his long and detailed reply. This took him no less than five minutes and, when he had finished, he slammed the receiver down and strode back down the street, past security, and into the Ministry of Defence. It took him exactly the same amount of time - to the second - to get back to his office, as it had taken him to leave it.

He sat back at his desk, straight-backed and aloof, and his pupils rolled upwards again and seemed to vanish again. He convulsing and twitching once more, like a ventriloquist's dummy, for a couple of seconds, and then his pupils re-appeared. His posture became more relaxed and he calmly picked up his dropped pen and began to write once more.

As if nothing had happened.

*   *   *

133

'Don't be stupid.' scoffed Spence, 'I've been trying to forget that. And, anyway, you were quite adamant that it was all untrue.' he added.

Jody wasn't so sure now.

'Yes, yes, I know. But, I've been thinking.'

'Did it hurt?'

'I've been putting two and two together.'

'Well, don't.' frowned Spence. 'You were never very good at advanced mathematics;'

'Suppose the break-in *was* something to do with this dream of yours?'

'Look, Jody, you'd convinced me otherwise! Stop confusing me with your changing view-point tactics. I just don't want to think about it.'

'Suppose those murders at The Toad & Toucan had something to do with it?'

'I'd thought of that already.' sighed Spence, 'But, I don't want to get involved.'

'You *are* involved. It was your dream!' snapped Jody.

'Let the police sort it out - they're good at that. That's what they're *paid* for.'

'You're going to have to go through your dream once more. Re-live it.'

'I don't want to.' growled Spence, gritting his teeth and wishing God would choose now to smite him down with a freak bolt of lightening or a massive cardiac arrest.

Jody jumped up and snatched a pen and notepad off the bookcase. She almost threw them at Spence.

'Jode!' warned Spence.

'Only the relevant points.'

'I've had a hard enough time blanking it from my consciousness.' he sighed, but he knew Jody wasn't going to give up.

Why hadn't she been like this in the first place? They could've sorted everything out then and there. Now he was going to have to go back to it and that was going to be like returning to the leftovers of a perfectly scrumptious dinner the next day – cold, unappealing, and with the possibility of throwing-up.

'Go on, Spence, go on.' urged Jody, prowling like a predatory panther. Her black mood had lifted and her brain was whizzing with possible calculations and solutions. She just needed Spence's input. This would impress her father.

The Colonel had been decorated many times and was a well-known figure throughout the Ministry. He was, what is known as, a Very Important Person.

Jody was just a pale imitation of her father - that was the general consensus, especially after she had turned down the offer of going backwards. It was an odd thing.

She had been a 'field agent' and, okay, she'd made a few mistakes, but nothing major, and now the Colonel was trying to get her to accept an 'easier' job. She resented that. She resented the fact that he was bowing to pressure from the other Heads of other Departments. There was no way she was going to accept a 'desk job'. The harder they pushed, the deeper she dug her heels in.

However, solving something like *this* would, perhaps, put her on the map again. It would show everyone that she could handle the pressure. Damn it, she knew she was good - and so did the others - but she just needed to prove it again.

Reluctantly, and with some hesitation and trepidation, Spence started scouring his memory for the bits he could remember... starting with Lemon.

*　　　*　　　*

Incase you were wondering, Eric was asleep.

He'd been asleep for an age and showed no sign of waking up. He was dreaming of having nine more lives.

And what he would do with them.

*   *   *

Fool. Stupid, incompetent fool.

Lemon had the Colonel's report from Suzanne Addison.

It wasn't good.

All the Colonel knew was that Jody was alive. She had phoned in sick and, being as this was the Ministry of Defence, they'd checked out her fantastical story of why she needed the day off.

Two people had been shot at The Toad & Toucan. The wrong two people, as far as Lemon was concerned. What was Lee Morgan up to? An old score to settle? Why hadn't he finished off Jody Marianne Lane?

Emotions?

Yes, perhaps.

After all, Jody Marianne Lane was attractive. Lemon had gathered that much from the picture on her file.

Lee Morgan would have to be terminated from his job. And, being as his job was his life, he would have to be terminated along with it. Somebody would have to be sent out to find him. And fast. He was a loose cannon.

Fool. Stupid, incompetent fool.

They were so near now, so near. Nothing could go wrong, surely. She'd *have* to get rid of this Jody Marianne Lane. She was too close to the core.

Suddenly, a horrible thought flashed into her mind. Perhaps Spencer Tracy and Jody Marianne Lane were working together?

It would make sense.

She was involved with the Ministry of Defence and *he* was involved with Philip Dicks.

Why hadn't she thought of that before? Perhaps Jody knew about her father? And, subsequently, she knew about the others too?

It was a possibility and one that really couldn't be ignored.

Lemon's delicate hand clenched into a fist and crashed down on the nearest console.

This couldn't be happening. She'd have to replace them.

Kill them and replace them.

It would take up time and resources but it would be safer than just getting rid of them. That could raise questions. She'd get the requirements from the files. The organisation should get to work on it straight away.

This needed to be done before the big switch, which was only a matter of days away.

*   *   *

It was 2.02pm.

Spence had trawled through flashbacks and panic attacks to get the bits of information that Jody wanted. He was exhausted and frightened. It had all become so real again. His heart was pounding in his chest and beads of glistening sweat trickled down his forehead and melted into his stinging eyes.

Jody showed no sympathy. She was eagerly scanning the fevered scribbling that Spence had made. Some interesting points were cropping up but it was still so fragmented.

What was that name that had been in the parcel?

It began with a 'D', she was sure of that.

She cursed Spence under her breath for slinging his trousers in the wash. It was probably the only time he'd done it of his own accord and on any other occasion she'd have been delighted with his apparent initiative... but not this time.

'I'm going to make a pot of tea.' gasped Spence, struggling out of the chair and wobbling towards the kitchen.

Jody grunted and sat down.

Spence made it to the kitchen before his legs gave out. He collapsed neatly in a folded heap on the floor near Eric and breathed deeply.

This wasn't doing him much good. He'd had more incidents happen to him in the space of three days than he'd have wanted in the whole of his life.

Spence had only ever asked for two things from life - hot tea and hot totty, and in that order. What previous horrors had he committed in a past life for this one to be so bad?

He rolled over on to his back and stared at the ceiling.

It was white.

Spotlessly white.

He sat up and buried his head in his hands. It was no good. He just wasn't cut out for this sort of life. He struggled to his feet and steadied himself on the work surface. His legs seemed a bit stronger and he tested his weight on them.

Now, where were the teabags? He was having serious withdrawal symptoms. He craved tea. He needed tea. What he didn't crave, or need, was to step on Eric's tail. But he did.

Eric awoke and hissed in a most horrific manner, not best pleased at being awoken from his slumber and his dreams.

He'd only got up to his seventh life, the one where he was a secret feline agent, 007, and he was fighting the evil veterinary villain, Coldfinger. He had just been about to curl up with Coldfinger's beautiful but deadly assistant, Pussy Galore, when he'd be dragged back into real life by the pain in his tail.

He sloped out of the kitchen, cursing Spence and spitting liberally to show his contempt.

Spence still couldn't find the teabags.

Jody bounded into the kitchen like an Olympic Bounder and grabbed Spence. She spun him round to face her and he saw that her eyes were positively twinkling. She smiled at him, which unnerved him, and kissed him passionately.

'Mr Arthur Plinth!' she cried, still grinning.

'See, you're doing it again.' said Spence, 'You're calling out other people's names in the height of passion.' he sighed. 'And that happens to be the name of my old next-door neighbour, as well.' he added, slightly disgruntled.

'It was one of the first things you remembered. You wrote it down.' she cried, thrusting the piece of paper under Spence's nose.

'I wrote *what* down, exactly?' asked Spence, slightly thrown by the buoyant enthusiasm of his on-off-on-again lover.

Jody kept the piece of paper under his nose and jabbed it with her free hand.

'Here.' she snapped.

'Look, will you calm down, Jode.' suggested Spence, soothingly. He guided her slowly over to the kitchen table and sat her down, taking the seat next to her.

'Now, what did I remember about Mr Arthur Plinth?' he asked.

Jody stabbed the piece of paper again with her forefinger.

'Don't you remember?' she asked, excitedly.

'Yes. Apparently, I do. And I wrote it on a piece of paper.' said Spence, trying to act calm and rationally.

Jody looked at him, grinning and wide-eyed.

'Well, just tell me!!!' Spence yelled, in a final act of exasperation.

'You said that you remembered your next-door neighbour watching from the window.' said Jody, triumphantly.

'Is that all?' huffed Spence, 'Is that *all*?' he repeated, with particularly emphasis on the italics in his speaking. 'He's *always* watching me from his window. He watches *everyone*. He's even got a pair of *binoculars* - dirty pervert.' Spence added, overdosing on italics.

'No, no, no. You recalled seeing him watching you being kidnapped.' explained Jody.

Spence's eyes widened and his mouth dropped open.

'Of course!' he cried, staring Jody straight in the eyes, 'He can confirm whether the whole thing was a dream or not.' he realised, in almost abject terror.

The possibility of an actual confirmation was frightening. Jody realised this and tried to change direction quickly.

'Let's go round after a cup of tea.' she said, getting up and switching the kettle on. It had only just finishing boiling from the last time. Spence nodded in agreement. He picked up the piece of paper and studied his efforts. Jody looked around the kitchen in bewilderment as the kettle switched itself off.

'Now, where *did* I put those teabags?' she muttered.

CHAPTER 10
'KEEP ON RUNNING'

Mr Arthur Plinth was playing Solitaire with himself. Obviously.

His wife, Helen, was in the shed, in the back garden.

Mr Arthur Plinth was sat by the window with a little table on his lap. He looked up every now and then - more 'now' than 'then', to be honest.

On the windowsill he kept a notepad and pen to jot down anything that caught his eye. The pad was bulging at the seams.

Everything caught the beady eye of Mr Plinth.

After all, he was the self-appointed leader of the Neighbourhood Watch.

So, this meant he needed to be alert.

Alert and observant.

Alert and observant and aware.

In a word: Nosey.

If Roger Hargreaves had a blueprint for his Mr Nosey character, Mr Arthur Plinth would've been it.

Well, maybe not *exactly*.

Mr Plinth wasn't actually green with a huge long nose but there was a certain similarity there. What Mr Plinth didn't know about the comings and goings of Mulberry Road wasn't worth knowing.

Mind you, Mr Plinth kept it all to himself.

He could've reported the burglary at Number 176; he'd seen it happening. He could've reported Maureen Eccleston's car being stolen; he'd seen it happening.

And the kid who was stealing the bottles of fresh milk hadn't gone unnoticed. He'd watched the secret rendezvous of Mrs Piper with her younger lover and kept it quiet.

Mr Plinth was writing an exposé, you see - a sort of novel. He'd written several drafts and still he was adding more.

It was provisionally entitled: 'Mulberry Road - A Neighbourhood Watched'.

It was an absolute corker.

He felt sure that it would make the Top Ten best-seller's list. Critics and the readers alike would rave about it. He'd be a national celebrity, as well as the subject of at least fourteen 'invasion of privacy' court cases from Number's 164 to 178, Mulberry Road.

He was drawn out of his daydream by a hollow and dull sound. The big brass knocker on his front door was being knocked, in a big brass way.

Mr Arthur Plinth shouted for his wife.

'Are you expecting visitors, Helen?!'

Helen, his wife of ten years, was still in the shed.

He shouted again.

She still didn't hear him.

He carefully placed the lap-top tray on the floor and got off his chair and wrenched himself away from his vantage point. He shuffled to the door as quickly as his carpet slippers would carry him. Fixing the safety lock, he opened the door as far as the chain would allow.

'Hello.' he said.

He could see the face of an attractive woman. This wasn't good. He couldn't let the neighbourhood know that he spoke to attractive women. I mean, they'd all *seen* Helen.

'What do you want?' he asked, gruffly.

Her face disappeared, to be replaced by a face he recognised. This more recognisable face spoke to him in a breathless, urgent manner.

'Hello, Mr Plinth - it's Spencer Tracy. Not *the* Spencer Tracy, obviously. I'm not famous. Or dead. Yet. Anyway, I used to be your next-door neighbour until my house burnt down.' said Spence, as if it was an everyday occurrence.

'Yes, I know who you are, yes.' said Mr Plinth, narrowing his eyes.

'We'd like to have a chat with you.' said Spence, smiling.

'What about?' snapped Mr Plinth, beginning to inwardly panic.

'Nothing important.' lied Spence.

'Do you think we could come in?' said the attractive woman's voice.

There was a lengthy pause as Mr Plinth thought about it for a bit.

There was a lengthy pause as Spence and Jody waited for Mr Plinth to think about it.

Finally, Mr Plinth disappeared from the crack in the door and they heard the safety chain being dismantled.

'Quick, quick, come in before the neighbours see you.' he snapped, throwing open his front door and peering behind Spence and Jody with his beady eyes, surveying and double-checking the surrounding area.

Spence and Jody darted inside and Mr Plinth slammed the door shut with an alarming force. He shuffled back to his 'drawing' room at the front of the house and sat back down in his chair. Spence and Jody had followed him and stood there waiting for another order.

Mr Plinth scanned the street with his narrowed but all-seeing eyes and then turned on his visitors.

'Well, sit down, sit down.' he barked.

Spence and Jody looked around.

'Make yourself comfortable.' he added.

They couldn't.

The room they were stood in was sparse, uncluttered and very, very bare. There was no carpet, just polished floorboards, and the walls were whitewashed.

Mr Plinth was sat on an antique chair that looked like it had seen better days and there was nothing else in the room except a few stacks of books, piled high, and one big cushion. It wasn't particularly 'homely'. But, then again, Mr Plinth didn't come across as a particularly 'homely' person.

He turned his attention back to the empty street.

It was 4.30pm and the sun was sinking fast.

Spence and Jody decided to stay standing.

'We need a favour.' Jody blurted out.

'No favours. I don't do favours.' snorted Mr Plinth, his eyes fixed.

'More of a recollection.' said Spence, hopefully.

'A recollection? A recollection?' barked Mr Plinth, parrot-fashion.

'Something that happened a few days ago.' said Jody.

Mr Plinth turned sharply on them, his eyes ablaze and his brow knotted into a furrow. He switched his stare back and forth to each visitor until they physically began to cower. His eyes narrowed again, his face was filled with suspicion.

'Why would I know anything about what goes on around here?' he hissed, worried about the reasoning behind the unexpected visit. Surely they couldn't know about his novel? His precious novel.

'Because I saw you at this window.' answered Spence. He paused and ran a hand through his unkempt hair. 'At least I think I did - it's all a bit hazy. I'm hoping you can remember seeing me... if, indeed, you did see me -

144

which is highly circumspect... which is why we're here now.' he rambled.

Mr Plinth snorted, in a way that could only be classed as a derisory.

'Why would I remember that? Eh? Why would I take any notice of you? Hmm?' he whispered, in a most sinister way.

Mr Arthur Plinth was, to put it politely, creepy.

Jody heard a sound. It was the sound of her skin crawling.

'It's just a whim.' sighed Spence. 'It was quite unusual.' he added, feeling it necessary.

Mr Plinth looked him up and down and down and up. He nodded his head for Spence to continue. Spence obliged him.

'It was last Saturday.' he began.

'It was raining.' added Mr Plinth.

'Heavily, yes.' said Spence, trying to contain his excitement.

'Time?' asked Mr Plinth.

'Late afternoon.'

'Wait there.' said Mr Plinth, heaving himself out of his chair and shuffling out of the room before another word could be spoken.

Spence and Jody exchanged puzzled glances.

The seconds ticked by. They could hear creaking floorboards and distant shuffling.

'Where's he gone?' whispered Jody.

'How should I know?' Spence whispered back, shrugging.

'Toilet?'

'Can't you wait till we get back to your house?'

'No, not for me.'

'Well, I don't need to go.'

'Do you think *he's* gone to the toilet?'

'Who?'

'Mr Plinth.'

'I don't know. Ask him.'

'How can I? He's not here.'

'When he comes back from the toilet.'

'You said he wasn't going to the toilet.'

'No, I didn't - look, how do I know where's he gone?'

'Well, I don't.'

'Who cares?!'

'Oh, shut up, Spence!'

'Me?!'

The shuffling got louder as Mr Plinth returned.

Spence and Jody shushed each other and waited as he entered the room, his head bowed and his back arched slightly. He trundled back to his chair and parked himself comfortably into it. He shifted a bit, glanced out of the window - worried that he'd been away too long - and then ignored his two visitors.

A couple of extra-long minutes dragged by in an extra-long way.

'About last Saturday?' asked Spence, nervously.

'Yes?'

'I asked if you - '

'I know what you asked.' snapped Mr Plinth, viciously interrupting. There was a pregnant pause that seemed to last nine months.

Spence coughed politely. Mr Plinth reacted.

'Yes. Yes. I saw you. You were picked up by someone in a black car.' he confirmed, in short, sharp sentences.

Spence gulped.

'It's true.' he spluttered.

'Of course it's true.' snapped Mr Plinth.

'What?'

'Are you suggesting that I made it up?' added Mr Plinth, turning on Spence.

'No.' said Spence, somewhat surprised.

'Anyway, *you* were the one being collected - you should remember.' finished Mr Plinth.

Spence took a step closer to Mr Plinth, took his hand and shook it warmly. Mr Plinth shrank away from him and pulled his hand away from Spence's firm grip.

'Good day to you both.' he concluded, making no attempt to get up.

'We'll show ourselves out, shall we?' said Jody, a little too sarcastically.

Mr Plinth didn't reply. He was too busy peering out of his window. He sat hunched over but strangely alert - like a cat waiting to pounce on an unknowing rodent. His hands clutched the arms of the chair like small talons.

Jody took Spence by the arm and dragged him out. They opened the front door and strode into Mulberry Road.

It wasn't dusk but the streetlights were switched on. Spence was jigging around as if his clothes had been filled with itching powder. He wasn't sure whether he was excited or not.

His dream was reality.

'Come on, Spence, let's get home and let this sink in.' said Jody, trying to calm Spence down.

'I'm not going mad, I'm not going mad.' he chanted, quietly to himself. Jody wasn't sure anyone would believe him, the way he was acting.

They walked down the street, hand in hand, as the first sequinned stars twinkled in the approaching black, velveteen sky.

*   *   *

It was 4.40pm.

Big Man #1 and Big Man #2 were sat in their car outside Jody's house. They were sat there because nobody was at home. This also applied to their brains.

There was only one tape in the car - an old album by the Spencer Davis Group - that had been slightly chewed up by the ancient car stereo. Still, they persevered with it and listened to a slowed-down, speeded-up, muffled-sound, mono-sound, stereo-sound, bad tape-recorder-remix version.

It was awful.

Still, Big Man #1 and Big Man #2 appreciated music as much as they appreciated sitting in a car, waiting for their target to turn up. They were both bored and drumming separate rhythms on various parts of the car in reach of their fingers. Not necessarily in time with the music.

Big Man #1 looked in the rear-view mirror for the seventh time that minute. He could see two dark figures walking towards the car. He nudged Big Man #2, incase it was Spencer Tracy and that female who'd got all feminist on them at the door.

The figures, holding hands, passed under a weak streetlight just before they reached the car.

Yes, it was them.

Action stations.

When the walking pair became adjacent to the passenger door, Big Man #2 swung it open with considerable force. It hit Spence and cannoned him into Jody, who cushioned his fall onto the concrete path.

Big Man #2 moved fast for a large man. He grabbed Spence by the collar and yanked him up off Jody.

Big Man #1 hadn't got out of the car. He had started the engine, ready for a quick escape. He leant across and pushed the back door open, on the pavement side.

But, before Big Man #2 could sling the struggling form of Spencer Tracy into the back seat, Jody had sprang up from her fallen position and swept Big Man #2's legs from underneath him. He fell to the ground with a grunt and instinctively let go of Spence.

Spence rolled away and scrambled to his feet, as he was pulled backwards by Jody.

Big Man #2 made a desperate lunge and half-gripped Spence's ankle. Jody lashed out with her foot and Big Man #2 recoiled in pain. Without a word, Jody ran back down her road, dragging a heavily breathing Spence behind her.

Big Man #1 didn't even have time to get out of the car and help. He leant across and shouted for Big Man #2 to get back in the car.

Big Man #2 did just that, hauling himself hastily into the passenger seat. Before he'd closed the door, the car had shot forwards and gone into a hand-brake turn.

The sound of the tyres screeching echoed around the peaceful estate. They ended up facing the same way that Jody and Spence were running. Wrestling with the steering wheel, Big Man #1 set the car off in pursuit of their escaping quarry.

'Come on, come *on*!!' Jody urged, literally dragging Spence as he stumbled rather ungainly behind her fleeing form. Spence was too out of breath to reply.

They came out of Hillview Estate and back on to the main road. Pausing momentarily, Jody made a lightening decision and set off again, with Spence in tow.

A couple of seconds later, the chasing car shot out on to the main road, skidding across like an out-of-control ice-skater.

Four cars swerved to avoid its mad path and narrowly avoided connecting with each other.

Big Man #2 jabbed a finger at the fleeing figures in the semi-darkness and the car was pointed in the same direction again.

Jody's head was snapping backwards all the time, like a nervous twitch, to catch a glimpse of their mystery pursuers. She saw the car shoot out after them and heard the horns and the tyres of the other cars harmonising in anger.

They'd been spotted.

She cursed under her breath and pulled Spence off the pavement and into the stream of oncoming traffic. They somehow avoided being hit and made it to the other side.

As Spence tripped up the kerb, he heard the crunching of metal against metal and the smashing of glass as cars met each other forcefully. The car that was following them skidded to a halt and made a dent in the side of a brand new BMW. The driver got out, red in the face with rage and indignation, and was silenced by a swift right jab top the chin as he leant into the passenger-side window.

Scraping along the side of the BMW, Big Man #1 steered their car through the small pile-up and off after Jody and Spence.

Even though Big Man #1 and Big Man #2 would have been slightly disadvantaged in a normal car-to-car chase (they were driving a clapped-out, Vauxhall 'not-so-super' Nova), they had the easy advantage in a car-to-foot chase.

'They're gaining on us.' puffed Spence, between sucking in huge gulps of air.

Jody couldn't be bothered to reply.

It was painfully obvious they were the underdogs in this chase. She just had to get them to the end of this stretch of main road; then there was a park to the left and another housing estate behind that.

Not far now, she thought.

Not far now, thought Big Man #1.

They were closing fast on the fleeing figures. He wrenched the steering wheel to avoid the oncoming car and mounted the same pavement that their prey was pounding along. The wing mirror flew off as he got too close to the railings that kept the general public from entering the Collinson's Parcel Company's grounds.

'Take it easy.' squeaked Big Man #2, clutching the dashboard with his fat fingers to steady himself.

Big Man #1 was focused. He didn't even hear Big Man #2's high-pitched moan. He was gradually gaining on them, getting closer and closer.

He avoided crashing into a streetlight, with an inch to spare.

Big Man #2 avoided letting go of his bowels, with an inch to spare.

'Nearly there, nearly there.' chanted Jody, under her breath.

Spence was nearly on the ground; his legs were buckling underneath him as his feet pounded the pavement with all-too-uncomfortable irregularity. Spence stumbled rather than ran. He'd always done this, ever since he was a child. He'd never seen the need to run anyway. So, subsequently, he hadn't practised it much. This gave him a curious stumbling motion when he was ever forced to do some actual running.

Like now.

He knew he was seriously hampering their escape. This was probably jogging speed for Jody.

The Vauxhall Nova was almost upon them.

Big Man #1 was having difficulty keeping it in a straight line on the loose gravel that made the pavement seem like they were driving on marbles. They'd had two more near misses with two more streetlights and brushed the railings enough to leave a new set of Go-Faster stripes all the way down one side of the car.

Big Man #1 switched the headlights on to get a clearer view and the two running figures in front loomed large. He gunned the car forward and came within touching distance of Spence when, suddenly, the prey veered off to the left and out of sight.

Big Man #1 hit the brakes and skidded into a 180-degree turn.

The Davies-Lambert Memorial Park.

That's where they'd gone. It was going to be easier on foot.

He didn't bother turning the engine off, kicked the door open and shot out of the Nova, leaving Big Man #2 somewhat startled.

'Cut 'em off!' he shouted, pointing across the park to the other side, where more terraced houses stood guard like a row of emotionless sentries.

Big Man #2 ungripped his fingers from the dashboard and crawled over to the driver's seat. He jammed his foot on the accelerator and the car jerked forward like it was about to vomit.

The open driver's door hit the nearby streetlight as Big Man #2 turned the car to point in the right direction again. It slammed shut and Big Man #2 almost lost concentration. He drove the car straight into the road, unaware of the approaching traffic, which had - yet again - to swerve in order to avoid the battered Vauxhall Nova, and set off to make it round the park before Spence and Jody got to the other side.

Spence tripped.

He didn't trip over a clump of recently-mown grass, or a hillock, or an Ant's Nest, or a Mole Hill.

No.

He tripped over his own feet.

He crashed to the floor and pulled Jody backwards. She fell awkwardly and twisted her back. Spence ate a mouthful of grass and bruised his nose. He'd knocked the wind out of him, which was a pretty easy thing to do, being as he hardly had any breath left in him. He rolled over on to his back and gulped in some air.

Jody jumped to her feet and a spasm of pain shot through her side, like a burning flame.

She ignored it.

In as much as you *could* ignore a burning flame.

Grimacing, she kicked Spence to get him up off his back. She glanced behind and saw a large figure gaining on them.

'Get up, you jackass!' hissed Jody, realising that one of the attackers was now on foot too. She didn't even think about where the car had gone - if, indeed, it had gone anywhere at all. She yanked Spence by the arm and almost pulled it out of the socket.

Spence yelped and struggled to his feet.

The large lumbering figure was almost upon them.

'We've got to split up.' she barked, pushing Spence away. He stumbled off to the right and she turned to sprint left.

The large figure had automatically turned to chase Spence. They, obviously, weren't concerned with her. She spun back round, ignoring her screaming back muscles, and made a running leap at the large figure. Wrapping her arms around his broad shoulders, the weight of her leap combined with the little weight she had on her frame, threw him off balance and brought him to the ground.

She rolled off and got to her feet first.

Spence had heard the thud of the two bodies behind him and stopped. He turned back to look, hands on his knees and bent-double, and took as many breaths as he could without passing out. Jody saw him stop

'Spence, you twit! Keep on running!!' she cried, not believing Spence's stupidity. He must have had all his common sense extracted at birth.

She never saw the left hook that felled her. But, it was a good one. She'd have to admit that, when she eventually came round.

The main, and most important, thing she'd be taught in acquiring her black belt in Martial Arts was: 'Be Alert At All Times'.

She'd just failed her re-test.

Spence didn't have the breath in him to shout a warning to Jody of the impending left hook. He squeaked one instead, at about the precise volume of a mouse with laryngitis.

He watched Jody chopped down as the powerful fist of the big, burly man felled her like a woodcutter. He knew she wasn't going to get back up again straight away. He could see that by the way her body had fallen. 'Limp' was too strong a word.

He panicked and ran.

Unfortunately, he panicked and ran right *at* the big, burly figure.

This was something that Big Man #1 wasn't expecting. It took him a while to register.

By the time he had registered Spence's intention, Spence had rugby-tackled Big Man #1 - quite spectacularly.

Both men were up again at the same time. They circled each other slowly. It was then that Spence began to wonder why he hadn't just run away. Big Man #1 wasn't called Big Man #1 for any old reason.

Spence was now worried.

His adrenaline shrank away in shame for making Spence behave so nonsensically. This allowed Spence to think quickly.

He turned and ran away.

And instantly tripped over once more.

This time, Jody's dormant form was the obstacle and not his own feet.

Spence and Lady Luck were somewhat volatile lovers. He hurt his bruised nose again and could hear Big Man #1 laughing.

This wasn't a good sign.

He felt Big Man #1's hands on his shaking shoulders so he lashed out with his legs, looking like a naughty five-year old having a tantrum.

Spence's foot connected with something soft and fleshy.

Big Man #1's hands were instantly retracted and Spence could hear his breathing speeding up. He was surprised that there was no sound. Still, he wasn't going to wait around for one.

He slapped Jody a couple of times and noticed a flicker of recognition on her face. He shook her roughly and her eyes snapped open. She got up on her elbows and shook her head, her hair whipping Spence in the face.

'Where am I?' she asked, her eyes narrowing to see through the darkness.

Spence pulled her to her feet and her legs wobbled slightly. He didn't answer her question, just set off to get away from Big Man #1, who was currently writhing in agony on the grass, his arms folded over his aching stomach that came from a painful groin kick.

They half-ran and half-stumbled across the park. As they began to reach the other side, Spence spotted the Nova, parked on the corner of a side-alley, in between two houses. He steered Jody the other way and they collapsed in some bushes near the road.

Spence looked back and saw no sign of Big Man #1.

Big Man #2 didn't seem to have spotted them either. This was good.

Unfortunately, they were trapped between them both, in some rather conspicuous bushes. This was not so good.

Jody seemed to be regaining her senses and she clutched her head gently.

'What hit me?' she moaned.

Spence peered out of the bushes again and saw Big Man #1 staggering across the park towards the road. His face was a mask of pain. He ran over the road and almost fell over the bonnet of the Vauxhall Nova.

Big Man #2 got out and propped him up.

'Did they come this way?' gasped Big Man #1, feeling incredibly sick.

'No.' said Big Man #2. 'What happened?' he enquired.

'Bloody little beggar didn't fight by the rules.' hissed Big Man #1, grimacing.

Spence motioned to the woozy Jody and they crept out of the bushes and scurried back through the park at break-neck speed, using the various tress and shadows cast by them as cover, glancing back all the time until they were out of sight of the two big, burly men.

They leant against the railings of the Collinson's Parcel Company and both sighed heavily.

It was 5.06pm and it was very dark.

'Back to your house?' enquired Spence.

'I don't think so.' answered Jody, rubbing her back vigorously to try and get rid of some of the pain at least.

She slid down the railings and sat awkwardly on the pavement.

'Well, where then?' asked Spence.

'How should I know?' snapped Jody. 'We can't go back to my house tonight. It's just too obvious.' she added.

'It's so obvious that they'll never think we'd do it.' said Spence, glimmering with an idea.

'Only a complete idiot would fail to re-check my house.' scoffed Jody. The traffic zoomed past and drowned out the rest of the conversation.

Jody put her head in her hands.

Spence sat down beside her and copied her. To passers-by, they looked like a couple of down-and-outs, a pair of tramps.

They were dirty, tired and temporarily homeless.

*   *   *

Big Man #1 climbed into the passenger seat with some difficulty. He closed the door as gently as he could and breathed out. He wasn't going to even attempt the seatbelt.

Big Man #2 started the engine and they sat there for a moment, looking as far across the park as the darkness would allow them.

'What shall we do now?' asked the high-voiced Big Man #2, looking for words of wisdom from his counter-part.

'Don't ask me.' gasped the temporarily high-pitched Big Man #1.

'We could check the house again.' suggested Big Man #2.

'Only an idiot would go back there. That's the first place they'd assume we'd look. No. I think it's best to just call it a night. They'll just check into a Travelodge or something.' said Big Man #1, aching for a relaxing, soothing soak in a hot bath.

Well, his most important parts of him were aching for a relaxing, soothing soak in a hot bath and he wasn't going to ignore their advice. He never had in the past.

'Okay.' agreed Big Man #2, allowing the car to crawl out of the side-alley at a slow speed. 'Fancy a pint?' he asked, hopefully.

'No, thanks.' said Big Man #1, using his cupped hands as a kind of shock absorber as the car hit a pot-hole in the road. 'Although I quite fancy your sister.' he added.

'Me too.' agreed Big Man #2, without thinking.

The Vauxhall Nova drove over another devious pothole and the sound of Big Man #1's pain was encompassed in one word.

A word that started with the letter 'F'.

CHAPTER 11
'PRIVATE INVESTIGATIONS'

It was 8.19pm.

Spence and Jody had been wandering around aimlessly. They'd bought some snacks from the local garage and munched away like ravenous animals.

They weren't sure what to do.

They certainly couldn't go to the police. They didn't have any evidence at all, aside from the bruise that was developing on Jody's jaw-line, and they couldn't go home because, as any idiot knows, that's the first place that Big Man #1 and Big Man #2 would look.

Ahem.

There was a Bed & Breakfast a mile down the road. It was never full, as far as they could remember. But, that was probably because it belonged to Mr Martinus and his wife. They were snobs. Nobody was allowed to stay there unless they possessed a Gold AMEX card.

Subsequently, nobody *did* stay there.

'Let's go and see your Dad.' suggested Spence, spitting crisps over his muddy trousers. It was the only thing he could think of. He didn't get on with the Colonel at all but he was sure to help them.

Jody swallowed the last of her mineral water and frowned as the throbbing muscles in her back returned for Round 10 of their Championship bout.

'He'll be working tonight.' muttered Jody.

'So?' said Spence, 'You work there too, remember?' he added.

Jody sighed.

'I *suppose* it's a good idea.' she reluctantly admitted.

She wasn't entirely convinced but tiredness and pain had set in, which meant she really couldn't think of anything better. They got up from the hard ground and made their way back into town.

*　　　*　　　*

Colonel Jack Lane was at the Manning Estate. He had left early from the Ministry and gone straight there. Lemon had sent for him and he had come. He had no choice in the matter, really.

In the dark basement, a ring of bright light emitted from the computer screens and Lemon looked like a ghost, sat enclosed in the circle of technology.

'Has the work started?' she asked, not looking up from her chosen terminal.

'Work has begun.' stated the Colonel, matter-of-factly.

'Good.' she said, a hint of a smile flickering on her cold and beautiful features.

'We estimate the reproductions to be finished by morning.' added the Colonel.

'I want them ready by dawn.' snapped Lemon.

'It will be done.' answered the Colonel.

'Dismissed.' said Lemon, looking up as the Colonel spun on his heel and rigidly marched out of her sight.

Her eyes sparkled.

The light from the monitors reflected off them and gave the illusion of a mischievous glint.

Only an illusion, mind you.

*　　　*　　　*

Spence and Jody had made it safely back into town. They were on the look-out for Big Man #1 and Big Man #2 and had seen no sign of them.

This was because Big Man #1 and Big Man #2 were in their respective homes, watching their respective televisions and drinking their respective alcoholic beverages.

Spence and Jody were still under the misconception that Big Man #1 and Big Man #2 were working for Lemon.

It was all very confusing, really.

It was now 8.45pm.

And Tuesday nights weren't particularly exciting in town. This was a relief to Spence and Jody. The streets weren't busy and the amount of people they passed would not have been enough for a quick game of mixed doubles.

Not that they were contemplating a quick game of mixed doubles.

Far from it.

Mind you, they do say that men think about it once every seven seconds. Tennis does things to you, I suppose.

'I haven't got my security pass.' said Jody, suddenly.

'What?!'

'I haven't got my...'

'I know. I heard you. My reaction was more of an exclamation than a enquiry. So, how do you propose we get inside?' hissed Spence.

'I'm not sure.' Jody replied.

They were nearing the front entrance, the barrier and the large-looking security guard with his equally large-looking semi-automatic weapon.

'I suppose I could just try telling the security guard who I am and that I've forgotten my security pass.' said Jody.

'That's true.' thought Spence, out loud. 'Your Dad can just verify who you are.' he added.

They walked up to the front gate of the Ministry and were stopped by the guard, who was right to be slightly suspicious of these two tramp-like figures. It was in his job specifications.

Fortunately, he didn't shoot and ask questions later. In fact, he didn't even ask if they were '*Friend or Foe?*'

Spence was quite miffed about that.

Jody explained the situation and the guard became even more suspicious. This too was in his job specifications. He was good at the 'getting suspicious' thing. That's why he'd got the job.

He walked into his little hut and phoned through to the interior.

'He's very thorough.' whispered Spence.

'It's probably in his job description.' Jody whispered back.

The guard returned.

'Colonel Lane is not at liberty to see you now. Come back tomorrow.' he barked.

'Oh, he's gone home.' corrected Jody, reading between the lines.

'If you come back tomorrow, you might get to see him.' stated the guard, ignoring Jody's remark. However, he knew for a fact that Jody's remark was true. This he found suspicious. It was more than his job's worth not to.

'Look, I do work here.' stated Jody.

'She works here.' repeated Spence.

'Just let me speak to whoever is in charge tonight and they'll verify this.' she added.

The guard wasn't at all happy with this. It seemed like a ploy.

A very suspicious ploy.

Nevertheless, he wasn't going to be rude.

'Bugger off.' he hissed, changing his mind.

'Pardon?!'

'You heard me. Clear off. Before I set the dog on you.' he added, in a somewhat threatening manner. He was fed up with being suspicious and now felt like being assertive. It was another thing that his job specifications had stated.

'You haven't got a dog.' said Jody.

'Ah, but can you take that chance?' asked the guard, grinning in an evil way.

'Yes. I work here. I told you that.' said Jody, getting fed up.

'She works here. She told you.' repeated Spence.

'Shut up, Spence.' snapped Jody. Spence shut up.

'Okay, okay. I might not have a dog...' said the guard, disgruntled.

'You haven't.' muttered Jody.

'Right, yes, I haven't *technically* got a dog but I have *actually* got a semi-automatic weapon.'

'Are you going to set that on us, then?' scoffed Jody. 'Is it your substitute pet? You've taught it to roll over and play dead too, I suppose.' she added, sarcastically.

'I'll make *you* roll over and play dead if you're not careful. Have I made myself clear?' hissed the guard, getting agitated. He was being wound up. This wasn't in his job specifications. He tried to stay calm.

'Go on, then.' said Jody.

'Go on then, what?' frowned the guard.

'Shoot us.' goaded Jody.

'Shoot us?!' gulped Spence, clutching Jody's arm in a restraining way.

'Shoot you?' questioned the guard.

'What's the matter? Chicken?' smiled Jody, leaning casually on the barrier.

'Right. Right. I'm calling security.' huffed the guard, getting flustered.

'You *are* security.' said Jody.

'I'm putting a call through!' he warned, stepping back inside his hut and picking up the telephone.

There was a short, heated exchange with whoever was on the other end of the line. Jody waited patiently for the guard to return. Spence tried to wait patiently too but found he was better at waiting nervously. So, he stuck with that. No point them *both* waiting patiently, he thought. Spence used logic like a fish used a bicycle.

'Now, listen. You two better just wait here. Or else.' said the guard, returning to the barrier, just as flustered as when he had left it to use the phone.

He narrowed his eyes and clenched the muscles in his jaw, in a vain attempt to look menacing.

It didn't work. He just looked constipated.

Jody leant against the barrier and folded her arms. She smiled her broadest smile at the guard. Just to annoy him.

It worked.

'And stop leaning on the barrier!!' he shouted.

Jody didn't.

Spence leant against the barrier too.

In his head.

Physically, he was standing quite a long way from it but mentally, well, he was just as brave as Jody. Oh yes.

It was 9.02pm.

And cold.

The wind had picked up considerably and was creating a particularly chilly evening.

The three figures stood motionless outside the Ministry of Defence as the wind swirled round them. It was whipping up leaves and litter and making them waltz together.

The moon was in crescent form and the stars were sparse, covered by hovering clouds that held more water than the South West Water Authority.

Which, to be honest, wasn't hard.

A puddle held more water than the South West Water Authority.

If the sun shone for more than four days, an official drought was called and an official spokesperson went on BBC South West News and said, in an official statement, that: 'Officially, there is an official water shortage.', in a manner that suggested it definitely wasn't their fault and most likely was the fault of the public for daring to fail to dehydrate.

If the sun shone for a week, hosepipes and sprinklers were banned. Anyone seen using them would face severe punishment. Torture and death weren't out of the question. It didn't matter if it had rained for a whole year, non-stop, before the sun shone for a couple of days.

For some unexplainable reason, which would ultimately involve money and Director General's salaries, they never seemed to collect enough water in their reservoirs. This allowed them to put Water Rates up by 25% each year.

It was 9.08pm when a figure approached from the Ministry of Defence.

He was a trim and uniformed figure, with a neat moustache, neat hair and neat eyebrows. He kept rubbing his hands together, which was odd as he was wearing a pair of leather gloves. He walked in military strides and military boots. He breathed through his nose like a snorting bull. The cold air exposed this by the great shafts of white that billowed out of his flared nostrils and melted away in the increasingly colder atmosphere.

He reached the barrier and the guard abruptly saluted him. The salute was returned. Jody hadn't seen him approach, as she had her back to him. She turned slowly.

'Hello, Mr Courtney.' she cheerfully bellowed.

'Hello, Miss Lane.' replied Mr Courtney.

The guard looked worried.

'Having trouble with some vagrants, are you?' snapped Mr Courtney to the guard.

The guard nodded, in a not very convincing manner.

'Well, where are they?' he asked.

The guard pointed in the general direction of Spence and Jody. Spence was now at Jody's side. He felt a lot more confident now, especially as Jody seemed to know this obviously higher-ranked visitor.

'I was hoping to get inside.' said Jody.

'The Colonel's gone home.' said Mr Courtney.

'Yes, I know.' said Jody, 'I had that information delivered, in a round-a-bout way, by Mr Security Guard, here.' she chuckled. 'I just wanted to collect something from father's office.' she added.

The guard was slowly retreating to the relative safety of his little hut. He wanted to re-read his job specifications again, just incase he had to re-apply.

'Right. Open the barrier.' barked Mr Courtney. The guard fell over himself in the hurry to raise the barrier. Spence and Jody walked past the guard.

Jody ignored him.

Spence couldn't resist a smug glance.

Mr Courtney made a brisk pace back to the Ministry building. The evening was losing temperature by the minute. His cheeks were already turning a crimson red colour and he'd left a boiling cup of coffee in his office. He smoothed his moustache down and the wind ruffled his hair in a playful manner, which Mr Courtney didn't appreciate.

Mr Courtney didn't appreciate a lot of things, unless it responded to orders and then carried them out with military precision.

Mr Courtney wasn't married, surprisingly.

Once inside the Ministry of Defence building, Mr Courtney passed on the obligatory 'Visitor's Pass' to Spence and then took his leave of them, striding back to his office like a man with a mission.

A mission to drink a steaming cup of coffee.

Spence and Jody made their way through the maze of corridors to Colonel Lane's office. It was quite a long walk. Neither of them spoke.

They got to the door. A brass plaque showed them it was the right one.

'Jody. Why are we here?' asked Spence.

'What do you mean?' replied Jody, with a question.

'Well, we know your father's not here. So, why are we here inside?' he asked, again.

'My father's office is equipped with sleeping quarters.' grinned Jody.

'Oh, clever!' said Spence.

'We can't go back to my house and we can't afford to go anywhere else, can we?'

'No, that's true.' nodded Spence.

Jody punched in her father's code on the electric lock and the door beeped. She turned the handle and they both walked in to the Colonel's private office.

Spence flopped down on to the leather couch and promptly slid off. He picked himself up and sat down again, more carefully this time.

Jody went and sat behind her father's desk. She nosed through the various odds and ends that were scattered in front of her.

It was too tempting not to.

'Are we going to tell your father about all of this Lemon business?' asked Spence, putting his feet up and snuggling down into the leather.

'There's not much to tell, is there?' mumbled Jody, more interested in the contents of the files in front of her. 'We haven't really got any specific evidence, as such.' she added.

'We've spent the last few days avoiding getting killed and you say we haven't got any specific evidence!' scoffed Spence.

'Well, nothing *substantial*, then. Just a few leads.' said Jody, half-heartedly.

'Why did we bother coming here to find him, then?' grumbled Spence.

Jody glanced up from her father's desk and fixed Spence with one of her 'looks'.

Spence ignored it.

He'd got very good at ignoring her 'looks'.

'It wasn't my idea to come here.' he said. 'You suggested it.'

'You agreed.'

'There wasn't much else we could do. Besides, it was a good way of getting a bed for the night.' said Jody, flicking through the bottom drawer of the desk and finding another file to sort through.

'We've got a witness.' Spence piped up.

Jody wasn't listening.

She'd become engrossed in the file she'd found in the bottom drawer of the Colonel's desk.

'Arthur Plinth.' said Spence.

'Philip Dicks.' muttered Jody, her brow creasing.

'No. Arthur Plinth - the Neighbourhood Watch chap.'

'Philip Dicks.' Jody repeated, at a louder volume. She slammed the file down on the desk and spread the pages out in front of her. 'Spence, come and look at this.' she breathed, not quite believing her eyes.

Spence swung his feet off the leather couch and stood up, wearily. He sauntered across the office and slouched behind Jody, peering over her huddled form.

'What is it?' asked Spence, scanning the pages briefly but not attempting to actually read them. He could see that Jody was doing that. No point them *both* reading the pages, he thought.

Spence was logical in a way that Mr Spock could never be.

'Philip Dicks worked for us.' she gasped.

'Worked for *us*?' queried Spence.

'The Ministry of Defence.'

'How do you know that?' asked Spence, taking a bit more interest.

'It's here, in this document.' said Jody, pouring over the pages with intensity.

'What did he do?' asked Spence.

This was a real lead; a real, tangible lead - the sort that hold dogs away from main roads and from humping other dogs when taking them for a daily constitutional.

'It doesn't say. Most of the stuff is censored. I think he must have been involved in something pretty big and pretty hush-hush.' said Jody.

'This is the evidence we need.' grinned Spence.

'I can't approach my Dad with this.' said Jody, 'I'm not supposed to be delving into his personal documentation.' she added.

'He's probably involved.' said Spence, excitedly.

'Or the more reason for keeping it to ourselves.' muttered Jody, gathering up the papers and putting them back into their folder.

Spence spun the chair round so she was facing him.

'Or the more reason to inform him. If he's involved, he'll help. At least he'll know what the whole thing's about.' blurted out Spence.

Jody wasn't so sure.

'No. Not yet.' she muttered. 'Let's try and find out a bit more information before we approach him.' she added, putting the file back in the bottom drawer and slamming it shut.

'We can't.' hissed Spence.

'Why?'

'We haven't got anything else to go on.' he moaned.

'We'll let ourselves be captured.' said Jody.

'You what?!' exclaimed Spence.

'Those men that were after us - well, after *you* - tonight. They'll take us straight to Lemon.' explained Jody, a plan forming in her mind.

'Oh, yes, great.' scoffed Spence. 'As plans go, that's up there with JFK's decision - after a heavy night of drinking - to take the open-top car to Dallas, as he needed to clear his head a bit.'

'It'll be fine.' reassured Jody.

'For you, maybe. They're after *me*, remember.' moaned Spence, sitting on the window-sill behind him.

Jody jumped up from her chair, too his face in her hands and kissed him passionately. She broke off and Spence looked shell-shocked.

'Trust me.' she sighed, breathless and dripping with sexual energy.

She kissed him once again.

His heart let off little fireworks and his stomach had more butterflies in it than on an entomologist's wall. She led him to the leather couch and pushed him down on to it.

'Well, if you put it like *that.*' grinned Spence.

CHAPTER 12
'WHO ARE YOU?'

It was 8.30am on Wednesday morning.

Spence and Jody uncoiled themselves and, bleary-eyed and aching of body, struggled to get up from the leather couch they had slept on.

The sounds of hustle and bustle of daily office routine could be heard all around them.

Jody adjusted herself and attempted to focus on the clock. She looked for the big hand, then the little hand, and ended up following the second hand.

Spence clambered over her and stood up, stretching his legs and trying to get some feeling back into his right arm; the arm that Jody had decided to sleep on. He yawned in an exaggerated manner and almost passed out. The sudden intake of air-conditioned oxygen had startled him somewhat.

Jody finally took note of the time and sprang to her feet, nearly knocking Spence off balance. He leant on the Colonel's desk to steady himself and activated the fan. It blew cool air into his face and his fringe lifted off his forehead as one huge piece of hair.

He staggered backwards away from it and fell over Jody's crouched form. She had knelt down to tie up her shoe-lace and, in the grand tradition of French theatrical farce, Spence had fallen over her and ended up back on the leather couch again.

It only needed for him to drop his trousers as the Vicar walked through the door and the whole charade would be complete.

Jody rubbed her back and glared at Spence. Her muscles still hadn't recovered from the awkward fall she'd had in the park and a night of sexual gymnastics had added to the strain.

They both made it into an upright position, finally, and looked at each other for a couple of seconds.

'What are we doing today?' asked Spence, wearily.

'Giving up.' replied Jody.

'Well, if three times in one night wasn't enough for to satisfy you...' started Spence, grumbling.

'No.' frowned Jody. 'We're going to find Lemon by giving ourselves up.' she explained.

Spence realised his mistake.

'Oh yes. Of course. Silly me.' he spluttered.

'We can practice your rubbish sexual technique again some other time.' she added, opening the office door and peering into the empty corridor.

Spence smoothed the leather couch to rid it of the human indents and muttered to himself.

'You've managed to get there every other time.' he grunted, just loud enough to be heard.

'Faked it.' added Jody, matter-of-factly.

She turned and walked out of her father's oak-panelled office, striding off down the corridor with a purposeful gait, leaving Spence in her wake. She was grinning to herself as she heard Spence scuttling after her.

'Well, I've faked every one of mine.' he retorted, triumphantly and not very convincingly.

Jody ignored him as she set off down the first flight of stairs that lead to the foyer.

Spence huffed in a disgruntled manner, adopted the usual attitude of a typical male when it comes to making love, with a 'Not-My-Problem-If-You-Fail-To-Be-Satisfied-By-My-Amazing-Nether-Regional-Activities'
thought process, and hurriedly scurried along behind her like an obedient pet.

Not only did Jody wear the trousers in their relationship, she also had the matching jacket and tie.

In the evolution of life, Jody had reached the ethereal stage.

Spence had just clambered out of the primeval ooze.

*   *   *

Lemon was impressed.

She didn't show it but she *was* impressed.

Standing before her were Spencer Tracy and Jody Marianne Lane. She nodded at Suzanne Addison and her personal assistant smiled.

Lemon typed in a short code on one of her computer keyboards.

Spencer Tracy and Jody Marianne Lane flickered into life. Their pupils rolled upwards and their eyes were pure white for a couple of brief seconds. Then, their pupils returned and they both blinked in unison.

They were android replicas.

Robotic doppelgangers.

And damned fine ones they were. Her technicians had done an excellent job.

'We thought they could go to work straight away.' said Suzanne Addison. She had consulted with the technicians.

Lemon raised one eyebrow.

'Do the jobs that their real counter-parts are employed in.' added Suzanne Addison, her pulse quickening slightly.

She didn't like it when Lemon raised an eyebrow. That signified discontent. Her pulse began to race as she noticed that Lemon had now raised the other eyebrow.

Lemon was enrolled in the Roger Moore School of Acting.

'And if they encounter the *real* ones?' whispered Lemon, so calm and cool. Her voice was more soothing than an all-over body massage… but not so much fun.

'The ideal opportunity to dispose of them.' said Suzanne Addison, her voice getting as close to matter-of-fact as she could allow it to get.

Lemon didn't speak.

Suzanne Addison could actually hear her own heartbeat. It was speeding.

Lemon nodded slowly, her silken hair falling across her perfect features. She flicked it back off her face casually, almost in slow motion.

Suzanne Addison breathed a secret sigh of relief. Lemon had agreed. And she was still her personal assistant.

A *living* and *breathing* personal assistant.

Coming out of Lemon's headquarters was always a huge achievement for Suzanne Addison. She always felt like her life hung in the balance almost every time she had to come into contact with Lemon. It was quite frightening and did nothing for her nerves, even though it did wonders for her regularity.

How could someone so physically perfect in every respect be so unnervingly scary? Lemon was the Hannibal Lector of supermodels. She looked like an angel and acted like a demon.

'Carry on.' sighed Lemon, averting her gaze and turning her attention back into her circle of terminals. Suzanne Addison tried not to hurry as she left the cellar.

The two android replicas followed her.

*   *   *

It was 8.56am when Spence and Jody arrived back at Jody's house.

Jody fumbled for her spare key, which she'd hidden somewhere in the soil at the bottom of her hanging basket.

She couldn't find it.

'Oh, sod it.' she huffed, giving up, 'You find it, Spence. You don't mind getting your hands dirty.' she muttered, picking clods of earth out of her nails.

Spence obliged by delving his hands into the hanging basket's array of flowers.

'I've always wanted to get my hands in your plants and rummage around.' he chuckled.

In the spirit of Queen Victoria, Jody was not amused.

They were an odd couple, Spence and Jody. To outsiders, they appeared to be constantly arguing and bad-mouthing one another.

To people that knew them, they didn't *appear* to be constantly arguing and bad-mouthing one another.

No.

They actually *were* constantly arguing and bad-mouthing one another.

Spence was the lit fuse to Jody's dynamite. If she was the Empire State Building, he'd be her King Kong.

Spence eventually found the key, but not before destroying Jody's floral arrangement. He handed it over to Jody who leant on the door to put the key in. The door opened under the pressure.

'Oh brilliant.' hissed Jody, sarcastically. 'We destroy my only attempt at being horticultural and then find that we left the door open.'

'We didn't leave the door open.' said Spence, recalling the last time they left the house, which was to see Mr Arthur Plinth.

'Oh, even better.' hissed Jody, even more sarcastically. 'You're now suggesting I've been burgled. Again.' she added.

Spence peered into her house.

'I'm not suggesting anything.' he said, 'I'm just thinking that we could be in luck.'

'Ah, yes. Luck.' snapped Jody. 'This must be that new meaning of the word LUCK that no-one but you has heard of!' she snarled, striding into her house.

'Luck, luck, luck.' she muttered, poking her head around the kitchen door. 'Doesn't that rhyme with fu - '

Eric pounced on her, interrupting her expletive.

'Owwww!' she cried, prizing the cat's claws out of her, 'Get off my leg, Eric!' she yelled.

Eric obliged.

Spence tried not to laugh. Eric had obviously heard the sound of his master's voice from the front door and then mistaken Jody's leg for his, as she had entered the kitchen first.

'Hello there, Eric!' said Spence, greeting the feline swine with a loving pat on the head.

Eric wasn't impressed. He knew Spence was being patronising. Spence knew he was being patronising too. They had quite a patronising relationship.

Eric did all the things that were expected of a cat - purring, rubbing up against his 'owner's' legs (and Eric used the 'owner' word in its loosest form), and sitting on laps. But, he did them all in a very patronising way - proving that he didn't agree with bourgeois convention.

Likewise, Spence did all the usual things that were expected of an owner. He fed the cat, stroked the cat, cursed the cat and wormed the cat. But, he too was as patronising as a University lecturer.

It made for an interesting life.

'I'm going to check upstairs.' said Jody.

'Hold on, hold on.' said Spence, grabbing her by the arm before she could leave.

'Okay. You can check upstairs and I'll check the back garden.'

'No, no, no. I never said I wanted to check upstairs. You're the one with the black belt, Jode. The only reason I have a black belt is to keep my trousers up.' he spluttered.

'Well, what then?' snapped Jody, yanking her arm out of Spence's un-vice-like grip.

'Look, you suggested we get captured by Lemon's lot.' explained Spence. Jody looked interested.

But, only slightly.

She wasn't sure whether he was stalling for time or actually had something relevant to say. Mind you, she felt like this at the start of *most* of Spence's conversations.

'This could be those two big blokes from yesterday.' he whispered, winking.

'That was either a rather clichéd and out-dated conspiratorial wink you've just attempted, or you've suddenly developed a nasty nervous tick.' grinned Jody, lightening up a little.

'It was both.' grinned back Spence.

Jody hit Spence playfully and they began to play-fight with each other. The sexual chemistry was fuelled by the size of Spence's Bunsen Burner.

Meanwhile, Eric the cat - bored with the meaningless human conversation - had padded off to the living room and was studying Big Man #1 and Big Man #2, who were crouched uncomfortably behind the sofa.

Stupid fools, he thought to himself. They'd been there since dawn this morning and they hadn't moved, apart from when Big Man #2 had got cramp and had hopped around the room, holding his foot, and howling like a banshee.

Eric had been studying them with some intensity. They were the same two that had interrupted his sleep the other night when Spence had been warned to pay them some money. But, they weren't the same two who had arrived on that same night a little while afterwards and who Spence had written a cheque for.

I wonder what happened to the other two, thought Eric. Probably used the blank cheque and flew off for a life of luxury in the South Pacific.

Of course, Eric didn't realise that Spence had about as much money as a sixteen year-old Saturday Shoe Shop Assistant. He had food on a regular basis, and none of that cheap muck either, so Eric assumed that Spence was rich.

He could hear Spence and Jody still chatting in the kitchen and so could the hidden men. He jumped up on the bookcase in a series of unbalanced leaps and bounds, thinking it might be a good vantage point with which to view what might happen next.

He temporally forgot his vertigo and ability to *not* land on all fours when he fell and just surveyed the living room.

Eric waited for Spence and Jody's entrance.

As did Big Man #1 and Big Man #2.

And they waited.

There was no more chatting now from the kitchen. It had been replaced by what sounded like someone's strange asthmatic panting.

Eric watched Big Man #1 and Big Man #2 exchange a look of confusion, so he decided to investigate.

He struggled down off the bookcase, landed heavily on the carpet - which cushioned his fall slightly - and limped out of the living room and to the kitchen.

The panting got louder and seemed to be accompanied by a weird groaning sound now. It sounded like a TARDIS, with chronic bronchitis.

The sight that greeted Eric when he slunk into the kitchen was not a pretty one, by cat standards. To be perfectly equal, it wasn't a pretty one by human standards either.

It was the act of procreation, on a kitchen table, done very badly.

Eric felt nauseous and slunk back out again. He had always thought that the day he was neutered, they should've done Spence as well.

*　　　*　　　*

Mr Pertwee, head of Data Section F, handed some more work to Spencer Tracy.

Not *the* Spencer Tracy, of course.

Or, indeed, the famous Spencer Tracy.

Confused much?

There was something strange about his laziest employee. He was working.

Yes.

Working.

Mr Pertwee was slightly unnerved by this.

He was also dressed smartly, with his hair brushed, his desk clear, and wearing a tie properly for once – something that Spence had an irrational fear of.

Mr Pertwee didn't like this transformation. Who was he going to shout at now? Spencer Tracy had been his release valve. People talked about stress, Mr Pertwee said he worked with it and it was called Spencer Tracy.

Still, he wasn't going to grumble. Just wait and see how long it lasts - that's what his instincts told him.

Spence had even said 'Thank you' when he'd received the bundle of files to input. That's what had originally aroused Mr Pertwee's suspicion.

In all the years that Spence had worked for Mr Pertwee, he'd said 'Thank you' about as many times as Mr Pertwee had had relations with a woman... without paying or having to inflate her first.

All of this thinking was making Mr Pertwee's brain hurt. And Mr Pertwee never liked thinking in the morning.

Especially at 9.10am.

On the other hand, Jody Marianne Lane (not *the* Jody Marianne Lane, of course) was busy doing nothing in her office across town. She'd asked her secretary to hold all calls and not to disturb her. This, effectively, meant she had nothing to do, apart from waiting for the *real* Jody Marianne Lane to turn up. But, she guessed this wasn't going to happen.

Well, she'd been programmed to guess that this wasn't going to happen.

It was more than likely that she would encounter her nemesis after office hours, at their shared home.

Well, she'd been programmed to think it was more than likely.

This version of Jody Marianne Lane was going to be as busy as a not particularly busy person today.

*   *   *

Big Man #1 and Big Man #2, ears cocked, could hear the definite signs of rigorous tea-making. This implied to them that the *other* rigorous activity that they'd had the misfortune to hear was over.

They hoped.

'I think they've finished.' whispered Big Man #1.

180

'I should hope they have.' whispered back Big Man #2, in his high-pitched voice.

'Look, I'm getting a bit fed up with waiting to surprise them.' admitted Big Man #1, 'Let's just go and get them now.' he added.

Big Man #2 held him back.

'What if they haven't... um... quite... erm... how can I put this? Reached the top of the mountain?' he stuttered.

'What?' frowned Big Man #1.

'Scaled the dizzy heights?' implied Big Man #2, winking.

'Are you feeling alright?'

'Hit the peak of performance?'

'Stop spouting rubbish.'

'Pressed the right buttons?'

'You're beginning to annoy me.'

'Died a little death? Excuse my French translation.'

'You'll be dying a little death in a minute, if you don't shut it.'

'Made it to the end of the tunnel?'

'What *are* you on about?' hissed Big Man #1, wrenching himself away from Big Man #2's sweating grip and standing up.

Big Man #2 jumped up too.

'They might not have finished bumping uglies like there's no tomorrow!' he hissed, under his breath, making the necessary (or unnecessary) motions to accompany his summing up.

'Do you have to be so crude?' snapped back am offended Big Man #1. 'You could've put it another way.' he added.

If this were a movie, Big Man #2 would now have been doing an over-exaggerated and over-exasperated double-take towards the camera. But, it isn't. So, he wasn't.

'Let's go and grab them, then.' sighed Big Man #2.

Big Man #1 couldn't think of a suitable comic innuendo, so they both turned to leave for the kitchen and both nearly fell over Eric the cat.

Eric had witnessed the start of the 'stand to attention, legs apart, trousers down!' action and had made a hasty exit from the kitchen. As far as he was concerned, he *hoped* that Spence and Jody got caught. He certainly wasn't going to warn them.

He had originally considered jumping up, claws out, and settling on Spence's bare behind but he'd a feeling it would be like a particularly unpleasant rodeo ride.

So, instead, he'd walked out of the kitchen and settled down in a ball, in the hall, too sleep. And to be a nuisance to anyone that happened to walk out or into the kitchen.

Eric chose his sleeping spots with calculated precision and maximum annoyance. He was as blatantly irritating as the onset of chickenpox. But, no amount of Calamine lotion would get rid of Eric.

Big Man #1 and Big Man #2 entered the kitchen, with the lumbering gait of those Egyptian Mummies in the Hammer Horror films of old.

Spence and Jody were sitting at the kitchen table now, drinking a cup of tea each and looking rather red-faced and dishevelled.

Spence caught sight of the intruders first, spitting out his tea and letting go of the cup with surprising ease. Big Man #1 cuffed him round the back of the head with some considerable force.

Spence dropped like a stone and so did the cup. They both smashed to the ground at the same time. Luckily, Spence's head wasn't quite as easily breakable as the cup of tea.

Jody didn't have time to move either. Her Martial Arts training counted for nothing when the nearest heavy object - which happened to be the chrome-plated toaster - was used as a cosh.

Lying together, on the kitchen floor, Spence and Jody looked like a pair of rag-dolls.

Eric slept on.

*   *   *

The time was now 11.43am.

Spence and Jody were awake, with headaches. The sort of headaches where you swear that your brain cells have taken up dancing lessons, in an attempt to beat some sort of world record for the longest and loudest continuous tap-dance.

They were both sat in the dimly-lit office of Mr Letts, slouched in uncomfortable chairs.

Big Man #1 and Big Man #2 were hovering behind them.

'Money.' barked Mr Letts. 'That's all I'm asking for.'

'And I'm telling you that I've all ready given you a blank cheque.' sighed Spence, rubbing his temples.

'You're pushing my patience to the limit.' Mr Letts grimaced.

'Look, these two idiots accosted me, twice, in my bed, a couple of nights ago.' said Spence, motioning behind him to the two big, burly shadows.

Mr Letts paused, took a drag on his cigar and blew smoke rings. Well, *tried* to blow smoke rings. He'd never managed it once.

Smoke *shapes*, he could manage. But, smoke *rings*? Not a chance.

It didn't annoy him anymore, though. He didn't feel any less of a 'villain' because he couldn't blow smoke rings. Those expensive therapy sessions had cured him of that.

'You're telling lies.' mumbled Mr Letts. He leant forward, into the arc of light that emanated from his table-lamp. 'And I don't like people who tell lies.' he added, menacingly.

There was another pause.

This was supposed to create tension. Mr Letts relied too heavily on *film noir.*

It just made Spence and Jody fidget.

'I'm asking for my money, Mr Tracy. You burnt my house down and I want some significant compensation.' said Mr Letts, threateningly.

'Did you not have house insurance?' asked Jody, in a somewhat sarcastic manner.

'I did not burn your house down.' said Spence.

'I say you did.' said Mr Letts.

'Did not.' Spence retaliated

'Did.'

'Did not.'

'Did.'

'Did not.'

'Did.'

'Did not.'

'Did.'

'Did not.'

'I'm not arguing with you, Mr Tracy.' hissed Mr Letts.

'You are.'

'Am not.'

'You are.'

'Am not.'

'You *are.*'

184

'Am *not*.'

'You - '

'Shut it.' snapped Mr Letts, interrupting.

He jabbed his cigar towards Spence and frowned heavily.

'£125,000 pounds.' he announced.

You could hear Spence gulp.

'Where am I going to get that sort of money from?' squeaked Spence.

'Just get it. I'll give you until the weekend.' said Mr Letts, settling back in his chair again.

Spence shook his head in disbelief.

'I'm telling you, I gave you a blank cheque.' said Spence. 'Perhaps Lemon didn't tell you.' he added, hopefully.

'Lemon?' enquired Mr Letts.

'Don't give me that. Don't tell me you're not working for Lemon. It's no use feigning ignorance. I *know*. I've met her.' said Spence, confidently.

He gestured to Jody.

'*We* worked it out. We *know* she exists.' he added.

'I'm very happy for you.' said Mr Letts. He had no idea what Spence was talking about.

Spence grinned, showing a fine set of teeth.

Mr Letts grinned back, showing a fine set of gums.

'Now sod off out of my office.' he added, losing the toothless grin.

Big Man #1 and Big Man #2 grabbed Spence and Jody from behind and hauled them roughly out of their seats.

*   *   *

It was 12.05pm.

Lunch break - not only at the Data Input Centre, but also at the Ministry of Defence.

Spencer Tracy and Jody Marianne Lane left their desks and made their way back to Jody's house on the Hillview Estate. They both had an hour and a half for lunch. They both needed to find their human counterparts. They both weren't programmed to be hungry.

*   *   *

It was 12.05pm.

The real-life Spencer Tracy and Jody Marianne Lane were shoved out of a door and onto a busy street. The daylight hurt their eyes after the darkened office and they staggered blindly about for a few seconds.

The busy street ignored them. It was a typically English busy street.

Regaining their sight, Spence and Jody looked back at the door they'd been pushed out of.

It was a perfectly ordinary door, in a perfectly ordinary building, in a perfectly ordinary street, in the perfectly ordinary centre of town.

The sign across the building's front said: 'LETTS PROPERTY DEVELOPMENT AND HOUSING'.

It was nothing if not informative.

Spence didn't know what he'd expected; an out-of-town warehouse, a deserted dock, a run-down shack in the countryside, perhaps? It must be a cover for Lemon, he thought.

Jody had the very same thoughts.

'Where am I going to get £125,000 from?' was Spence's first sentence in the open air.

Jody shrugged. She was getting confused. If Lemon only wanted money then what had Spence done? And what a strange co-incidence that she owned his rented house. This was just too complicated. Was this all he was being chased for? He'd supposedly seen Lemon *before* his house got burnt down.

Her head hurt.

'Let's go back home.' she sighed, linking arms with Spence. They marched off to find the nearest bus stop.

Their stomachs rumbled in unison with the steady stream of traffic.

*　　*　　*

It was 12.25pm when they got off the bus.

It took them another five minutes to reach Jody's house. This would make it 12.30pm. But, then, you could have probably worked that out for yourself.

They trudged up the drive to Jody's door. She fumbled in her pockets for the spare key that they'd found earlier. Spence produced it from his pocket. But, before she could use it in the lock, the door opened.

Eric trotted out.

'That was impressive. Even for Eric.' marvelled Spence.

Eric stopped in front of them, seemed to study them for a moment, and then arched his back. The hairs all over his body stood to attention and he hissed and spat.

'Calm down, Eric.' chuckled Spence, wondering what was the matter with his feline chum.

Eric skipped away from Spence's outstretched hand and made a break for the tree in Jody's front garden.

'What's the matter with Eric?' asked Jody. Spence shrugged.

'I don't know.' he replied, looking rather puzzled. They turned to look for him.

Eric the cat was now nowhere to be seen.

They turned back to the open door and framed in the doorway stood two people. Two people that looked very familiar.

'Since when have you replaced the glass in your front door with mirrors?' asked Spence, turning sharply on Jody.

Jody turned slowly towards Spence.

'Since never.' she gulped.

Their eyes widened. They turned back. They were still there.

Spence reached for the front door and slammed it shut.

'I think the words I'm looking for are 'RUN' and 'AWAY'.' he whispered, spinning Jody round and heading back down the drive.

Jody didn't reply. She couldn't. Her bottom lip was dragging along the ground.

'Shut your mouth and start running.' snapped Spence, hearing the front door open again, behind them.

They shot off down the road, running as fast and as haphazardly as people in old black-and-white news footage.

It wasn't the first time they'd run away from themselves.

But, never quite so literally.

CHAPTER 13
'UNDER PRESSURE'

Richard Delgado was putting the finishing touches to an ear.

A human ear.

Well, what *looked* like a human ear, anyway.

He sat back and admired his work. He often did this. He was a great admirer of his own work. He was also a great admirer of himself - he had an ego the size of Milton Keynes.

He was a funny sort of man; short in stature and big in nose. He was balding, bow-legged and bearded; a man at ease with alliteration.

'One small dab of flesh-tone pink for man, one giant shell-like for android-kind.' he muttered, chuckling to himself.

The ear he was working on was placed gently into a small box, wrapped in cotton wool, and stored with other similar-sized boxes.

He rummaged through a pile of invoices on his workbench and found a memo from Philip Dicks. He couldn't, for the life of him, remember reading it. Or, indeed, receiving it.

Still, he hoped it was good news.

If the prototype wasn't found soon, he'd be in serious trouble. And serious trouble was something he didn't want to be in. He hadn't got where he had today by being in serious trouble.

No, sir.

If a job was worth doing, it was worth doing well - that was Richard Delgado's motto.

And he also had an A-plus in Sucking Up.

This helped.

Spencer Tracy and Jody Marianne Lane spent the afternoon in a kind of daze. Neither of them wanting to speak about what they'd witnessed.

They had spent most of the afternoon sitting in the park, on a bench, in total silence. The words 'riveting' and 'conversation' were somewhat alien to them throughout this sullen afternoon.

Had they just seen themselves? And, if so, who were *they*? It was more confusing than Chinese proverbs.

It was now 4.45pm and starting to get dark.

Out of the two of them, it was Jody who made the first move. She got up and pulled Spence to his feet by liberal usage of his clothes.

'Come on.' she sniffed, setting off for the main road.

'Where are we going?' asked Spence, prising Jody's hand off of him and then attempting to straighten his tie, forgetting that he didn't have one on away from work.

Spence had made it a policy of his never to wear a tie if he could get away with it but still always felt like he should be and was, in fact, wearing one. It was one of his many quirks that some people would deem as endearing, whereas other people would see them as downright irritating.

He'd been forced to wear a regulation school tie at the Grammar School he'd attended and he'd rebelled by wearing it as a belt instead.

He'd also worn it around his ankle a few times too.

Well, there was nothing in the school rules that told you *where* you had to wear it - just that it was an essential part of the uniform. In the same way, reasoned Spence, that meat is an essential part of a Vegan diet.

Spence hated ties more than he hated his old headmaster. In fact, his old headmaster - a cheerfully bald man who went by the name of Mr Slaphead (not his *real* name, obviously) - was very much like a tie; long, thin and permanently knotted.

'I'm going to see Father.' stated Jody.

'Oh.' said Spence, half-listening. He paused. 'Why? Have you got a pair of binoculars handy?' he exclaimed, over the roar of a passing motorbike.

Jody did what she always did when Spence gave her a glib answer.

She ignored him.

*　　　*　　　*

It was 5.00pm, exactly.

On the dot.

To the very second.

Richard Delgado had officially finished his day's work. But, after reading the memo from Philip, he decided to reply. It was a matter of urgency. If the M.o.D. found out that his prototype had gone missing, he'd be subject to an internal inquiry, which was as painful and intrusive as it sounds.

Philip had a lead.

This could be the bit of good fortune that had been lacking in his investigations so far. It was an old memo too; five days old, to be precise.

Why hadn't he seen it before? Paperwork wasn't Richard Delgado's forte, unless he was making paper aeroplanes - he was good at those; with paper-clip nosecones, adjustable wing-flaps, a tall tail fin and a set of distinctive markings.

A scientist's life was never dull.

*   *   *

It didn't take Spence and Jody long to reach the Colonel's house. It seemed very welcoming in the darkness of early evening.

Lights shone out of all the windows, no curtains were drawn and you could see right into the front room from the road.

The Colonel was sitting, straight-backed and rigid, at his computer. He didn't seem to be typing anything, just sort of staring at the monitor. His face was white from the glow of the screen.

Spence and Jody walked up the drive and tapped on the window.

The Colonel didn't break his concentration.

Jody knocked on the window a little bit harder. The Colonel's head turned slowly away from the screen and faced Spence and Jody. He stared blankly at them.

Jody almost screamed.

Spence almost fainted.

The Colonel's eyes were white. Pure white.

Spence and Jody were rooted to the spot. The Colonel's face turned back to the computer screen and he then stood up and left the room.

'Christ.' gasped Jody, starting to breath again, in short, shallow breaths.

'Did you see his eyes?' asked Spence, leaning against the window. 'They were... well, they were... not there.' he stammered. Jody frowned at him, pulling herself together.

'Don't be stupid.' she snapped. 'It must've been the reflection from the computer screen.' she added, trying to convince herself as well as Spence.

The front door opened and a beam of light illuminated the drive.

192

The Colonel poked his head out into the beam and looked across at Spence and Jody on the lawn.

His eyes were normal.

'What an unexpected surprise!' he barked, in his usual clipped, emotionless manner - making his exclamation sound like it was the last unexpected surprise he wanted to deal with at that very moment. He was probably one of the most unwelcoming men that had ever existed.

'Come in, come in.' he ordered. 'Don't stand on the lawn. You'll damage it.' he added.

Here was a man with pride in everything, even his lawn. There were no flowers on it and it certainly wasn't aesthetically pleasing, but it was neat, tidy, trimmed and green, without a weed in sight. It was a probably the perfect lawn.

Spence and Jody tried to creep off the lawn as gently as they could. He stood back and let them through the front door.

They entered the Colonel's headquarters. The furnishing was sparse but functional, the decor was plain, and the place was spotless. He ushered them through into the front room.

The computer screen was blank. It was the first thing that Spence and Jody noticed. It was the first thing they looked at. It was as pure white as they'd imagined the Colonel's eyes were earlier.

The Colonel switched off the computer and the humming of the internal fan subsided slowly as the power drained away. He had pressed the only coloured button on the keyboard just before he had turned it off and something flashed across the screen that was unreadable to Spence and Jody.

*　　*　　*

193

The monitor in front of her lit up as a message flashed across the screen, too fast for the human eye to read.

Yet, she read it.

She sighed. It was a long, sensual sigh.

Her fine hair fell across her face as she bowed her head. She caressed the keyboard that was nearest to her, running her fingers over the letters and numbers as if she were blind. She had received the message and now she must act on it.

It was a simple decision.

As she typed away, the other monitors that surrounded her glowed with ferocious intensity, demanding her attention. She had a shimmering aura around her, created by the flashing screens.

What had started out as a feeble annoyance had now turned into a large irritation; she was determined to put an end to it once and for all. She thought about leaving her technological den and dealing with everything herself but that wasn't feasible.

Two more days before her plans came into fruition. She couldn't chance it.

Lemon communicated with her androids. They would have to do the job this time.

*   *   *

Jody finished telling the Colonel about it all.

She had blurted out nearly all they had discovered, been involved in, got mixed up with, and uncovered. It sounded jumbled and incoherent and made little sense but it was a relief to get it off her chest.

Spence would've rather got something else entirely off her chest, but could never undo the catch at the back

194

(and certainly not in the presence of her father!). Spence always did this. In times of social intercourse - especially if it was serious - his mind would turn to the *other* form of intercourse.

And even more so if he was with Jody.

He watched her dishevelled hair fall over her shoulders and cascade like a muddy waterfall down her back. Her deep green eyes were anxious and wide, like two precious emeralds – they were as priceless as his love for her. He felt wonderful when he was around her.

Spence wasn't tall but he towered over Jody. He could envelop her with a hug. Not that he got to give her many hugs. She was a feisty firecracker and it was usually her that looked after him.

Still, he pretended to be the dominant one.

His mind was slowly turned back to what was being talked about as he overheard the name 'Philip Dicks' mentioned. He panicked and assumed that Jody was going to tell her father about the document in the Colonel's office. He was about to make some glib comment to interrupt Jody's storytelling when the doorbell did it for him.

Three chimes echoed around the house and faded away so softly.

'It all can be explained away, my dear - it's probably nothing more than a freakish co-incidence.' said the Colonel, with an air of flippancy. He got up and walked out of the front room, leaving Jody in mid-sentence.

'He doesn't believe us.' Jody sighed, her forehead creasing into a frown. Spence stroked his fingers across the furrows. He gently kissed her on the lips.

'Don't worry.' he said.

He didn't know why he had said it. He was more worried than she was. It just seemed the right thing to say.

Plus, the Colonel was a decent enough chap. He'd do something about it, even if he didn't truly believe in it. He adored his daughter. Spence knew this, purely by the looks he was given every time he was near her. The Colonel was good at those. He could make Spence feel so small. And Spence was paranoid enough about that, as it was

'We'd better get going. Father was obviously expecting visitors.' said Jody, trying to pull Spence to his feet as she got up too.

The visitors entered the front room.

Spence saw them first. He gulped.

'Yeah.' agreed Spence, his mouth suddenly becoming very dry. 'He was obviously expecting *us*. Look, we seem to have arrived a little too early.' he added.

Jody looked at Spence quizzically and then followed his fixed stare.

She saw the visitors.

It was the very same 'visitors' that had visited her house earlier.

It was them.

A spitting image of them.

And one of them had a gun.

Jody shoved Spence out of the way as she saw the trigger-finger tighten. He fell over the settee and out of sight. As she felt the bullet whistle past her ear, she fell to the floor. It was highly-polished and smelt of wax.

She pulled at the rug and it unbalanced the other Spence and Jody. The gun went off again and a map of Africa on the wall gained a smoking hole.

Jody rolled across to her double and wrenched the gun from its hands. So intent was she of doing this that she didn't notice the foot from the other Spence in her midriff. It knocked the wind out of her and she doubled up.

The real Spence popped up from behind the settee and attacked himself – literally, not metaphorically.

The sight of Spence struggling with himself was not something new. He often struggled with himself, but usually it was just a case of tight trousers.

Jody shot herself.

Her double jerked in an odd manner and stood still. No blood.

Jody got to her feet and was then bowled over by two helpings of Spence. She went to shoot and then froze.

Which was which?

She shot the one that was winning, straight through the head.

Sparks of electricity flashed and the losing Spence jumped away. She'd got it right.

Well, it had been pretty obvious, really. The day Spence won a fight would be the day of the re-emergence of Elvis Presley from his enforced exile by aliens in Area 51.

The Colonel entered the room and surveyed the mayhem. Jody pointed her gun at him. Her hand shook with rage and with fear. She looked into his eyes. There was no sparkle.

He walked towards her.

Her finger trembled and the pressure on the trigger increased.

Spence turned away. She wouldn't do it, he thought. She can't. He thought right. He knew this as he blacked out. The Colonel's walking stick had connected with his neck in just the right place to cause instant unconsciousness.

*   *   *

It was now 7.34pm.

Richard Delgado posted the letter. The last collection went at 7.45pm.

It had taken him a while to find Philip Dicks' address but at least it was all done and dusted now.

Mulberry Road.

He liked the sound of that.

It sounded like the sort of road you'd find in children's stories. Richard Delgado liked children's stories. If he hadn't have become a scientist, he would've liked to been a writer of children's stories. He'd had a good idea for a series of books called 'Science Is Fun'. Of course, if he'd ever written them and had them published, he would have been prosecuted under the Trade Descriptions Act.

He walked away from the Post Box and hoped Philip Dicks would have some good news for him soon. The prototype mustn't fall into the wrong hands, he thought.

Namely, any hands other than his own, in Richard Delgado's mind.

His whole idea was such a perfect one; dispensable androids as fighting machines. Cool, calculated and not affected by human emotion. It would save human lives too. This was his argument. No soldiers would get killed in battle, just androids.

Richard Delgado wasn't at one with defending or championing his inventions. He just invented. That's what he was paid to do. There were so many intricacies and conversational webs that evolved around his latest invention that it would be impossible to say if the idea was right or wrong, moral or immoral, black or white.

As long as he got the wage-slip at the end of the month, he was happy.

Richard Delgado was a man in love with money.

When you're the top scientist and one of the highest-paid employees of the Ministry of Defence, you *would* be in love with money.

It would be hard not to be when you saw the amount of noughts that appeared after each figure on his wage-slip.

*   *   *

It was about 8.18pm when Spence regained his sight and came to his senses.

The room span and slowly came into sharp focus. He was lying on the settee. He tried to sit up and the throbbing in the back of his head shot right over his cranium and into his temples with some force.

Jody was stood over him.

'You took a nasty knock.' she said, ruffling his hair. Spence tried to grin but it hurt to do so.

'The Colonel?' he managed. His throat felt dry and the words sounded odd.

Jody didn't answer. Spence didn't push the issue.

He pulled himself up by his elbows and half-sat, half-squatted on the settee. His head was really pounding and he felt extremely nauseous. He looked around the room.

They were still there. Their doubles. In exactly the same position as he remembered. Jody was stood. Spence was on the floor. It was such a surreal thing.

Jody saw what Spence was looking at.

'They're some kind of robots.' she said. 'I didn't study them too closely.'

'Oh.' was all Spence could manage.

'You going to have to get some sleep, Spence.' said Jody, putting him back into a vaguely horizontal position again. 'That bump on your head is pretty big.'

'That's no way to talk about my nose.' smiled Spence, closing his eyes. The second that his eyes closed, he was asleep.

Jody brushed his fringe off his forehead and sat on the floor. She leant against the settee and buried her head in her hands. Her body shook as she began to cry, quietly but uncontrollably.

*   *   *

Postman Pat had been a postman since leaving school. Since 1981, however, his life had been a living hell. If he could get his hands round the neck of the twit who'd come up with the idea for that stupid kid's programme, he'd squeeze and squeeze.

It was Thursday.

He looked at his watch.

8.56am.

He should be finished by 9.00am.

Should be.

The slower he did the round, the more money he got. Over-time was the way to go. So, he was on his third street out of seventy. Well, he was getting ever near retirement age. That was his favourite excuse.

Mulberry Road.

What a stupid name for a road, he thought. He always thought that. Mind you, he'd never come across a street, a road, or a cul-de-sac that he didn't think was stupidly named.

Postman Pat wasn't at all like the kid's programme, apart from the name, obviously.

If he'd had a black-and-white cat called Jess, he wouldn't have greeted it like his fictional namesake. There would've been no hearty 'Hello there, Jess', unless the sign language for 'Hello there, Jess' was a swift kick up the backside.

He bent a 'Fragile - Please Do Not Bend' envelope to get it through the door of Number 169.

He hated Mr Arthur Plinth.

Always spying out of his front window - as if he was invisible and no-one could see him doing it. Ever since he had been on this postal round, Mr Arthur Plinth had been sat at his window. It didn't matter how early he got to his house.

He shuffled away from his front door as he sorted out the rest of the letters for the rest of the houses. He had one for No.171, addressed to a Mr Philip Dicks.

Postman Pat scratched his head as he couldn't recall that name from memory. He hadn't had any post for No.171 for a couple of days. As he looked up to see where he was going, he remembered why.

There was no No.171. It was a pile of gutted rubble.

There was a sign stuck in the front lawn with a company name emblazoned acrros it: 'LETT'S PROPERTY DEVELOPMENT AND HOUSING'.

In front of it was a small, pad-locked box saying 'Correspondence'.

Postman Pat shoved the letter in the box and tutted to himself. As he glanced back briefly, he saw the pinched face of Mr Arthur Plinth watching his every move.

Postman Pat gave a cheery wave... using only his middle finger.

*   *   *

Jody had mapped out what they were going to do today.

Spence still felt a bit unsteady but he didn't want to tell Jody that. After all, it was just a minor bump on the head. A minor bump on the head that hurt like the world's worst paper-cut.

He was off to see his Bank Manager and she was off to the Ministry of Defence. He needed a loan of substantial monetary value and she needed a loan of that file they had seen before.

Spence decided to overlook the fact that the Colonel seemed to have disappeared. He didn't want to ask Jody about it. She seemed wound up and tight-lipped enough as it was.

The Colonel's house was in quite a deserted area, so it took a while to reach any main road. They split up and agreed to meet back at the Colonel's house in the early afternoon.

*   *   *

The Colonel had his orders.

New orders.

It was going to be a busy day. But, then, busy days were what he enjoyed. At least, he used too.

It was very complicated.

The Colonel was an android. The first one that Lemon had built, in fact, and his programming was too intense. She had programmed it *too* well.

All her other androids knew they were androids... except the Colonel.

He drove his car to the outskirts of town. A crumpled man was scuttling along the pavement, into the biting wind. It was another day that threatened a storm.

He glanced up momentarily as the Colonel pulled up beside him. The Colonel nodded and opened the passenger door. The scuttling man graciously bowed his head and slumped in the empty seat, out of the cold morning.

'Morning, Colonel.' he gasped, catching his breath. 'Thanks for the lift.'

'Morning, Mr Delgado.' answered the Colonel, not even looking at his new companion. 'My pleasure.'

*   *   *

Jody had left Spence at his Bank (who billed themselves as 'The *Listening* Bank', in an attempt to appear caring) and made her way, at a pace that could only be described as leisurely, towards the Ministry of Defence.

She'd stopped off at her favourite cafe, right opposite, and had ordered a calming cup of coffee and a couple of rounds of buttered toast and raspberry preserve. She loved this little, up-market cafe. There was something very old-fashioned about it, almost Victorian.

She was trying to forget about her father. He had betrayed her. Somehow, he was mixed up with this whole Lemon thing.

But why?

And what was he going to get out of it? Perhaps it was a secret operation by the Ministry of Defence. Why didn't she know?

Christ, it was cold.

Another customer opened the door to leave and a chill wind swept through the place, moving the staid, starched, lace tablecloths into some sort of synchronised flapping and causing the people sat around them to shiver and pull their coats tighter about themselves.

She felt the last buttered piece of toast stick in her throat and wished she hadn't eaten so much. She drained her coffee cup and looked at her watch.

It was 10.19am.

She'd been there for over an hour. She kicked her chair out from under her, causing the regulars to look over disapprovingly, and went to pay the bill.

Spence would probably be finished by now. She hoped the Listening Bank lived up to the name. He needed a loan of £125,000.

And quick.

Mr Letts wasn't a man to be trifled with. It was best not to ask questions. Just pay him. Then, this whole sorry business would be over. For him, at least.

She hazarded a guess that the rest of it had something to do with the Ministry of Defence and her. Was it some sort of test? How the hell would she find out? It was all too many questions, pinging around her brain like a bluebottle in a jam-jar.

*   *   *

Spence *had* finished at the Listening Bank.

They had - for the time he was there - been the Laughing Bank instead. He had more chance of winning the Nobel Peace Prize than securing a loan for £125,000 from them.

One look at his bank balance had made their minds up.

He didn't know what to do now.

He could go back to the Colonel's house or straight to the Ministry of Defence and wait around for Jody. He opted for the Colonel's house.

His mind was made up for him as he exited the Listening Bank and the first droplets of rain hit his aching head like falling sledgehammers.

*   *   *

The Colonel had taken Richard Delgado for an early morning swim, which was strange as Richard Delgado had never learnt how to swim.

*   *   *

Jody was having trouble with the same guard as before. She'd, apparently, clocked in 10 minutes ago. This didn't make sense. Still, this was the story he was sticking with and he was really *sticking* with it.

'Look, I'm here *now*, so let me in.' she hissed, showing him her official pass for the third time - even though she hated the photo on it.

The guard shrugged.

'I've all ready let you in.' he sighed. He didn't seem to find it strange. 'And being as you didn't clock out again, I can't let you back in.' he added.

Jody frowned and looked seriously confused.

He continued.

'You may well have come back out again, but you didn't officially clock out - so, you left unofficially - therefore you are, officially, still inside the building. It's not my fault if you forget to clock out. I suggest you go and ring your extension and let them clarify the error. Then - and only then - I'll allow you entry.'

'You really are a perfect fool, aren't you?!' snapped Jody, pocketing her pass.

'No.' replied the guard.

'No, you're right. You're not.' she agreed. 'Nobody's perfect.'

Jody left the gate and stormed off in the direction of the nearest public telephone. It was a good five minutes walk away, so she increased her pace to cut down the time. As she turned the corner, she bumped into Mr Courtney.

'Aha.' she cried.

'Hello there, Miss Lane.' smiled Mr Courtney, doffing his hat.

'I'm on my way to work.' she said, linking arms with him.

'You were going the wrong way.' he frowned.

'Not anymore.' she grinned, pulling Mr Courtney along.

The guard saw the couple approaching and his spirits sank. It was going to happen again. Damn that little woman. She was so cunning. His Grandma had always warned him off little women. And she had been so right, God rest her soul.

Mr Courtney and Jody sailed past the guard and through the main barrier. The guard saluted Mr Courtney. Jody resisted returning the salute with a two-fingered one of her own.

Once inside the Ministry of Defence, she said her goodbye's to Mr Courtney and made her way up to her office. She could go to the Colonel's after she had found out what the mix-up at the gate was about, she thought.

*   *   *

Spence had gone back to the Colonel's house, getting soaking wet in the process, and had flopped down on the settee as soon as he had entered the front room. His head was swimming and his neck was aching. He couldn't even be bothered to make himself a cup of tea, which was highly unusual.

Tea was more important to him than... well, most things. It was something he couldn't do without, unlike his splitting headache. He glanced around the room. There was something wrong. His brain registered an abnormality.

'Oh no!!' he exclaimed.

Jody wasn't there.

And nor was he.

The doubles had gone.

He jumped up off the settee, weaved his way across the front room as his natural balance tried to counter-act the swimming feeling in his brain, and fell out of the house into the wet weather.

He had to warn Jody.

*   *   *

Jody swept up the corridor and into her secretary's area. The secretary jumped to her feet. She just stood and stared.

Jody stopped and stared back.

'What's the matter?' asked Jody, unnerved by the secretary's reaction to her arrival.

'Miss Lane.' gurgled the secretary, stumbling over the words as if the English language was something she'd only just learnt that morning.

'As far as I can tell.' smiled Jody, checking herself up and down in a comical way. It didn't amuse the secretary. She turned white and sat down heavily in her chair.

'Are you feeling okay?' asked Jody, raising an eyebrow.

'Miss Lane.' repeated the secretary.

'I think you'd better take the rest of the day off.' said Jody.

'You're *here*.' she squawked.

'Well, this *is* my office and you *are* my secretary... for the time being.' Jody barked, getting more irritated. 'Pull yourself together, woman.' she added.

The secretary didn't reply. So, Jody left her and opened the door to her office.

Somebody was sat at her desk.

The chair was swivelled round to face the window but she could distinctly see their hands on the armrests. She marched over to the chair and spun it round to come face to face with *herself.*

*   *   *

Spence was severely out of breath and his head was pounding a little bit harder than his heart, but not much. He leant on the barrier and took some huge gulps of wet air. His fringe was plastered over his eyes and his clothes were stuck to him like a limpet.

The guard walked up to the gate and waited for Spence to speak. Spence couldn't find his voice between the involuntarily fish-like gulping that his lungs required his torso to engage in. The guard didn't recognise him. But, Spence recognised the guard.

Suddenly, the impending storm that was hanging in the air was overshadowed by another noise. Sirens began wailing like sirens are apt to do and there was a flurry of activity. The guard was distracted and ran back to his hut. Spence struggled over the barrier and jogged out of sight behind some bushes.

The guard didn't return to the barrier. He stayed in his hut, on the telephone, and appeared to be extremely agitated.

*   *   *

The last thing Jody's secretary needed to see was her employer's identical twin.

She stood in the doorway as they grappled with each other.

One of them was obviously winning.

The secretary ran out of the office and pressed the alarm in a state of panic - the alarm that you only pressed in *very* serious emergencies; like the onset of a Nuclear War.

She heard the smashing of a window as the sirens tried to out-wail each other and poked her head around the office door to see the triumphant Miss Lane facing the broken window, wind whipping her hair around like Medusa, the rain soaking the carpet and chair that were too near the broken pane, and no sign of the identical twin.

This was when the secretary fainted.

*   *   *

Jody Marianne Lane lay on the roof of the lower building, gazing up at the window of her office above.

She didn't blink.

The other Jody Marianne Lane studied her from the office window and, satisfied that it was a job well done, walked backwards - out of sight.

Now she could blink.

And blink she did.

The rain streamed out of her eyes and down her cheeks. Her back screamed at her and she felt sure it wasn't going to stop until she moved. She did. It didn't stop. It was the same sort of twisted pain that she'd had a couple of days ago and hadn't fully recovered from.

She sat up and thanked the planners of the Ministry of Defence for building that extension. It had cushioned her fall.

Well, cushioned her fall in as much as she wasn't dead - which she would have been if there hadn't have been an extension there.

She moved very carefully - nothing seemed to be broken and she had a few bleeding cuts - as there were huge shards of glass dotted around her that looked dangerously lethal.

The sirens deafened her and she could hear the shouting and clattering of feet of soldiers below.

She crawled across the roof and out of sight of her office window. She made some quick calculations in her head and worked out that she could probably make it to her father's office from where she was. It would mean scaling a few walls and jumping a few spaces between buildings, but she could probably make it.

No.

Definitely.

There was no *probably* about it.

Probably was for wimps.

Spence's middle name was 'Probably'.

*   *   *

Spence knew the way to the Colonel's office and just hoped that Jody was there. If she wasn't, then he'd be in serious trouble.

Mind you, it wasn't anything new.

Spence had been in serious trouble, on and off, ever since he'd been at school.

He wasn't given a second look by the hordes of people that were swarming about the building like headless chickens. He entered the Colonel's office with a hefty shoulder-barging action.

The door wasn't locked. He hadn't bothered to check.

So, not only was his head hurting, his lungs smarting, his feet aching and his skin red raw from the rain, but his shoulder now had incredible shooting pains through it.

Spence had once considered leaving his body to Medical Science when he died. They would've asked for a refund.

He found the file he'd seen with Jody, with ease. It was in the exact same place as they had left it. The Colonel obviously hadn't been back to his office since then.

He was about to make a hasty exit when he heard a knocking on the window. He looked round and saw Jody's drenched form. He pulled open the window and helped her through. She was seriously bedraggled.

'What were you doing out there?' he asked, shocked at her appearance.

She looked tired, drawn and was covered in cuts. Little pieces of glass were weaved into her matted hair and she collapsed into his arms as if she were made of jelly.

'I met myself... again.' she said, muffled by Spence's dripping wet frame.

'Yikes.' said Spence.

He flinched for a second.

What if *she* was the double?

She could be lulling him into a false sense of security before killing him. At any moment she could win his confidence and then... well... he couldn't afford to take any chances.

He gently prised her away from him and squeezed her breasts.

She slapped him hard across the face.

He felt the stinging pain reverberate through his entire body and he staggered a little.

Yep.

211

That was the real Jody.

'What the hell did you do that for?' she asked, crossing her arms.

'I thought you might've been false.' explained Spence, not entirely convincingly.

'I would've expected you to know my boobs by now!' she huffed, adjusting her cleavage.

'No, I thought you might've been your double.' corrected Spence. 'I know *those* are real! And a very nice double they are' he added, pointing at her chest.

Jody frowned and then burst into sweet laughter. Only Spence would have thought of finding out that way.

Spence laughed with her, nervously at first. He half expected another slap across the other cheek.

He held up the document and smiled.

'Let's get out of this place.' sighed Jody, taking the Philip Dicks document off Spence and walking out of the Colonel's office, trying not to limp. Spence followed her and watched her behind, wiggling.

He was thinking about it again. And we're not talking about tennis.

CHAPTER 14
'HEARTBREAKER'

It was nothing short of utter chaos in the Ministry of Defence.

Jody cut through the swarm of people milling around corridors with the determination of a bull in a china shop. Spence followed her closely with all the determination of a sheep in a field.

He still had his eyes fixed on her pert behind. It was perfectly sculpted and breathtaking in its curvature. It was a mini-masterpiece.

Jody stopped abruptly and Spence barrelled into her. She nearly lost the file.

'It's the Colonel.' she hissed, not moving a muscle.

Spence looked at Jody and he instantly frowned.

She had just called her own Father by his military title; something she'd never done before. He didn't know why and he could tell she wasn't sure of anything to do with him anymore.

The Colonel was striding out of the building and soon was out of sight.

'Come on, let's follow him.' whispered Jody. She set off again, at a considerably faster pace and still limping slightly.

Spence followed.

They came out of the Ministry and into the fresh air.

The cold, fresh air.

The wet, cold, fresh air.

It slapped them in the faces like a jealous lover and took their breath away.

Rain was still pelting down like rain is apt to do and there was a strong wind kicking leaves around like a playground bully and ruffling their hair like a particularly annoying relative.

'Let's get home and fetch my car.' grimaced Jody, biting her lip as the pain in her back increased.

Spence nodded, brushing his fringe out of his eyes.

'Then we'll go to the Colonel's house.' she added, making her way towards the front gate.

She'd done it again.

She'd called him the Colonel.

Spence was rather worried by this. But, not as worried as he was about the other feeling he had; a gnawing, unsettling, sickly sensation in the pit of his stomach.

He sneezed.

This confirmed it.

He was *definitely* catching a cold.

* * *

The Colonel had his orders.

As did Jody and Spence.

Not the *real* Jody and Spence, of course.

They were to report back to the Manning Estate. Half of their task was completed. Jody was dead; killed by the fall from the window of her own office. Spence could be dealt with soon.

It was all working out rather well for them, so they thought.

* * *

It didn't take the real Spence and Jody long to return to her house. Well, to return to her car at her house.

Jody jumped in and started the engine up, she let Spence in the passenger side and, before he was even seated comfortably, she skidded round the close and out on to the main road. She was heading for her Father's house.

Eric the cat had decided to get cosy on the windowsill and from this vantage point could also see what was going on in the world. He saw Spence and Jody get into her car and pull away.

So, they had no concern for him at all, then.

He hadn't been fed properly for a couple of days and was getting quite grumpy. His lazy eyes began closing again as a couple of birds fluttered outside the window, on purpose - safe in the knowledge that there was a protective glass screen between them and Eric.

Eric decided he was in need of a catnap.

The rain ran down the window like melting wax and Eric drifted away on the sound of pounding water.

Meanwhile, Jody was driving like a maniac. This was nothing new to Spence. Jody *always* drove like a maniac. She was to driving what Charles Manson was to happy families. She drove the car with all the accuracy and concentration of a blind archer. Speed limits were alien to her. She had more points on her licence than was strictly allowed.

But, because she worked for the Ministry of Defence, these little discrepancies were sometimes overlooked.

It was now 2.12pm but it seemed more like 2.12am.

The sky was overcast and black, darkening the daylight and giving the whole atmosphere an air of menace. It was the sort of day when you curse yourself for leaving the washing out on the clothes-line.

'Slow down, Jode.' soothed Spence, pressing his foot down on an imaginary brake pedal as they narrowly missed becoming one with a Keep Left bollard.

Jody shot him a look.

As she did so, she forgot to stop at a Give Way junction. Luckily, there were no cars coming their way.

'And would you mind telling me why we're in such a rush to get to the Colonel's house?' Spence asked, still feeling the effects of the Colonel's stick on the back of his skull.

'We've got to find out what's going on.' hissed Jody, wrenching the wheel to the right and almost mounting the mini-roundabout.

'We don't *have* to.' sighed Spence. 'We could just stay at home and have a cup of tea.' he suggested, quietly.

So quietly, in fact, that Jody failed to hear it.

This was Spence's intention.

He knew Jody well and when she was in this sort of determined mood it was best to let her get on with it. Still, she could've got on with it without him.

Spence tried hard not to be a coward but somehow always came back to being one. It was such an easy thing to be. Spence liked easy things. That's what had first attracted him to Jody.

She screeched to a halt on the opposite side of the road to the Colonel's long drive, just out of sight of the house. Spence glanced at Jody out of the corner of his eye, wondering what was going to happen next. She reached into the back of the car and picked up the folder they had taken from the Colonel's office.

But, before she could even open it, a car pulled out of the Colonel's drive and sped away. Jody had recognised the Colonel driving and Spence had seen the passengers sitting in the back. This was why his skin had turned a sickly white colour.

It was him and Jody again, sitting in the back of the Colonel's car, as bold as you like.

He didn't have time to say anything to Jody as she had thrown the folder in his lap and crunched the car into first gear. She jerked the car forward and set off in pursuit.

*   *   *

Mrs Woodnutt, of Endsleigh Gardens, liked to take Elvis for a walk down by the canal. Elvis was her black Labrador. He'd got his name because he looked like he had a quiff, as well as maintaining a consistent diet of cheeseburgers and home-cooked fries.

It was usually quite tranquil down by the canal and she could let the pressures of daily life float away from her.

Mr Woodnutt, her husband, had died nearly four years ago now and he had been an avid supporter of the canal walks every afternoon - he had also been an avid supporter of Elisabeth's Massage Parlour, which had been raided on no less than twenty occasions - the majority of times when he had been there.

Mr Woodnutt had died in Elisabeth's Massage Parlour of a massive heart attack. The Elisabeth of the Massage Parlour's title had been with him when it had happened, giving him his regular massage.

In the nude.

That had been Constable Burden's statement in the official Police Report.

As far as Mrs Woodnutt was concerned, the enquiry in her husband's affairs was falsified.

Mrs Woodnutt was the perfect wife - ignorant, forgiving and far too trusting.

Elvis had been let off his lead and was down by the canal's edge, trying to drag something out of the murky water.

More litter, thought Mrs Woodnutt. It saddened her to see the canal used as a dumping ground. It wasn't like that when she was young. She struggled down the bank to pull Elvis away from the floating debris. She looked at what he was trying to rescue from the canal.

There was something vaguely familiar about the sodden shape. It had two arms, two legs and a head.

It was a human body.

What would they think of dumping there next?

She paused.

A human body?!

Mrs Woodnutt screamed in the key of 'C'.

*　　　*　　　*

The Colonel was obviously driving somewhere very far away, thought Spence. They'd been travelling for an hour now, keeping a discreet distance from their quarry, and Spence was a nervous wreck.

Jody's erratic attempts at driving were hard enough to manage at the best of times but, coupled with following another car, driving through windy country lanes for an hour and visibility being so poor because of the disgusting weather, it was downright terrifying.

All these country lanes looked exactly the same to Spence. He wouldn't have been at all surprised to discover that they'd been travelling in circles.

Eventually, the Colonel's car pulled up by some huge, iron, ornamental gates. They opened with a squeaking sound that could be heard over the wind and rain.

The Colonel's car drove through and the gates squealed shut again. Jody had stopped her car and was all ready getting out. She turned and saw Spence, arms folded and still wearing his seatbelt.

'Come on, Spence. Where's your sense of adventure?' she hissed.

'I left it at home.' he muttered.

'Come on.' she urged him.

He sighed and reluctantly undid his seatbelt. As he opened the car door, the wind and rain hit him full in the face, like a wet kipper.

'Botheration.' he muttered, stepping into a puddle. He slammed the door shut as if he'd been practising. Jody was up near the gates all ready. She was way too eager for his liking.

Spence lived by two words: 'Easy' and 'Life' - more often than not they were coupled together. He didn't need excitement, escapism, entertainment or enjoyment.

No.

These were signs of weakness, as far as he was concerned. They also all started with the letter 'E', and Spence didn't much like the letter 'E'. He'd got enough of them for his Secondary School Exams. And the teachers had mocked him, as teachers so enjoy doing. Mock, mock, mock, they had gone.

Spence had reached the gigantic gates and peered through the delicate ironwork. His stomach flipped over like a tossed pancake and he tugged on Jody's arm.

'Get off me, Spence.' she moaned, trying to wrench her arm away.

'I've been here.' he whispered, still tugging at her arm. 'This is the big house in my dream.' he gulped.

'This is the dream that we've established *wasn't* a dream.' said Jody.

'Whatever.' muttered Spence.

They both stood in wet silence for a minute, clinging on to the gates and staring up the long, long driveway to the long, long house at the end of it.

Thunder rumbled in an ominous manner, far in the distance. It was either thunder or it was Spence's stomach. They made a similar sound and at a similar volume.

'What are we waiting for, then?' asked Jody, staring at Spence.

'What?'

'Let's go up there and have a look around.' she smiled, excitedly.

Spence usually adored Jody when she smiled. She had a lovely smile, all teeth and dimples. But, for some reason, at that particular moment in time, he was having trouble remembering why he found it so lovely.

'Have do you propose we get through these gates?' scoffed Spence. 'Wait until we become thin enough to squeeze through?' he added, sarcastically.

'We can go *over* them.' sighed Jody.

Spence looked at the height of the iron gates. They obviously hadn't been designed for people to go *over* them.

'After you.' he graciously bowed.

'Spence, you know you'll have to go first. I'll have to guide you or you'll never make it over.' said Jody. 'You couldn't even climb over *my* gate properly.' she chuckled.

Spence muttered something under his breath and struggled to find the first foothold. After three slippery attempts, he got started.

Halfway up, he got stuck.

At the top, he got vertigo.

Halfway down the other side, he fell off into some blackberry bushes.

Jody never stopped smiling.

Spence picked the thorns out of his clothes and skin, brushed off the blackberries and noticed that the juice had stained his shirt. He was now covered in scratches and deep, red blackberry juice stains. He wondered what the opposite of 'Yippee' was.

Jody nibbled on a few blackberries and watched with increasing amusement as Spence tried to kick the bush, in a rage. He got his foot entangled and fell in again.

*   *   *

Eric purred.

He was dreaming of food; a big, fat, juicy fish, to be precise. Probably Salmon, or sardines, he wasn't fussy as long as it was part of the fish family. His pink tongue licked his lips and his purring got louder.

He sounded like a feline helicopter about to take off.

*   *   *

The big house was there in front of them. Spence and Jody crouched amongst the ring of forest that encircled the courtyard and drive. It also provided them with some shelter from the wind and rain, both of which seemed to be getting heavier.

'Well, now we're here, what are we supposed to do now?' whispered Spence, shivering as a falling leaf landed on his bare neck. Jody frowned at him.

'We've got to have a look inside, dummy.' she muttered.

'You say we've got to have a look inside and *I'm* the dummy?' mumbled Spence, in disbelief.

Jody ignored him. Not for the first time.

The mansion seemed to be deserted. At least, Jody couldn't see anyone through the windows (of which there were many). She didn't want to take any chances, though.

'We'll keep under cover of these trees and make our way round the back. There's bound to be a less conspicuous entrance somewhere.' she explained.

'Why don't I stay here and...' began Spence.

Jody grabbed his arm and yanked him out of his crouching position.

'Tell you what, better still, I'll come with you.' he added.

They made their steady way around the perimeter of forest and eventually came to the back of the big house. It didn't look quite so grand from the back. It actually looked quite shabby and run-down.

There were three separate doors at the back of the house, including a pair of wooden doors that were raised slightly from the ground.

Spence saw them and froze - they looked like some kind of cellar doors and he'd all ready been in that cellar once.

He prayed Jody wouldn't decide to choose those doors.

Jody was scanning the building and finding the safest door to make an attempt on. They'd have to break cover to get to any of them but some were easier than others.

Suddenly, Spence made a run for the door on the west wing of the house, crunching gravel under foot and diving under the windows as he approached it. He hadn't bothered to wait and see if Jody would choose the so-called cellar doors and had decided to choose ones that were as far away from those cellar doors as possible. She was bound to follow.

And she did... except she did it with a bit more stealth than Spence.

He had looked like a whirling dervish in his attempt to reach the door, whereas she looked like a gracious gazelle. Still, she'd been trained for this sort of thing, thought Spence. He'd been trained for running away from any form of public brawling and Traffic Wardens.

Whereas Jody was trained for not being seen, Spence was trained for not being caught.

There was a big difference.

'This looks the most promising door.' puffed Spence, still out of breath due to his burst of activity.

'Why?' asked Jody.

Spence hadn't anticipated a question. He'd tried to sound like he knew why so Jody wouldn't ask him that very question. He'd obviously been less than convincing. He decided not to answer.

When in doubt, don't reply.

Instead, he just tried the rusted brass handle of the door and it turned slowly in his hand. The door opened a little and then stuck. He tried to budge it with his shoulder and it opened a little more, scraping across the tiled floor on the inside. Spence squeezed himself through the narrow gap and Jody followed.

It was cold, dark and damp inside. They were in some sort of corridor. The black and white tiles underfoot were cracked, uneven, and missing bits. It took just two seconds for Spence to trip up on one.

'This way.' whispered Spence, taking charge.

Jody smiled a wry smile. She'd go along with his attempts to be brave for now.

He walked down the corridor, followed by Jody, and came to another corridor. At the end of this one was a door.

They went through the door into a huge room, clean and spotless and full of scientific equipment. It seemed to be some kind of laboratory. There was some structure in the middle of the room that looked like an operating table, a bank of powerful computers across one wall and the opposing wall was full of corpses. At least, Spence and Jody *assumed* they were corpses. They took a closer look.

'More androids?' asked Spence, running his finger over one of the plastic cocoons.

'Robot replicas.' suggested Jody, 'And I happen to recognise a few of them.' she added. Spence was shocked.

'What do you mean?' he asked.

'There are a few from the Ministry of Defence - no bigwigs, no really top names, just mostly underlings. The Number 2's of important departments.' she explained, pointing them out to Spence. 'I suppose the others are the same but from other places.' she added.

'Why go to all the trouble of replicating 'assistants'? Why didn't they just replicate the main, important people?' asked Spence, more as a question to himself than Jody.

'This is the deputy Prime Minister.' gasped Jody, stopping abruptly by one of the ghoulish cocoons. 'That's the Ministry of Defence *and* Parliament.' she reasoned.

'The rest must be from important places too, then.' guessed Spence.

'I suppose so.' agreed Jody.

There were three empty cocoons. Jody and Spence happened upon them at the same time. It suddenly dawned on both of them. This was the space for *their* replicas.

It was also the space for the Colonel.

Jody broke down. She steadied herself on the operating table and tried to stop sobbing. It was uncontrollable.

Spence had no idea what to do - how could he re-assure her? If the Colonel was an android, then where was the real Colonel? Alive or dead? He took her in his arms and she cried into his chest.

There was a click of a safety catch being removed.

Spence turned his head slowly and felt the cold, hard metal of a gun barrel against his temple. He couldn't see the carrier.

Jody was unaware as she was buried in his arms, trying to control her unforced release of pent-up emotions.

A voice spoke.

'No sudden moves.'

Spence almost laughed.

With Jody in his arms and a gun pressed against the side of his head how was he supposed to make any sudden moves?

The voice spoke again.

'Turn around slowly and start walking out of here.'

Jody had heard the voice this time and she slid out of Spence's arms, very carefully.

Their captor was an ordinary-sized man of ordinary-sized proportions. In fact, he seemed rather bland. He was wearing a long, white coat and black, leather gloves.

Spence felt the pressure of the gun evaporate from his throbbing temple and he turned slowly to face the door. Jody was pushed roughly in front of him.

'Get going.' hissed the voice.

Spence was shoved hard and he toppled into Jody, they both stumbled out of the spacious laboratory and into the dim corridor once again.

The voice from the ordinary man barked directions as and when they needed them.

They finally reached some steps that began to feel all too familiar to Spence. He could feel the palms of his hands go very cold and clammy.

Down the steps they were ushered and into a cellar.

There, sat behind a ring of flickering monitors, was Lemon, in all her glory. She looked up, her blonde hair was falling over her face and her sparkling eyes were just visible through the velveteen strands.

'What have we here?' she asked, grinning broadly.

'I found them in the laboratory.' said the ordinary man, from somewhere behind Spence and Jody.

'Why did you leave it unattended?' asked Lemon. There was no emotion in her voice, just pure monotone detachment.

'I had to answer a call of nature, didn't I.' replied the voice.

'Leave us.' barked Lemon.

The sound of footsteps from behind them indicated to Spence and Jody that the ordinary man had left and taken his voice with him.

The synchronised humming of the computers disturbed the silence that had fallen momentarily.

Lemon stared at Spence and Jody and they stared back.

'Well, it's good to see you again.' smiled Spence, trying to sound cheerful.

'The pleasure is all yours, indeed.' said Lemon. She had stopped smiling now.

There was another slight silence, which the computers interrupted.

'So, you've been in my laboratory, have you?' asked Lemon, not waiting for an answer. 'Seen anything of interest?' she added.

Spence and Jody didn't answer.

'Of course you have.' said Lemon.

'What have you done with my Father?' hissed Jody, through clenched teeth.

'Improved him.' came back the curt reply.

'You've killed him, haven't you?' spat Jody, showing more than a trace of emotion as her voice began to crack slightly.

Lemon chose to ignore her.

'You're supposed to be dead anyway.' said Lemon, standing up and leaning on the nearest two monitors. She pressed a button. 'Well, we'll soon see to that.'

'What are you doing here? Why all the replicas?' asked Spence.

Lemon smiled again.

There was something warm yet sinister about Lemon's smile. She was too perfect, too beautiful, too aesthetically pleasing. It just wasn't natural.

'You really want to know?' she asked.

'And why duplicate such insignificant people?' added Spence.

'My point is proved.' she said, sitting down again. 'To you they are insignificant, but to the running of the country they are essential. Nobody knows them yet they do all the real work. No-one rewards them and they get no credit. They melt into the background. Yet they always need to be there. It is simple, really. They can do most damage and yet would be the last to be suspected.' she explained.

The sound of approaching footsteps made Lemon look behind Spence and Jody.

'Ah, here is the Colonel.'

Spence and Jody turned to see the Colonel advancing on them, holding a gun in his hand. His expression was blank and he stared straight ahead of him.

'A perfect replica, just like all the others.' she sighed. 'Everything, including even family histories, has been catered for. They are all carbon copies with just one difference. I control them.' said Lemon, menacingly.

'They will live on, far longer than their human counterparts.' she added.

'The living dead? How lovely.' muttered Spence, sarcastically.

'Well, it's been nice meeting you again, Mr Tracy, and nice to meet you for the first time, Miss Lane. You will excuse me. I have work to do. The Colonel here will show you into the grounds and then you will to die. Goodbye.' said Lemon, cold as ice.

She began typing on the nearest keyboard and didn't look up again.

Spence and Jody were ushered back up the cellar steps by the Colonel.

It was a short walk from the cellar, through the Manning Estate, and out of the front door, but it seemed like an age to Spence and Jody. The Colonel followed them closely, in impassive silence.

Spence took Jody's hand and held it tight. It comforted him more than her but the gesture was there. They walked out into the biting rain.

It was dark now.

The sky was beginning to show the first signs of stars, peeping through the melancholy clouds that were trying to smother the sky into submission.

Into the grounds they marched, the Colonel steering them like a Shepherd with a particularly dangerous crook. They got deep into the woodland and stopped abruptly.

'Are we going to make a break for it?' whispered Spence.

'No point.' sighed Jody, her eyes were full of rain and tears.

'Snap out of it, Jode.' hissed Spence.

The Colonel raised his revolver.

'I love you, Spence.' said Jody, her eyes were almost pleading as she looked at him. Her soft face glistened with the wet and the anguish was etched in her expression. She was so beautiful. Her dark hair clung to her face and her little nose was turning red with cold.

The Colonel tightened his figure on the trigger.

'Jode, we've got to do *something.*' grimaced Spence. He wanted to kiss her. He wanted to hold her. He wanted to take her in his arms and say that everything was going to be okay. She meant everything to him.

The Colonel fired.

Jody slumped to the floor.

Spence froze in horror.

The Colonel jerked slightly as he levelled the gun a second time. He seemed almost unsteady. His arm shook violently.

Spence turned to face him.

The Colonel tightened his finger on the trigger again. Spence frowned heavily and looked confused.

The Colonel fired.

He slumped to the floor, sparking and writhing. A small explosion sounded, a puff of smoke came out of his chest and he suddenly lay still.

Spence couldn't believe it.

The Colonel had turned the gun on himself and fired. He'd killed himself.

The rain pelted Spence with an unnerving regularity and soaked right through to his soul. He looked at the fallen Colonel. He looked at his fallen love.

What had gone wrong? Why wasn't *he* dead?

He recalled something Lemon had said moments earlier - about the detail of the androids, family histories, etc. Had the android really thought he had shot his own daughter? Were they *that* real? This was insane.

He collapsed to the muddy ground by Jody and tried to sit her up.

She was limp and useless.

His hands became red with her blood as he took her in his arms.

*   *   *

Eric was awake and hungry. There were no fish in reality. He was stuck in Jody's house and he knew full well there was a saucer of full cream milk awaiting him at Mrs Beevers' house.

It was too much to bear.

He'd take great delight in scratching Spence and Jody when they returned; totally on accident, of course.

But only after they'd fed him properly... preferably with fish.

*   *   *

Jody lay in Spence's arms.

The rain beat down on her lifeless body and Spence caressed her hair as if she could still feel him doing it. He kissed her on her cold lips and held her head to his heaving chest.

The pain was unbearable.

His looked up at the sky, eyes wide open, and the stars winked at him. The rain made his eyes sting and the wind whipped his hair about his face. Tears streamed down his cheeks as he silently grieved.

The moon peered out from behind the last of the black clouds and gently lit up the woodland in monochrome colourings. There was something strangely comforting about the moon. He closed his eyes and bowed his head.

Part of him was missing.

His reason to exist.

*   *   *

Eric knew it was evening.

Late evening, at that.

He decided to go back to sleep. If he couldn't taste fish, he might as well dream that he could. He curled up by the front door, hoping that Spence and Jody would return at some point, and closed his eyes.

*   *   *

It was Friday morning.

Eric was startled into consciousness by the morning papers being dropped on to him from the letterbox. He spat and spluttered, arched his back and made his hairs stand on end.

It didn't do any good.

The newspapers just lay there, lazy as you like. He tested his claws on them. That would teach them a lesson. They'd think twice about allowing themselves to be dropped from a great height on to Eric the next time.

Two similar outlines loomed into view through the frosted glass of the door. Eric hoped for a brief second that they might be Spence and Jody. He knew, from a second glance, they weren't.

The doorbell rang.

Eric heaved himself up on to all four paws and padded away to Jody's bedroom. It was the best window vantage point and, plus, her bed was incredibly soft. Being as he wasn't eating, he was making up for it by sleeping.

Eric was a nocturnal cat. He slept *all* the time.

The doorbell rang again.

Eric, with all the agility of an arthritic Mountain Goat, leapt up on to the windowsill. He pressed his nose against the glass and his cat's eyes waited for the callers to walk back down the drive, so that he could get a good look at them.

It was then that he spotted the bedraggled figure of Spencer Tracy.

*　　*　　*

'No-one's answering.' muttered Big Man #2, in his naturally high-pitched voice.

'Well, I can see that, can't I?!' hissed Big Man #1. 'That's just stating the bleedin' obvious, that is.' he added.

Big Man #2 rang the doorbell for a third time.

Big Man #1 knocked his hand away.

'Leave it now, just leave it.' he snapped.

'Look, I don't want to get in trouble with Mr Letts. I'm staying here until someone turns up.' ranted Big Man #2, reaching for the doorbell again.

'I'll go and sit in the car, then.' said Big Man #1. He was cold from the biting wind and wet from the pouring rain. The car was just too inviting. If Big Man #2 wanted to catch pneumonia, that was his problem. And *he* certainly wouldn't have any sympathy for his partner.

None at all.

Well, he might buy him a Lemsip, maybe.

Big Man #1 turned to go back to the car and saw Spencer Tracy trudging up the drive. His head was bowed and he was shuffling like an old man. His hands were dug deep into his pockets and he wasn't exactly dressed for the weather. This was too good to be true. Mr Letts had asked for Spencer Tracy and here *was* Spencer Tracy.

Big Man #1 elbowed his partner, who swivelled round - fists raised - ready to punch his counterpart very hard for putting him off his fourth attempt at ringing the doorbell, when he saw why he had been elbowed. Their quarry was walking right towards them. It couldn't have been simpler. *They* couldn't have been simpler.

Spence glanced up, peering through his rain-plaited fringe, and caught sight of the two big, burly men stood at Jody's front door. He shuffled to a halt. They were approaching him. This was just what he needed. He sighed loudly and shivered violently.

Without a word being spoken, he had Big Man #1 and Big Man #2 flanking him and they all walked in unison to the car at the end of the drive.

*   *   *

Eric watched in vain as Spence was bundled into the back of a car.

Well, he sighed, there went his meal ticket. Still, perhaps Jody would be home soon. Unless she was going to get picked up by two big, burly men too. It would probably be her idea of heaven, thought Eric, compared to Spence.

He fell off the windowsill and on to Jody's comfortable bed. He'd wanted to spring off the windowsill with all the elegance of a black panther but Eric was to springing what Tigger was to keeping still.

Not very good at it.

He clawed the bed and settled down for another catnap. The rumbling of his stomach complimented his purring perfectly and the rain that washed down the window added that final touch.

He drifted off into the land of dreams; somewhere over the rainbow... trout.

*   *   *

233

It was 10.03am.

Spence was sat in the office of Mr Letts, of 'LETTS PROPERTY DEVELOPMENT AND HOUSING'.

Again.

He really wasn't in the mood for this. His mind kept flashing up images of Jody Marianne Lane and his soul was screaming in pain. There was a nagging ache in his stomach and he felt constantly sick. He was freezing and soaking wet. The rain felt like it had seeped through to his very bones.

Mr Letts seemed quite agitated.

'Mr Tracy, or should I call you Mr Dicks? Hmmm?' hissed Mr Letts, puffing on his cigar in a manner which suggested he wasn't inhaling any of it at all.

Spence's brain snapped into gear.

Mr Dicks? What was this, some kind of sick joke?

Either Mr Letts was working for Lemon or he wasn't. It was just too closely inter-linked. Christ, why hadn't *he* been killed yesterday evening?

Why?!

'I received this little letter yesterday, Mr Tracy. It was delivered to the house you were renting and is addressed to a Mr Dicks. Ring any bells, Mr Tracy? Have you been using a false name? Answer me, damn you!!' shouted Mr Letts.

He'd lost his cool.

There was something in the suspicious brain of Mr Letts that suggested a scam, a con, a devious plot to rob him of money. He couldn't work out how, but he just knew that there was something odd going on. And he didn't like it.

Spence hadn't looked at him once, either. This was a sure sign of a suspicious character. He stroked his beard, rather too hard.

'Look, just give me the letter.' snapped Spence, suddenly jumping out of his chair and slamming both of his hands on the table.

Mr Letts was startled and fell back into his chair, dropping his cigar into his lap. He grabbed hold of the arms as Spence leant over the table towards him.

'Don't mess with me, Me Letts. I am *not* in the mood.' hissed Spence. He snatched the letter off the desk and pocketed it.

'I... I...' tried Mr Letts.

'Have a nice day.' said Spence, narrowing his eyes.

Mr Letts was genuinely afraid.

Big Man #1 and Big Man #2 were waiting for some sort of order.

None came.

Spence walked to the office door and swung it open. He turned and stared at Mr Letts.

'Expect your £125,000 at the weekend.' he snapped. He didn't know how he was going to get it but he felt it was a nice departing line.

Mr Letts nodded. The cigar was burning into his trousers and he couldn't feel a thing.

Spence slammed the door shut.

The genuine Picasso print, purchased from the indoor market in 1975, crashed to the floor.

Mr Letts suddenly became aware of the cigar.

Big Man #1 and Big Man #2 suddenly became aware of the intense discomfort Mr Letts was now feeling.

The noise was deafening.

*   *   *

Spencer Tracy arrived back at Jody's house and almost fell inside. He was tired, drained and his emotions were running riot.

He stumbled into the kitchen and filled the kettle up with water, plugged it in and switched it on. If anyone needed a cup of tea, it was Spence. He fished the letter out of his pocket and tore it open.

Sure enough, it was addressed to Philip Dicks.

Spence felt a chill shoot through his body and didn't know if just *reading* the name scared him or if the cold was seeping into him more than he realised.

Before delving into the letter properly, he scanned it quickly to see who it was from. The signature was scribbled but just about legible.

Richard Delgado.

Now, *that* name was ringing bells in his memory.

Delgado? That was the name inside the parcel. This really wasn't a good thing at all.

The kettle boiled and he made a very sloppy cup of tea. Something brushed against his leg and he jumped a mile.

It was Eric.

Good, old Eric.

He stroked him and was got scratched and bitten in the process.

Bad, old Eric.

Spence reached for a tin of cat food, pulled the top off and put it on the floor. Eric stuck his nose straight into it.

Spence sat down at the table and read through the letter, taking huge gulps of his steaming hot tea as he did so. His hands were shaking badly and it was difficult him to do both of these things but he managed. It seemed to be a rather odd letter; more of a reminder, almost.

Oh bugger.

He'd left that file in Jody's car.

Arse.

236

Still, how was he supposed to remember that? If he'd been able to drive, that wouldn't have been a problem, as he'd have brought the car back with him. As it was, he'd had to walk for what seemed an age before he could start hitching lifts back to Hillview Estate. Jody's car was still in a country lane somewhere.

He bit his lip.

He could feel the tears welling up in his stinging eyes and he struggled to hold them back. The pain was intense. He concentrated on the letter again.

Philip Dicks seemed to be working for the M.o.D. as Delgado's sort of right-hand man. Something about the urgency needed to recover some sort of prototype. He didn't really understand it. Perhaps, if he had read the file from the Colonel's office, it would've made more sense.

Perhaps not.

He put his tea down on one of the morning papers he'd picked up off the doormat as he'd entered Jody's front door. He'd almost tripped over them first.

As he plonked his cup of tea down on The Daily Bugle, he caught sight of one of the headlines.

Someone had committed suicide.

Someone from the Ministry of Defence.

Someone called Delgado.

He knocked his tea over in his haste to pick up the paper. He scanned through the story quickly and made up his mind. A plan began to form in his weary mind and he was determined he would succeed.

First, he needed to get rid of his android double. And the chances were, because Lemon seemed to be *that* sort of meticulous person, his double would be doing what he should be doing now.

Working.

He looked at his watch.

It was 11.45am.

If he hurried, he could meet himself for lunch.

*   *   *

Mr Pertwee called lunch early today. He didn't have any real reason. Sometimes he called lunch early and sometimes he called lunch late. It was up to him. His section left their computer terminals running and all headed for the exit, as one big ball of people.

Outside, it was still raining heavily.

Half the staff wound up in the canteen and the other half wound up in McDonalds, or *got* wound up in McDonalds; the service being so impeccably *good* and so incredibly *quick*. Ahem.

Spence sat on the wall, near the under-pass, where everyone walked to get to the big yellow 'M'. He turned to face the other way as colleagues scurried past, ignoring the solitary, lurking figure. He tried not to catch anyone's eye and kept a lookout for himself. If these replicas were so perfect, he'd be heading to McDonalds too on a Friday.

Friday was Toad-In-The-Hole at the canteen and that reminded him far too much of his sex life to eat it for lunch.

Most of Mr Pertwee's section had walked past. Spence didn't know whether to go into the canteen or stay outside in the freezing cold. His mind was made up for him when he saw his mirror image walking towards him.

As he got level, Spence shoulder-barged into it and felt himself re-bound off.

Oops.

The android turned on its assailant and apologised.

How very polite, thought Spence, and promptly rugby-tackled it. They both fell over the small wall and into a clump of sodden flowers.

The android was up first and didn't attempt to fight. It attempted to run away.

He *has* been programmed realistically, thought Spence. He grinned to himself and launched into another rugby tackle. Spence had played a lot of rugby when he was younger.

And thinner.

And fitter.

He brought the android down to the floor again. Now, how do you disable an android? He kneed it in the groin as hard as he could. Not a flinch.

Spence felt his knee explode with pain and he grimaced.

They rolled across the mud of the little raised island of foliage and fell off, back on to the pavement. Struggling to his feet, Spence pulled the android up and rammed it against the wall of the under-pass. The android caught sight of Spence's face for the first time and its expression changed dramatically.

It looked shocked.

This, in itself, shocked Spence. But then, of course, the android assumed that Spence was a corpse.

An animated, angry corpse that was now pinning it up against a brick wall.

Spence slammed the android twice into the wall. This was harder than he'd thought it was going to be. And that was Spence's main problem. He hadn't actually *thought* about it at all. Otherwise he would have brought some vital android-disabling equipment, like a giant magnet, perhaps.

The android suddenly began to fight back.

This was what Spence was dreading. Androids don't, as far he could work out, feel much pain. Spence did. Even the smallest pain like a stubbed toe could disable Spence for hours.

The android retaliated by slamming Spence into the opposite wall. So, Spence returned the compliment. They staggered back and forth across the under-pass like a pair of out-of-control ballroom dancers.

Spence chopped the legs away from the android and crashed to the ground with it, as he wasn't letting go for a minute.

He head-butted it.

Bad mistake.

Spence had never head-butted anyone, or anything, in his life and shouldn't have started at that exact point.

There was something of a metallic ring to the connecting heads and Spence felt a sharp pain sear across his forehead. He reeled backwards and allowed the android time to get up.

The android really began to put the boot in now. Huge kicks were landing in Spence's midriff and Spence was losing breath faster than any Government broke its election promises.

Fortunately, two men were walking through the under-pass and saw what looked to them both like a rather cruel mugging. They did something very un-English.

They *didn't* ignore it.

One man pinned the android's arms behind its back and the other man lifted Spence to his shaky feet. It was then that the un-English thing wore off.

Both good Samaritans suddenly realised that they were holding the *same* person. They returned very quickly to being English, letting go of both men, mumbling some sort of apology and half-walking, half-running off - without once looking back.

As Spence gulped in air with huge movements that were obviously very painful to him, he had a vague idea.

An idea that was so far-fetched, it might just work. And, he didn't care now if it didn't.

The identical twins stared at each other. Spence walked forward, offering the hand of friendship. This confused the android.

What was he supposed to do now? Accept a *draw*?

The android hesitantly put out a hand for Spence to shake.

Spence took it with both hands, rolled backwards - using his feet to lever the android up - and flipped it over his head. The android sailed through the air and crashed into the wall. Spence was up first.

He dragged the android by a leg into the biggest puddle he could find and held the head underwater, sitting on its back and pinning its arms behind him.

Obviously, the android wasn't going to drown. It wasn't a human. Still, if he could maybe make it short-circuit in some way?

He'd noticed that the android was curiously dry - something which the rest of the staff that had passed by weren't. It was only a very small hunch but, the again, there was nothing about Spence that wasn't small. Apart from his premature middle-age spread, of course.

The android began to struggle quite violently and Spence had trouble staying on its back. The rain seemed to beat down harder and his vision was blurring and focusing alternately. The android was *really* struggling now.

For a brief, alarming second, Spence had visions of it being a real person. Perhaps it wasn't an android at all and some organically grown thing. He almost laughed. Sometimes, he really was quite stupid.

Suddenly, there was a fizzing noise and the large puddle seemed to bubble. The android seemed to be convulsing now, rather than struggling.

There was a popping noise and Spence jumped back off the android. It stopped moving. Smoke poured from the back of its neck. Spence bent down and turned it over.

The eyes were blank.

White.

No pupils.

Spence found he was holding his breath. He let it out with a sigh. Reaching into the android's clothing, Spence pulled out a perfect replica off his own wallet, identity card and a picture of Jody. He paused momentarily and put it back inside the android's pocket.

A single tear trickled down his cheek, intermingling with the rain on his skin.

He was dead.

Well, his *android* was dead. If androids actually died.

And once it was discovered, theoretically, *he* would be dead too.

Perhaps.

This really was doing his head in.

He wished he *really* was dead. The pain of Jody's death was still eating away at his insides. He stumbled over to the small wall nearby and sat down on it, breathing heavily.

He looked at the sky; it was grey with clouds and so, so ominous. There was something portentous about such a sky. He looked for any sign of the sun. It was nowhere to be seen.

He closed his eyes and Jody's face appeared in the blackness of his eyelids. His head felt so heavy and he bowed it low, covering his face with his hands.

Lemon was going to pay. Oh yes. She was most definitely going to pay.

Spence began to cry.

CHAPTER 15
'DANCE WITH THE DEVIL'

Lemon flicked her hair out of her flickering eyes and realised that the Colonel wasn't responding to her call, at all. This wasn't a good thing. She pressed another button on the closest keyboard and sat back in her seat.

Her eyes scanned the monitors and seemed to almost glow with the reflection. Within a few seconds, the android version of Jody Marianne Lane had appeared before her.

'Return to the Ministry. Find the Colonel. Then return back here.' ordered Lemon.

The android's white eyes rolled back to normal and it turned and left the cellar.

Lemon looked across her monitors again. Why wasn't the Colonel responding? A malfunction would have showed up. Her face showed no sign of the anger she felt.

She sat still and impassive, radiating a kind of fatal beauty. The time was fast approaching. The time she had so meticulously planned for.

Her time.

*   *   *

Spencer Tracy sat in the passenger seat of Shaw's Rent-A-Cab and didn't say a word. His driver was Alan Wisher, who *did* say a word. Quite a few words, in fact.

Alan Wisher was nothing if not talkative.

It was fair to say that Alan Wisher enjoyed the sound of his own voice much more than Spence did. Spence had tried to ignore him but found he couldn't. He had one of those voices that was so irritating, so annoying, and grated on your nerves so much, that you just couldn't *help* listening to it. It was like being forcibly hypnotised, through your ears.

Alan Wisher was a divorcee. He had one son, Gary, who was now attending 'big school' and who he got to see on every alternate weekend. He also had a new girlfriend, Liz, who was - according to Alan - a 'right goer' and somewhat of an 'animal' in bed. Spence had declined the need to see his scratches as proof. He was also thinking of having his nipples pierced, and contemplating going to either Barcelona or Blackpool for his holidays. It was probably going to be Blackpool. Barcelona was so over-rated, cheap and tacky, according to Alan.

All of this Spence found out, in alarming detail, before they'd even got five minutes away from Hillview Estate. It was enough to make you go mad. And Alan Wisher wasn't finished yet. Oh no. Not by a long chalk.

Spence prayed for some sort of divine intervention. A lightening bolt from the heavens, directed at Alan Wisher's tongue would be the ideal solution.

He steadfastly watched the windscreen wipers sway in unison across the rain-pelted windscreen. The droning quality of Alan Wisher's voice was quite unique. He was a talking sedative. Spence felt so tired. He scrunched his eyes up and blinked twice, very hard. How he was going to find the big house again, he didn't know. If he could get dropped off where he was first picked up on his long hitchhike back to civilisation, he should be able to re-trace his steps, he reckoned.

In the pouring rain.

And chill wind.

Great.

Still, he had Jody's car to look out for as a kind of landmark. His body ached and throbbed and his head had a dull, nagging, pounding pressure all over it. He definitely was catching a cold and he definitely needed some sleep.

Alan Wisher was now giving his views on black people. Spence inwardly sighed and tried to look interested.

*   *   *

Mr Franklin was tall and thin, with eyes that could only be described as 'bulbous'. If Mr Franklin didn't have some kind of thyroid problem, then Mr Franklin was lying. Or his pants were too tight.

Mr Levene, on the other hand, was short and stocky. His eyes were normal, if a little bloodshot.

It was just 3.00pm when they arrived at the Manning Estate. They were ushered into the 'conference' room by Suzanne Addison, Lemon's personal assistant, and then left alone.

'Seems a well-run organisation.' muttered Mr Franklin, his big eyes looking around the large room with increasing interest. It was his first time inside the Manning Estate and he was quietly impressed with the size of it.

Mr Levene nodded in agreement. He too had never actually been inside the Manning Estate and was suitably taken by the scale.

Mr Franklin and Mr Levene were the majority share-holders and biggest company directors of two separate companies based in Europe. Mr Franklin's company was something to do with mechanical goods and Mr Levene's company was big in electrical engineering. Both were competitive, both were business-led, both were scrupulous, both were under-handed, both were devious, both were cunning and both were generally what power-crazed executives should be.

Power-crazed.

They admired and respected each other. Therefore, they hated each other's guts.

*   *   *

Spence recognised the stretch of the road in front of them. Alan Wisher was talking about the French, in a very derogatory fashion. Spence wondered if he should take the gamble and let Shaw's Rent-A-Cab drive on. Perhaps he would recognise more of the country lanes and it would save him the long, weary walk. He suddenly realised that Alan Wisher was actually talking *to* him, rather than *at* him.

'You heading for the Manning Estate, then?' repeated Alan Wisher. Spence sat more upright in the passenger seat.

'Where?' he enquired.

'The Manning Estate. Big house, big grounds, used to belong to old Lord Manning - don't know who it belongs to now, of course. Probably some corporation who use it for their stupid 'think tanks' and their team-building...'

'Yes, yes. That's where I'm going.' interrupted Spence. He took a gamble.

'Oh. Right.' he paused. 'You should have said that in the first place.' he added. There was another slight pause. 'You work there, do you?' he asked.

Spence looked blank.

'Only I was pulling your leg about the business thing; probably a good thing, after all. I mean, Lord Manning had let it go, you know? Couldn't afford the upkeep of it, I suppose.' said Alan Wisher, changing his viewpoint, just incase Spence was a big business executive who would leave a big business executive tip.

'Yes.' was all Spence could reply.

He was just hoping that this Manning Estate was the big house he had just returned from. 'How do you know about this Manning Estate, then?' he asked.

Alan Wisher was slightly taken-aback. He hadn't anticipated a *conversation*. Usually, his paying customers allowed him to give them his pearls of wisdom and heady insights into the world at large without attempting to converse with him as well.

'My Uncle used to work there. He was a sort of handyman. Used to do the odd jobs around the house, you see.' said Alan Wisher. 'Until Lord Manning couldn't afford that sort of thing anymore. Sad, really. Uncle went on the dole. Never came off it. Died five years later, a broken man.' sighed Alan Wisher.

Spence had stopped listening after the words 'My' and 'Uncle' and was watching the road intently. He definitely remembered it. These winding country lanes weren't as similar as he at first thought.

It took them another five minutes and a lecture from Alan Wisher on the state of the Social Benefit System, and how it should be radically reformed, to reach the Manning Estate.

Spence got the taxi to pull up next to Jody's car, still parked in a hedge at the side of the road. He was genuinely surprised that it was still there. As far as he could remember, it was unlocked and the keys were still in the ignition.

'That your car is it?' asked Alan Wisher. 'Been out on a bit of a bender, eh?' he chuckled.

Spence couldn't be bothered to answer him, incase the reply he gave ended with the word 'Off'.

The fare was quite hefty and he shoved a load of crumpled notes into the outstretched hand of Alan Wisher.

'Thanks very much.' said Alan, 'I won't bother counting it.' he grinned, presuming there was a tip amongst it.

Spence hoped there was enough to cover the actual fare.

The rain soaked his back straight away as he got out of the car and nodded as cheerfully as he could to Alan Wisher.

'Take care of yourself, sir.' said Alan Wisher.

Spence slammed the door shut and Shaw's Rent-A-Cab (No.12) drove off.

Spence sneezed.

His hands and feet automatically began to lose temperature and feeling. He jogged up to the gates and found that they were open. He looked around quickly. There didn't seem to be anybody about. So, he ran through and straight into the trees that made the natural corridor that wound its way up to the house. It didn't take him long to reach the gravel courtyard.

Parked by the front of the house were two cars.

Expensive cars.

The sort of cars you promise you'd never buy if you got rich but then do once you are. They were top-flight businessmen cars, complete all the mod-cons that nobody really wants and seldom ever uses after the first test drive.

He knew what he was going to do next was falling the wrong side of foolhardy. Still, he just didn't care. The tiredness had numbed his brain and he was still trying to control the pain of losing Jody and being able to do nothing about it.

Until now.

He walked, bold as brass, straight through the front door. He was assuming he could pass as his own android.

Luckily, there didn't seem to be anybody about.

He had found a suit at Jody's house, just before the taxi had picked him up. It was his, he was sure of that. He vaguely recalled Jody buying it for him. It was black, with a tartan lining. It was actually quite smart. He had decided to wear it. He couldn't find another white shirt and kept the one on that he was wearing, complete with blackberry stains and dirt patches.

He had thought long and hard about a tie and decided, against his better judgement, to wear one. Even though he hated ties with a passion, this wasn't about him.

This was about Jody.

For once, Spencer Tracy looked passable.

He opened the nearest door and found himself in a large room, complete with four large walls, a large ceiling and one large table. Seated at the table were two men. They were also in suits. He nodded to them. They nodded back. He took another risk and entered the room. They stood up as he approached them.

'Mr Franklin - of Rothchild Mechanics.' said Mr Franklin, grabbing Spence's hand and pumping it vigorously. Spence smiled weakly.

'Mr Levene - of Yeoman Electric.' said Mr Levene, shaking Spence's hand by grasping it with both of his. Spence carried on smiling weakly. He had no idea what to do.

'And, pardon my ignorance, you are?' asked Mr Franklin, sitting back down in his chair. Mr Levene sat down next to him. Spence felt he ought to do the same. So, he did.

'I'm... ' Spence racked his brains. 'I'm...' he tried again.

Before he had chance to be found out, the door to the room opened again and Suzanne Addison walked back in. She seemed unfazed to see an extra person sitting at the table. She nodded a greeting to Spence, who nodded one back.

There really was too much nodding going on, thought Spence. It really can't be good for the neck.

'I have spoken with Lemon.' said Suzanne Addison, leaning casually on the back of the nearest chair. 'And the arrival time will be 8.00pm - on the dot. She will inform the rest of the conglomerate in due time.'

'We're to be back here by 8.00pm tonight.' repeated Mr Levene, typing it into his personal organiser.

'The actual switch will take place at 9.00pm.' added Suzanne Addison.

'And the ransom demands?' asked Mr Franklin.

'Will be relayed at the exact same time as the switch.'

'9.00pm?'

'9.00pm.' confirmed Suzanne Addison. 'If that is all, gentlemen, I shall take my leave of you.' she added. 'I'm sure you can find your own way out.'

She left as swiftly as she had appeared.

Mr Franklin and Mr Levene automatically got up from their seats, nodded their farewells to each other and to Spence and promptly left. Spence hadn't moved. He was breathing heavily and perspiring rather badly.

It took him a couple of minutes to regain his composure.

Ransom demands? And some sort of 'switch'? It still didn't make any kind of sense to him. But, then again, Spence didn't have much sense to begin with. Or he wouldn't have walked right back into the scene of the crime, as it were. He wished he'd thought things through now.

Revenge was sweet; when you knew what you were actually doing. That's why it was usually described as cold and calculated revenge and not badly-planned-and-no-idea-how-to-go-about-it revenge.

He got up from the table and made his way back out into the hall. There didn't seem to be anybody about. The only thing that he could think of to do was return to the laboratory. It was the most important part of Lemon's set-up. If he could somehow disable the android replicas, then he was in with a fighting chance.

The switch!!

That was it.

The switching of the people with their android replicas. That's what was going to happen tonight. He'd have to work fast.

He left Manning House through the front door and made his way round to the back of the building. He soon found the door he'd entered by with Jody. It took him a couple of tense seconds to force the door open. He could feel his strength ebbing away. He needed some sleep, food, and a nice hot cup of tea.

The wind tore through his clothes and made him shiver uncontrollably and the rain pelted him like a Roman stoning. It wasn't the sort of weather in which you'd contemplate taking an evening stroll with your beloved, unless you *really* hated her, of course.

Spence didn't take long to find the laboratory. He stepped in cautiously.

And fell over.

Spence was allergic to the word 'stealth' in the same way as Elizabeth Taylor was allergic to the word 'marriage'. Luckily, the laboratory was empty. He picked himself up from the polished tiled floor and shivered. Not from the cold this time.

Where once had been a row of androids was now a row of empty cocoons. They had all gone. He was too late.

Spence went wild. It was not a pretty sight. Summoning all his last reserves of strength, and acting mostly on adrenaline, he took the laboratory apart in a way that the *'How To Dismantle A Laboratory In Six Easy Steps'* booklet had not thought of.

Sparks flew, glass was smashed, expensive equipment was brought down in price, tubes were pulled out, liquid was allowed to run free, and so on and so on.

When he had finished, he collapsed in a crumpled heap in the middle of the mess. In between huge gulps of air, he spotted a lone computer. It shone out like a beacon.

Spence knew a thing or two about computers, being a Data Input Operator. He struggled to his feet and lurched over to it. The computer was slightly damaged but not broken. He switched it on and allowed it to boot up.

Maybe, if he could ruin Lemon's plans *this* way... well, it would be like beating her at her own game.

*   *   *

The android double of Jody Marianne Lane obeyed orders and returned to the cellar.

Lemon was not pleased.

There was no sign of the Colonel at the Ministry of Defence. What had happened to him? There was a nagging doubt beginning to gnaw away at Lemon's supreme confidence. She ignored it. Nothing could go wrong.

No.

Nothing.

Her anger welled up and she turned to take it out on the android Jody. Order the stupid thing to kill itself, she thought. After all, she had no use for it now.

As she went to give the final order for Jody, she was aware of a flashing light on a nearby console. It stopped her in her tracks. She swivelled round to face it. The flashing indicated an intrusion.

Someone was tampering with the computer in the laboratory.

Someone who wasn't aware of the security bypass.

Someone who would have to be dealt with.

Lemon turned to the impassive form of Jody and barked some new orders. For once, her cool voice seemed to crack and there was a distinct urgency in the tone.

Lemon was, for the first time, beginning to worry. It was something entirely new to her and she didn't like it one bit.

Jody turned and walked out of the cellar.

*   *   *

In the wrecked shell of a laboratory, Spence was engrossed in the flickering monitor. The files he was scanning through were mind-blowing in the extreme. He bowed his head and studied the keyboard again.

As he scrolled through the memory, he didn't hear his attacker enter the laboratory. She was relatively silent. The only warning he got was the constriction in his windpipe as two arms locked round his neck and squeezed tight.

He pushed himself backwards without thinking, throwing himself and his unseen attacker off balance. They both stumbled away from the computer and through the debris, locked together, finally coming to a halt when they crashed into the opposite wall.

Spence was struggling to breathe. He could see large black dots looming into his vision. He twisted round suddenly and nearly broke his own neck in the process. It seemed to do the trick, though. His attacker had to release the grip slightly to get a better one and, in that split-second, Spence was free.

He snapped his arms upwards and broke the now tenuous hold of his foe. He felt the kick in his midriff too late and his breath left him like an express train. He fell back and over the operating table. He grabbed hold of a still sparking lead to pull himself up off the floor and narrowly avoided electrocuting himself.

Finally, his eyes alighted on the face of his attacker and his heart skipped a beat.

It was Jody Marianne Lane.

He stood, open-mouthed, leaning on the operating table. Jody ran at him and dived across the shiny table, sliding into him.

They both crashed to the floor amongst the rubble of technology. Spence felt a sharp pain in his side as he landed on some shattered glass and he rolled over on top of Jody. Her hands were searching for his neck again and he wrenched himself free. He crawled away and noticed a handgun lay on the desktop, near a smashed cabinet. He lunged for it.

For a brief moment he had the gun in his hands.

But, only for a brief moment.

Jody lashed out and he let go of the handgun. She got to it first and Spence made a break for the door.

The searing pain hit his senses first before he heard the sound of the shot. His shoulder sent messages of pure pain seeping through his mind. He swirled round and crashed into the door, sliding down it on to the tiles. He glanced at his shoulder and could see a dark stain appearing on the arm of his jacket, there was a hole in the material too.

He looked across at Jody, still with the smoking handgun pointing in his direction.

This was it.

Spence waited for his life to flash before his eyes, waited for the pre-title sequence stunt, the opening titles with the semi-naked ladies dancing in shadows, the roller-coaster plot-ride of thrills and excitement, and then the final credits with the title song playing over them.

Unfortunately, Spence's life wasn't anything like a James Bond movie. It was closer to a half-hour situation comedy.

But, he didn't get anything flashing before his eyes.

Jody took a step forward, to get better aim.

Spence gritted his teeth.

He'd been waiting for death all his life and, now it stared him in the face, he didn't know if he wanted to meet it.

As she stepped forward, Jody's foot slipped on a cylindrical piece of mechanical equipment that threw her slightly off balance. She stumbled sideways and Spence threw himself sideways.

The resulting bullet bit into the door-frame and Spence hauled himself to his shaking legs. He fell across the intervening space and knocked Jody's gun-arm away. He grabbed her by her hair and, with his other hand, grabbed the hanging pipe that had steadied him earlier.

A shooting pain flashed through his shoulder as he tightened his grip on the sparking ridged pipe.

Jody turned the gun to point at Spence's face, just at the same time that Spence connected the sparking end of his 'weapon' with Jody's neck. He jumped backwards as the sparks consumed her and she shivered violently.

The gun went off again as her fingers automatically tightened around the trigger, the bullet whistling past Spence's ear.

He turned away.

He couldn't bear to see her go again.

There was a thud as her inhuman body hit the floor. He turned back round and fell to his knees. Crawling over to the defunct android, he could feel the tears flowing.

Yet again, he cradled Jody's head in his arms and looked into unseeing eyes. The immense pain came back to him and his face scrunched up into a mask of anguish.

*　　　*　　　*

It was 8.03pm and the boardroom meeting was in full swing.

Spence had got down into the cellar without anyone noticing. He looked around.

No sign of Lemon. Good.

She would probably be in the meeting with the others.

His face contorted into a grimace as the pain in his arm got worse. It was so difficult to ignore it. He'd wrapped some cloth round it and pulled it tight to stem the flow of blood but it was still giving him real discomfort.

The winking monitors guided his path as he came down the cellar steps. He made his way to the ring of computers and sat behind them. It took him quarter of an hour to patch into them and discover how and why they were connected. It took him another quarter of an hour to give out new orders to the army of androids.

He stumbled across the Manning Estate accounts and smiled to himself. It took him just a few happy minutes to transfer £250,000 into his bank account. His bank manager would be astonished. He'd take great delight in going back to the so-called Listening Bank and withdrawing all that money to put into another Bank. Maybe the one with the motto of 'The Bank That Likes

To Say Yes!'. Or possibly, with £250,000 to deposit, the bank that liked to say 'Yeeeeessss!! Nice one, son!!'.

He glanced at the clock, ticking away on the third monitor.

It was 8.43pm.

Spence wiped the computer files completely and set off a virus in them that shot through the system like a bowl full of prunes.

He sat back and caressed his aching arm gently. He allowed himself a few minutes of quiet satisfaction as he watched the monitors scroll the information as it cleared them from the main memory.

*   *   *

It was now 9.00pm and there was a hushed silence in the boardroom.

Intense faces looked at the single black telephone that sat in front of Lemon at the head of the table. Any second now it would ring. The ultimatum would've been sent, via the computers.

Who would be on the other end of the line? The Prime Minister, perhaps? It would be nice to hear him grovel.

The seconds ticked by. The air became noticeably more tense.

Where was the call? The androids should have taken over by now. The country was held to ransom. Wasn't it?

Lemon got up from her chair.

All faces turned on her.

'Gentlemen.' she said, 'I will return in a few minutes.'

There was instant mutterings and mumblings as Lemon strode out of the room. She slammed the door shut with some considerable force. The mutterings and mumblings grew into chattering and moaning. It didn't seem to be going to plan.

Lemon made her way back to the cellar. Had she forgotten some last minute detail? Had she forgotten to send the email? There was a gnawing, nagging feeling that was really bugging her.

She swept down the steps into the cellar and could instinctively feel that there was something really wrong.

Running her fingers along the monitors as she sat down, enclosed in her circle of technology, Lemon tried to enter the mainframe database but she couldn't.

She tried again.

Still nothing.

She tried once more.

The screens were blank.

Her perfect face creased into rage and her eyes narrowed. She looked around the cellar. The semi-darkness seemed to leer and sneer at her, mocking her very existence.

Spence stepped out of the shadows.

Lemon didn't seem to move, she didn't seem startled or surprised. She slowly and carefully reached for her concealed gun, hooked underneath the main computer stand; the same trusty gun that had dispatched Lord Pembridge and Philip Dicks. Now, it would dispatch Spencer Tracy, once and for all.

Her hands grasped nothing as it dawned on her that Spencer Tracy was pointing a gun at her; the same gun that had dispatched Lord Pembridge and Philip Dicks.

'You seem to have me at a disadvantage.' she said, her voice smooth and silken.

'We are all going to die.' hissed Spence, breathing heavily. The pain was increasing from his shoulder and he was sweating profusely.

'A very philosophical thought.' smiled Lemon. 'Though, I think you'll find that most people know that already.' she added, still smiling.

'At 9.15pm, this place is going to go up like a rocket.' said Spence.

'Explain yourself.' said Lemon, intrigued at how calm Spence appeared to be.

'This whole place is rigged with explosives. I ordered your precious androids to return and carry out this simple task. The ones that couldn't make it back will self-destruct. Everything will be gone, up in smoke, in just five minutes.' whispered Spence.

'Is that so?' Lemon sighed. She was still smiling. It was such a beautiful smile.

Spence tried to ignore it but he couldn't; in the same way as he was finding it increasingly difficult to ignore the pain in his shoulder.

'You're not afraid to go up with it?' she asked him. Spence shook his head and grimaced.

'I have nothing to live for.' he muttered, sadly.

'Of course, of course.' soothed Lemon. 'Your lovely *friend*!' she hissed. 'Dead.' she added, still smiling.

Spence felt his hand start to shake. His finger tightened on the trigger.

Lemon suddenly got up from her seat. She did so with a graceful ease and she began to walk towards him. Spence couldn't take his eyes off her; the dazzling smile, the beautiful face, the swaying golden mane.

'I'll shoot.' he warned.

'What does it matter?' said Lemon, still smiling, 'We'll *all* be dead in a minute. You just said so.'

Spence pulled the trigger and saw the bullet bounce off her ribcage. He fired again and saw the spark of the ricochet. He pulled the trigger again and again. She didn't stop walking towards him. It was like a bad erotic dream mixed with the 'Terminator' movie.

The gun clicked and clicked as Spence kept pulling on the trigger. There were no more bullets.

Lemon was upon him.

She wrenched the gun from his hand and threw it aside. She pushed him back against the wall and pressed up hard against him. Her hands were on his face, pinning his head back.

'How... how...?' he gasped, as she pressed her body into his.

'I am the *prototype.*' whispered Lemon, kissing him with cold, dead lips.

Spence couldn't move.

She was an android.

The thought echoed around his brain like a tidal wave of sound.

Her hands moved off his face and onto his neck. She squeezed harder and harder. Spence couldn't breath. He couldn't even choke. His eyelids began to flutter.

Lemon broke off from kissing him. He looked into her empty blue eyes.

Spence's pupils began to dilate. In fact, everything began to feel very odd and out-of-place.

'I'm going to let you live these last few moments.' she whispered in his ear. She kissed him gently on the lips and the pressure on his windpipe decreased. He slumped to the floor, clutching at his throat and his torso heaved.

Lemon turned and walked away, into the shadows. Spence crawled to the bank of computers and hauled himself up.

It was 9.13pm.

There was now no sign of Lemon.

He staggered into the shadows and crashed into the far wall. It spun round and jettisoned him into a damp corridor. He paused to take a deep, deep breath and then began to run down the corridor. It seemed to be some sort of underground tunnel, curving upwards all the time.

His head pounded, his shoulder screamed with pain and his muscles were on the point of collapse. But, still he kept on. Stumbling along the tunnel, he could see no sign of Lemon up ahead.

Suddenly, he could feel the tunnel headed steeply upwards. He came out into the darkness of night. It was cold and raining but the air felt so good on his hot skin. He breathed in huge gulps of oxygen and looked around. He was in the grounds of the Manning Estate, but where?

He could make out the lights of the Manning House behind him and, as he turned, he caught sight of Lemon's fleeing form as the moon shone brightly for a brief second, before the black clouds smothered it again. He set off in pursuit. Not really knowing why.

There was a huge explosion.

The noise was deafening and the ground shook and shuddered violently underfoot. Spence was thrown to the ground and he lay there, dazed. He didn't look back but could hear the fire licking around the wreckage of the once-great house. He imagined the plumes of smoke wending their way skywards.

Dragging himself to his feet, he set off again, in the general direction he was running in before. As he reached a clearing in the trees, he knew what was going to happen. Sure enough, Lemon appeared and stood in his way.

'I spared your life once.' she hissed, the rain plastering her now dark, rain-drenched hair over her glistening face. 'But this time...' she spat the words out through gritted teeth.

'I never asked for any favours.' grinned Spence.

She dived at Spence and they both fell to the ground, rolling over and over on the leaf-carpeted ground. Spence had no idea what to do. There was no way he was going to win.

Why had he run after her?

Spence had done about as much pre-planning for this moment as the designers of the Titanic had done for the possibility of meeting an iceberg.

His hand alighted on a broken branch and he gripped it tightly. He swung it round to connect with Lemon's head.

She fell off him.

He shot to his feet and held the branch aloft, ready to bring it crashing down on her. She sliced away his feet and he crumpled, landing heavily on his bandaged shoulder. The pain rumbled through him like a steam train.

He howled in agony and dropped the branch.

Lemon was up and standing over him. She brought her foot down hard on the same shoulder. Spence recoiled and rolled away. He scrambled to his feet and started to run.

Lemon followed him.

There was no way he was going to escape.

He leapt a stream and clawed his way up the slippery mud of the bank. Ahead of him was the perimeter wall of the Manning Estate. He jumped at the vines that were growing up it and climbed his way to the top. He'd suddenly become as agile as a monkey. Fear gives you strange powers.

Pure, unadulterated fear.

He fell down the other side and twisted his ankle badly.

There was a sound of an engine.

He stumbled out into the road and straight in front of a motorcyclist.

Silas Holmes was thinking about breeding rabbits when Spence stepped out in front of him. He swerved to avoid the unexpected human roadblock and skidded into a ditch, flinging himself sideways off his machine to avoid damage to himself or his pride and joy.

Before Silas could even check if all was okay, he saw the human roadblock - which seemed to be some sort of a scruffy tramp - leap into the ditch beside him and pick up his motorbike.

Damn. He was going to be robbed again.

Silas Holmes hadn't had much luck with motorbikes. He'd owned twenty-two of them and twenty-one of them had been stolen.

This made twenty-two.

CHAPTER 16
'HEAVY SOUL'

Jody's bed was warm and comfortable.

Spence woke up with a start and reached for Jody. She wasn't there.

Instead, Eric was lay on his bad shoulder - on purpose. He pushed him off and sat up in Jody's bed.

It was morning.

The dappled rays crept through the curtains and turned the room a golden hue. Well, not really. He'd left the light on. He heaved himself out of bed and opened the curtains. It was raining and it was dark and it was seriously windy.

Saturday.

It wasn't what you'd call a good start to the weekend.

He switched the portable television on and flicked through the channels until he found BBC News 24, which rolled on and on with the same news for 24-hours, hence the cleverly thought-out name of the programme. The BBC were nothing if not educational and informative.

Some slick, garish-tied automaton, with plastic hair and funereal face, was reading off an autocue with all the personality of a dead pig. He turned the sound up and waited.

There must be something about the Manning Estate and about the missing people and about... well... everything? It wasn't something that could be ignored.

Was it?

Fifteen minutes later, he gave up.

He flicked through Teletext to see if there was any mention at all of Lemon.

Not a thing.

Though, he did discover a Celebrity recipe for Flapjacks, supposedly written by Eva Braun.

Yeah, right.

He switched the television off and sat with his head in his hands. He ran his fingers through his tangled hair and they got seriously stuck.

Eric was brushing against his legs. Not as a sign of affection, just because he had fleas and was trying to get rid of them.

Spence lay back on the bed and fiddled with the duvet. He stared at the ceiling and could make out Jody's face in the outdated Artex swirls. He closed his eyes and there it was again. His shoulder brought him back to reality.

Well, Eric jumping on his shoulder brought him back to reality.

If Eric was trying to preserve his nine lives, he was definitely going about it the wrong way.

Spence grimaced as he sat up and pushed Eric roughly off the bed.

Eric was, as established, not the most nimble or graceful of cats and landed on the carpet with a dull thud, legs spread-eagled. He let out a small miaow of disgust and trotted off, out of the bedroom.

The time was exactly 11.05am when Spence finally emerged from Jody's room. He sauntered slowly across the landing and stumbled into the toilet, dressed in nothing but his second pair of Winnie the Pooh boxer shorts - the ones with Eeyore on (which, he thought, was very apt as he always boasted that he was hung like a donkey).

He looked in the mirror and almost fainted.

The reflection staring back didn't look like him at all; less like him, in fact, that his android double. Instead, he was looking at a pale, drawn, and pinched face that had black rings under the eyes. His tatty fringe had curled and frizzed on the forehead like the remnants of a mouldy Pot Noodle and the lower half of his features were covered with, what could only be described as, some sort of a beard; a not-very-good sort of a beard that grew down his neck, where red weals from inhuman fingermarks were glowing like Rudolph's nose.

It would take a great deal of plastic surgery to bring *that* face back to resemble anything half-decent.

He decided not to even bother trying to spruce himself up more than he had to.

Splashing some cold water hastily over his skin and making it tingle; he rubbed his face with a towel to dry it and then ignored the mirror. He sauntered back across the landing and rummaged around in Jody's room for his old clothes.

He slipped into a pair of black jeans, which were a tad too tight for him, wrestled with a V-necked sweater before getting his arms through the right holes and reached for his trusty, battered Doc Martens. His trusty, battered Doc Martens that he'd had since the beginning of time. They were scuffed and grubby, tattered and old. They were slowly falling apart.

Spencer Tracy's Mum had always said that you could tell what a person was like by looking at their shoes. This was so true.

As he came down the stairs, clumping like Frankenstein's monster on each separate step, he heard the front doorbell ring.

Eric was asleep at the bottom of the stairs.

Spence tripped over him.

The doorbell rang again and Spence picked himself up off the floor, cursing Eric loudly. He opened the door and was greeted by Big Man #1 and Big Man #2. They didn't look particularly happy.

'Good morning.' grinned Spence, leaning against the door.

'That's open to discussion.' growled Big Man #1.

'And what can I do for you today?' asked Spence.

'It's not what you can do for *us*.' growled Big Man #1.

'No.' added Big Man #2, 'We've come to *do* for *you*.' he hissed, though his threat lost some of it's menace because of his squeaky voice.

Spence sighed.

'Mr Letts would like the money he's owed, I suppose.' said Spence.

'He gave you until the weekend.' said Big Man #2.

'And this is the weekend.' said Big Man #1, taking a step towards Spence, his fist raised and his eyes twinkling with the thought of dealing out a good bashing to this smug twit with the rubbish beard-growth.

Spence raised his hand to stop him in his tracks.

'If you'll allow me to get my coat and, of course, my cheque book, I will come with you to pay Mr Letts his required amount of money.' said Spence, turning to the hat-stand in the hall and picking a coat off it.

It was Jody's dark-green wax jacket that had been given to her by the Colonel when he'd invited her to come clay-pigeon shooting with him at the weekends. It had never been worn, until now. It fitted Spence slightly too snugly and, when it was on, he caught his reflection in the full-length mirror by the door.

Interesting.

It suited him as much as acting in the English language suited Arnold Schwarzenegger.

*   *   *

Mr Letts was smoking one of his cigars. He allowed himself as many cigars as he had clients to see. That way he could *always* look slightly menacing, as well as being able to keep up the horrendous wheezing that sounded as if his lungs were being played like an out-of-tune accordion.

He was quite surprised to see Spencer Tracy stride into his dimly-lit office. He was even more surprised to see him smiling.

'Greetings.' said Mr Letts, puffing vigorously on his cigar.

'Now, Mr Letts - how much money do I owe you?' enquired Spence, sitting down in the seat opposite Mr Letts.

Mr Letts liked this 'straight down to business' approach. This was a good start to any Saturday.

'I recall we agreed on £125,000.' rasped Mr Letts, his fingers beginning to itch at the mere thought of such a sum.

Spence took out his cheque book, snatched a pen off the desk and wrote out a cheque for the exact amount. He ripped it out of his book, kissed it and passed it over to Mr Letts.

'Cheques bounce.' Mr Letts muttered.

'This one won't.' stated Spence, 'I transferred some funds from a reliable source.' he added, remembering the delight he'd felt as he'd transferred the money via computer from Lemon's organisation.

And by 'transferred', he meant 'stolen'.

'Pleasure doing business with you.' said Spence, standing up.

'The pleasure is all mine.' grinned Mr Letts, truthfully.

Spence turned and shook Big Man #1 and Big Man #2, in order, and then strode purposefully out of the office.

Big Man #1 and Big Man #2 looked at each other, somewhat surprised. They were also slightly miffed, if truth be told.

It had been a long time since they'd given anyone a proper going-over and they had been looking forward to putting Spence into hospital. They'd also been looking forward to then visiting him in hospital and bringing him a basket of fruit and a funny 'Get Well Soon' card.

They weren't naturally malicious men; just incredibly stupid.

'Well done.' said Mr Letts, offering a cigar each to Big Man #1 and Big Man #2.

'Yeah.' said Big Man #1, taking the cigar offered. 'I suppose it was really.' he added.

Big Man #2 just nodded in agreement and accepted his own cigar.

Mr Letts relaxed back into his seat, fondled the cheque in the way that a perverted Uncle fondles himself when schoolchildren are around, stuffed it in his pocket, and took a long, slow, suck on his cigar.

The sound of him coughing drowned out the noise of the traffic outside.

∗   ∗   ∗

Silas Holmes - owner of twenty-two different stolen motorbikes in the space of twelve short months - was at the Police Station, reporting his twenty-second missing machine.

Police Constable Terence Walsh knew him well.

PC Walsh had dealt with every single one of Silas Holmes' reports of stolen property. It was a thankless task.

PC Walsh felt desperately sorry for the man.

Silas Holmes was probably the unluckiest man alive, when it came to motorbikes. PC Walsh felt some remorse. He also found it increasingly hilarious.

The rest of the force on duty had a running betting system on when Silas Holmes would next appear there. It had even been extended to *other* stations in the county and Silas Holmes had become something of a minor celebrity, without ever being aware of it.

The bets had been placed from all over the South West division.

If PC Walsh remembered correctly, Sergeant Daniel Sherwin would be the one with the windfall coming his way this time.

Lucky bugger.

'So, I'd appreciate it greatly if you could contact me as soon as any information comes your way.' said Silas Holmes.

PC Walsh put the finishing touches to the relevant forms and nodded.

'Certainly, Mr Holmes.' said PC Walsh.

'I'm just off to look at a quite spiffing Harley Davison I spotted on the way here.' grinned Silas Holmes.

He was the epitomy of the phrase: 'There's One Born Every Minute'.

'Racy little number, seemed to have a fair bit of poke in her.' he added, winking. Silas Holmes had money to burn and burn it he did.

PC Walsh smiled.

'Goodbye then, sir.' he said cheerfully, refraining from adding: 'See you again soon.'

'Cheerio, PC Walsh! Or should I say "Evening All"?' chuckled Silas.

'No.' muttered PC Walsh, 'Cheerio will be fine.' he replied, gritting his teeth.

Silas Holmes had been in the Police Station twenty-two times now and this was the twenty-second time he'd said that joke. He really should retire it off with some kind of decent pension plan, thought PC Walsh.

As Silas Holmes opened the one double-door to leave the Police Station, Spencer Tracy walked in, using the other. They paused for a moment and looked at each other, nodded a frowned greeting and then passed each other, racking their brains for some recollection of why they distantly recognised one another.

Spencer Tracy marched up to the desk and, when he got there, didn't quite know what to say. He'd come in on the off-chance. He thought about reporting an explosion.

But, that would've been silly.

Surely someone else would've done that.

Or reporting Jody Marianne Lane's murder.

Too painful.

Reporting Lemon, perhaps.

Too far-fetched.

He'd just been instinctively drawn into the Police Station and didn't quite know what he could tell them, aside from recounting the whole tale in its ludicrous entirety.

'Morning, sir.' said PC Walsh. 'What can I do you for?'

'I've got a strange story that may interest you.' whispered Spence.

'Really, sir?' said PC Walsh, slightly intrigued. 'Come through to the interview room and tell it like it is.'

he added, lifting the entry flap of the desk up and beckoning him through.

This should be good for a laugh, he thought to himself. There was nothing like a good nutter to laugh at before lunchbreak, chuckled PC Walsh. There were usually a fair few climbed out of the woodwork on a weekend; it seemed to draw them out like moths to a flame.

He wondered whether this would be the next Silas Holmes, on who the rest of the force could use for a bit of in-house gambling.

*   *   *

It was 3.30pm when Spencer Tracy was allowed to leave the Police Station.

He was slightly dazed and very confused.

A whole battalion of many different people had interviewed him and he'd had to go over the last week of his life in amazing detail, repetitively. His head hurt and his brain felt numb.

So, no change there, then.

There had been hushed telephone calls through to the Ministry of Defence, accusations, suggestions, and - finally - the ultimate weirdness... Spencer Tracy found out that he didn't actually exist. Well, they told him, quite bluntly so.

This had come as quite a surprise to him. He thought he'd existed quite well for thirty-three years but now found out that he hadn't existed at all.

He couldn't fathom this out.

Perhaps the computer records had packed up?

But, the Police had been quite adamant on this point. They had absolutely no record of him existing at all, anywhere, and had tried to get his *real* name out of him.

He'd explained that Spencer Tracy *was* his real name, however silly it sounded to them, and not some fake pseudonym that he'd picked up from watching old movies.

This revelation of his failure to exist had come from the top source as well. It had been the phone-call back from the Ministry of Defence that had prompted this accusation of his non-existence.

All very strange.

He walked out in front of a bus. And didn't notice. Luckily, the bus driver noticed.

Spence stumbled out of town and kept walking. The rain had soaked him through to the skin but he couldn't feel the cold. And the rain seemed to be getting heavier.

The Police had told him to return to his home and await an arrival from the Ministry of Defence. They'd wanted to check his story out too. He really didn't want to have to go over it again.

He found himself walking into Mulberry Road without thinking.

This was a stupid mistake.

His brain had been on automatic pilot and, instead of going back to Jody's house, he'd instinctively made his way to his old rented home.

He decided to take one last look at the gutted remains of No.171.

He looked up into the wind and his eyes blinked madly as he caught sight of Mr Arthur Plinth, *still* sat at his window.

Suddenly, he was aware of a big, black car pulling up beside him. He turned and saw the electric-darkened window slide effortlessly down.

A voice spoke from inside.

Perhaps they want to know directions, thought Spence, leaning closer.

'Get inside, Mr Tracy - we have a job for you.' said a silken voice.

Two big, burly men got out of the car and Spence gulped. He was getting seriously fed up with this. The words 'Vicious' and 'Circle' sprang instantly to mind.

Spence sighed, looked up to the heavens, brooding and dark above him, and raised a quizzical eyebrow.

'Oh God.' he muttered, even though he didn't believe in God. In fact, the irony hit him that, much like he didn't believe in the existence of God, the world around him didn't believe in his very own existence either.

Spence laughed, just a little too hysterically.

EPILOGUE
'HERE COMES THE RAIN AGAIN'

It was a monsoon. Well, a mon-maybe-soon.

It had been raining now for what seemed like Biblical proportions.

So much rain had fallen, in fact, that the South West Water Company had run out of excuses for saying that the reservoirs were still half-empty.

The local radio weather announcer had stated that dry weather was on the way and we would all see the last of this wet spell by the end of the weekend.

This prompted a mass exodus to the shops and a sharp rise in the profits of umbrella sales. The general public always knew who to trust.

The rain had become so heavy that drains were over-flowing, plants had drunk far too much and were toppling over, grass had the distinctly fatal consistency and quality of quicksand, and all the roof guttering was acting like junior versions of Niagara Falls.

Mr Arthur Plinth, a long-term resident of Mulberry Road and head honcho of the Neighbourhood Watch (because he was the only one who could actually be bothered to run it), was sitting in his front room. He referred to it as his 'Drawing Room' because he liked to believe himself to be Upper Class.

He was looking out of the window.

A window, he had just decided, that would benefit greatly by having a tarpaulin stretched out above it.

As the rain streamed down his double-glazing, he caught sight of a big, black car.

A big, black car with diplomatic plates on it.

It looked like a Government car.

Hush, hush. Top secret.

'Are you expecting departmental visitors, Helen?!' he shouted.

Helen, his wife of ten years, was in the attic, up in the roof. Not surprisingly, she didn't hear him.

He shouted again.

She still didn't hear him.

So, he turned back to try and see through the rivers of water that were running through his double-glazed vision. This would be ample fodder for his book he was writing: 'A Neighbourhood Watched'.

He caught sight of his old next-door neighbour - the annoying one with the annoying cat - being bundled into the back of the Government car by two big, burly gentlemen, who wouldn't have looked out of place at a convention for heavy steroid users.

He didn't think anything of it, which was a good thing.

Anyone who spots a big, black car with Government licence plates pulling up should ignore it completely. Two big, burly men getting out should make you really forget you ever saw it. And a man being bundled unceremoniously into the back seat - even if it's a relation - of this aforementioned car is not cause for ringing the Police.

That will just get you into trouble.

Or make you mysteriously disappear.

Fortunately, Mr Arthur Plinth knew this. This was why he was so good at running the local Neighbourhood Watch.

The rain still beat down with the regularity of a Bran Fibre diet.

The sky was still painted black.

The clouds were still gathered together like a packet of discoloured, out-of-date marshmallows.

The thunder still rumbled like the approach of a particularly impressive fart. And the lightening flashed down like a faulty strobe light in a bad school drama presentation.

It was pure Kafka-esque, vicious circle story-telling for Theatre Studies A-level students everywhere.

And with the possibilities of a sequel.

Acknowledgements...

Barnaby Eaton-Jones would like to thank, in no particular order:

The Family
Mum, Dad, and Sopho. They continue to be my guiding lights and constant support. And I still hear my late Grandad's laughter at all of my stupid jokes when I was young, which continues to inspire me to try and make people laugh today.

The Spouse
Kim Jones - her never-ending support, her patience, her twinkling sunflower eyes, her understanding and caring nature. If I wasn't already married to her, I'd have an affair with her, divorce her, and then marry her again.

The Teachers
Stephen Rix, Stuart Butler, and Dora Brooking - all of them had the ability to inspire and influence me at a young, impressionable age.

The Friends
Too numerous to mention but each and every one has shaped who I am in some way, by being there throughout my evolution.

AUTHOR BIOGRAPHY

Barnaby Eaton-Jones has had the debilitating illness M.E. since 1991 and still can't pronounce what it stands for. He is a Sagittarius, for those of you who believe in Astrology. This, apparently, means he is half-man, half-horse (unfortunately, it's the wrong halves).

When he isn't writing novels, he is writing rude graffiti and his home telephone number on toilet walls.

Amongst other things, he runs (with his wife) a touring theatre company called The OFFSTAGE Theatre Group (_www.offstagetheatregroup.com_) and a regular comedy improvisation show called 'Off The Cuff' (_www.off-the-cuff.co.uk_); as well as managing and appearing in a big band Blues Brothers tribute show called Blues Brothers Reloaded (_www.bluesbrothersreloaded.co.uk_). Not content with that, he is also one half of Crow Crag, an acoustic folk/rock duo (_www.myspace.com/crowcraggy_), and does the odd bit of teaching.

He likes Jaffa Cakes far too much and sometimes gets accused of being a human being.

'Lemon' was written in 1997 and edited in 2009.

Printed in the United Kingdom by
Lightning Source UK Ltd., Milton Keynes
141110UK00001B/247/P

9 781849 233897